# THE REDBIRD'S CRY

MYSTERY NOVELS BY JEAN HAGER

Featuring Molly Bearpaw

THE REDBIRD'S CRY
RAVENMOCKER

Featuring Chief Mitchell Bushyhead

GHOSTLAND
NIGHT WALKER
THE GRANDFATHER MEDICINE

# THE REDBIRD'S CRY

## JEAN HAGER

**THE MYSTERIOUS PRESS**

Published by Warner Books

A Time Warner Company

Copyright © 1994 by Jean Hager
All rights reserved.

 Mysterious Press books are published by Warner Books, Inc., 1271 Avenue of the America, New York, NY 10020.

A Time Warner Company

The Mysterious Press name and logo are registered trademarks of Warner Books, Inc.

Printed in the United States of America

First printing: April 1994

10 9 8 7 6 5 4 3 2 1

          Library of Congress Cataloging-in-Publication Data
Hager, Jean.
      The redbird's cry / Jean Hager.
        p.  cm.
      ISBN 0-89296-494-4
      1. Indians of North America—Oklahoma—Fiction.   2. Cherokee
Indians—Fiction.   I. Title.
PS3558.A3232R4   1994
813 .54—dc20
                                                    93-36320
                                                       CIP

*For*
*Courtney Anne Clark and Madeline Elaine Clark*
*With a heart full of love*

## Author's Note

While some factional disagreements among enrolled members of the Cherokee Nation of Oklahoma have resulted in lawsuits, the True Echota Band depicted in this novel is fictitious and is not meant to represent any actual group or organization. Likewise, all the characters who appear in the book are fictitious, including members of the True Echota Band, and any resemblance to real persons, living or dead, is coincidental.

As far as I know, no murder has ever occurred in the Cherokee National Museum, nor am I aware of any of the museum's exhibits having been stolen.

# THE
# REDBIRD'S CRY

# 1

Autumn in northeast Oklahoma is like an indolent beauty who's all dressed up with no place to go. She often dawdles through September, October, November, and sometimes lags right on through Christmas.

Leaves, drooping in the humid summer heat, revive and paint the countryside crimson and orange and yellow. In Cherokee County, where small towns nestle in valleys surrounded by wooded Ozark foothills, the trees flaunt themselves in a grand, flamboyant display.

Autumn's glory reaches its zenith in October, the season the ancient Cherokees call *Duna'na-dee'*, the harvest moon. Days may be warm, but by then the nights have turned chilly and invigorating.

On such a mid-October night, at twenty-five minutes after midnight, a car traveling south from Tahlequah turned off Highway 62 into the Cherokee tribal complex. The headlights blinked off and the car moved slowly through the lighted grounds of the Talking Leaves Job Corps Center, crept past the big sign that read "Cherokee Nation of Oklahoma," circled around the modern, brick tribal office building, and stopped behind the complex in the deep shadow of a pecan grove. The driver killed the motor and sat, scanning the surrounding area, seeing no one.

The engine popped as it began to cool, as loud as a gunshot in the silence. The driver, already on edge, jumped and gripped the steering wheel, then sat tensely still as more long minutes spun out. Nothing moved. No lights shone in any of the office windows, and no car approached the building.

Finally, the driver released the wheel and opened the glove compartment. Fingers curled around a can of black spray paint. Gripping the can, the driver eased open the car door and got out. The pungent smell of burned leaves hung in the crisp air. A car hummed past on the highway, the light from its headlamps dissolving long before it reached into the darkness where the driver stood.

To the west, a coyote howled at the moon, disturbing a dog who answered with frenzied barking. But the dog was too far away to worry about. Quick steps muffled by rubber soles took the driver away from the car to the south side of the office building.

For an instant, the driver hesitated. The leaders of the band would deny any knowledge of this. Some of the band's members even worked in the building, and the majority, if they favored any action at all, backed the official plan which dragged on and on through the courts.

It had been so for hundreds of years. The history of the Cherokee people was a series of humiliations and defeats by white men's laws in white men's courts. The Cherokees had learned the ways of the white man, and now they used what they'd learned against their brothers.

The driver didn't expect this to change anybody's mind on either side. At best, it would seem a puny protest. Almost childish. But as the first item on a carefully orchestrated agenda, it would be effective.

It might take a while for them to remove the message. They'd have to sandblast. In the meantime, the bold words would be there for all to see—and contemplate.

Black paint had been chosen deliberately. Black was the color of death. The can was raised, a thumb jammed hard against the plastic nozzle. Two-foot-high letters began to appear on the side of the building.

In a matter of moments, the message was complete. The writer stepped back. Light from the front of the building provided enough illumination for the message to be read. Those who mattered would understand.

PROPERTY OF TRUE ECHOTA BAND—TRESPASSERS BEWARE!

The plan was launched, no turning back now. The writer uttered one word. " '0 sda," good, and hurried back into the shadows.

Daye Hummingbird moved restlessly in her bed and watched the window turn slowly from deep slate to pearl gray. She could hear the beat of her heart; it throbbed in perfect time with the ticking of the bedside clock. She knew it was only her imagination that the beat was much louder than normal, but she had not been able to stop listening to it for the past half hour.

The week ahead of her was fraught with so many potential disasters, she wondered if she would sleep at all. If only she hadn't agreed to participate in the week-long exhibition of Cherokee arts and crafts at the tribal museum. Having done so, she should certainly have backed out when she learned, two weeks ago, that Wolf and his father would be demonstrating their Cherokee blowguns and darts. Ever since then, she had lived with an ominous sense of foreboding.

Well, it was too late now. The pre-opening reception was tonight, and the exhibition was scheduled to begin tomorrow morning.

Several thousand people were expected to tour the museum during the exhibition, and many of them would see her work for the first time. She should be able to sell a few pieces, and she needed the money. She taught three art classes at Northeastern Oklahoma State University, four blocks from her house in Tahlequah, but her part-time salary, with no fringe benefits, wasn't enough to live on. So it was crazy to consider giving up her place in the exhibition. Impossible. She couldn't let her fear of what Wolf might do drive *her* to desperate action.

She curled on her side and closed her eyes, hoping for an hour or two of sleep after a night filled with anxious imaginings. But it was no use.

Finally, despairingly, she untangled her naked body from the sheet and sat up, switching on the bedside lamp. The hands of the old-fashioned alarm clock pointed to six and ten. Not quite six o'clock.

Swinging her legs over the side of the bed, she reached for the paint-streaked shirt and jeans she had tossed in a chair last night and pulled them on, then slid her feet into terry-cloth scuffs. She padded to the kitchen to start coffee brewing, then to the bathroom to wash her face and brush the tangles from her thick black hair.

Wide dark eyes in a tawny face composed of classically beautiful features looked back at her from the bathroom mirror. With a conscious effort, she erased the worry lines from a high, normally smooth forehead. Wolf wouldn't create a scene with so many people about, she told herself.

But no one could really predict what Wolf might do.

The situation would be less volatile if Tom weren't going to be there too. But Tom, a lawyer, was the best Cherokee storyteller around, and besides, she would need his calm strength to get through the week. Judgments in several lawsuits, in which he had represented the Nation, had been handed down in recent days, allowing him to take a week off work.

In spite of her apprehension over the exhibition, a smile tugged at her lips. Tom Battle had been her lover for three months now, and he could still make her feel weak merely by walking into a room. His rangy good looks had attracted her in the beginning, but it was his kindness that held her. She had never known such a *good* man. He was the polar opposite of Wolf Kawaya, her ex-husband.

Opposites did not necessarily attract, especially when they were of the same sex. Wolf hated Tom; he'd hated him even before Daye left Wolf. Then, Tom had been nothing but a casual acquaintance to her, but try to tell that to Wolf. Although the divorce had been granted months before she started seeing Tom, Wolf persisted in blaming him for it. And for Daye's refusal to discuss reconciliation. Wolf's problems were always somebody else's fault.

Lately Wolf had stepped up the pressure, accusing her of being a traitor to her own family, who were all members of the True Echota Band. How could loving Tom be disloyal? Disloyalty was a conscious choice, but she couldn't command her heart.

Or her rational mind. Unlike her family, Daye invariably saw both sides of an issue. At times, it seemed more a curse than a blessing. She thought life would be easier if she could categorize every question in terms of black or white, right or wrong. It would dispense with a lot of the soul-searching, which sometimes interfered with her sleep.

In the conflict between the Cherokee Nation of Oklahoma and the TEB, both of whose leaders were passionately convinced they were the rightful rulers of the band—if not the entire Oklahoma contingent of the tribe—what she saw was a huge gray area. Both sides, it seemed to her, made some valid claims. It was a conflict that was rooted in two hundred years of wrangling between mixed-blood progressive and full-blood conservative factions of the tribe, with no clear-cut solution.

Her ex-husband simply wouldn't admit the possibility that an opposing view could have merit. Much less could he comprehend that, for Daye, her relationship with Tom was separate from other areas of her life. A thing apart, like a perfect jewel encased in velvet.

Her parents had difficulty accepting the relationship too, but they hadn't forced Daye to choose between Tom and them. They merely avoided the subject when she was around. Nor did Daye and Tom discuss the merits of the lawsuits in which he represented the Nation against the band.

Such avoidance was simply beyond hotheaded Wolf's comprehension. You either agreed with her ex-husband on all points or you were an enemy. She had reasoned and argued with Wolf until she was hoarse and finally had realized she was dealing with an obsession. At the end of their last meeting, Wolf had shouted, "If I can't have you, nobody can!" A cliché that might have been laughable in other circumstances.

She hadn't laughed. She had threatened to get a restraining order.

Since then, Wolf hadn't come to her door or tried to arrange a meeting elsewhere. But twice her phone had rung in the middle of the night and the caller hung up when she answered. She was sure it was Wolf. And several times she had seen him drive slowly down her street, as he stared at her house. Then he'd park nearby and just sit there, for an hour sometimes.

A few times, he'd followed her as she drove around town. She'd glance in her rearview mirror and there he'd be, staring back at her through his windshield.

She'd gone to the police, who had pointed out that there was no law to prevent Wolf's driving and parking on public streets.

An icicle of fear slid through her at the thought of spending the next week under Wolf's watchful, somehow menacing eyes. She tried to shake off the feeling. She couldn't become a recluse to avoid seeing him. She would simply have to ignore Wolf.

With a sigh, she turned away from the mirror and went to the kitchen for a mug of coffee, then to the small corner room where she spent so many of her waking hours. The room, with twin banks of windows on the north and east, and a skylight installed by Tom, was her studio. In dawn's milky light, the golden oak floor and white walls glowed.

Daye sipped her coffee and studied the painting in progress on her easel. A young Cherokee woman with a green shawl over her shoulders looked down serenely at the sleeping infant cradled against her full breast.

A little more black to deepen the shawl's folds, she mused, and some magenta on the horizon behind the mother and child. Maybe a line of trees in the distance. It was going to be one of her best works.

If she put in a few hours today, she could finish the painting and add it to her exhibit at the museum. Indian women were her specialty, and the mother and child would bring four figures.

Daye set the mug down and chose a brush from several lined up on the window ledge. With that simple action, she felt the knots of anxiety in her stomach loosening. She would lose herself in her work and forget about the reception and exhibition looming ahead.

# 2

Maud Wildcat stood at the stove and studied her grandson from the corner of her eye. It was nearly noon. She had finally succeeded in rousting Robert from his bed, a maddeningly frustrating task. She'd been trying to get him up since before she went to the grocery store at eight o'clock. Today was Friday, and school was out for a teacher's meeting. Robert had promised to help her this morning, then he'd stayed out until after two in the morning. That was becoming a habit.

Well, he was up now—barely. He sat slumped over the kitchen table, disgruntled, unwashed face propped in unwashed hands. He wore faded jeans with torn knees, deliberately torn. Ripping up perfectly good clothes was the latest fad at Tahlequah High School. The boy had not bothered to put on a shirt or shoes. She would never have allowed her own children to come to the table like that. She was going soft in her old age.

Robert mumbled under his breath.

"What?" she asked.

"Nothing," he said darkly.

Maud shrugged and turned back to the stove. She worried about him even more than she had worried about her son Lee, Robert's father, who had died five months earlier from a head injury received in a bar fight. Robert had always had an unruly bent, but Lee had been able to handle him. After Lee's death, the boy had gotten so out of hand that his mother turned him out of the house. There was only one place left for him to go. To Maud, who was more convinced than ever that sixty-three-year-old women had no business taking responsibility for rebellious teenagers.

She had always been able to forget her troubles when she was weaving, but now even weaving didn't blot out her apprehension over her grandson.

Robert sighed loudly. She ignored him and continued her silent litany of fears. The boy stayed out until all hours and came home reeking of beer. She suspected he used marijuana too. She'd found cigarette papers in his dresser. Some days she couldn't get him up in time for school, and his grades were slipping. He was a senior, but he wasn't going to graduate if he didn't take more interest in his studies.

It was clear to everyone but Robert that he was headed for trouble. When she tried to talk to him about it, he lost his temper and stormed out. She did not approve of what his mother had done, yet she was beginning to understand why Ruth had washed her hands of him. But if Maud did that, there'd be no one to talk sense to him and impose some semblance of discipline. Not that he paid much attention to the few house rules she'd established when he came to live with her, but she owed it to Lee to keep trying.

She turned off the burner under the oatmeal, dipped a bowlful, and set it in front of him. "Here," she said, "this'll stick to your ribs. We've got a lot of work to do this afternoon."

He gazed at the steaming oatmeal. "Yuk. I'm not hungry," he muttered and pushed the bowl away. Robert loved oatmeal. He was punishing her for nagging him until he got up. She had to admit, it worked. She fretted when he didn't eat breakfast. The first meal of the day was the most important, and it had always been her favorite. She was an early riser and needed nourishment before she tackled her household chores and whatever weaving project she was working on. She could not understand a growing boy who would turn down food.

She set the sugar bowl and margarine beside the oatmeal, then turned away with an air of indifference. "Suit yourself, but you'll be starved before we get all my things hauled out to the museum." Yesterday a neighbor with a pickup truck had moved her loom to the Cherokee Heritage Center in Park Hill, five miles from Tahlequah. Today she'd take boxes of her handiwork for display and the yarn and supplies she would need for finger-weaving demonstrations.

She ran hot water over her own breakfast dishes in one side of the sink and squeezed detergent from the bottle. The pin oak tree outside the kitchen window was a blaze of orange and red, so beautiful it brought a lump to her throat. Reaching up, she pushed the window open and stood for a moment, comforted by the colorful tree and the blue sky overlaid by a soft haze that made the sun fuzzy around the edges. The air was brittle but not really cold at midday, and she could smell the aroma of wood burned earlier in fireplaces to take the edge of chill off the morning. It seemed, in that moment, as if time had ceased and winter would be held forever at bay.

Robert stirred, shattering her enjoyment of the scene outside the window. She glanced over her shoulder. While she'd had her back turned, Robert had begun to eat his oatmeal. He hunched his shoulders and shuddered. "Brrrr. Close the damned window." He spoke with the surliness of one who was determined to pick an argument about something.

She pulled the window shut.

"What's the big hurry to get to the museum, Granny?" he grumbled, switching back to the real bone of contention. "Hell, we've got all day."

"You know I don't want that kind of language used in this house, Robert."

He muttered something else that sounded like a curse, which she decided not to hear, but he kept eating. She plunged her hands into the warm soapy water, having learned to say as little as possible when Robert was in one of his sulks. There was never any way of knowing what would set him off. She washed the dishes and placed them on a rack to dry, determined to keep her mouth shut while he finished eating.

But Robert was still bent on airing his complaint. "How can you associate with the people who killed my father?" he asked crossly, throwing his spoon down on the table. Sometimes even her silence irritated him. No, not her silence, really. She didn't think it had anything to do with her in particular. Robert was just mad. At life. At the world. At his father for dying. She stifled an impulse to hug him and say she understood. He would only push her away.

Since he seemed dead set on drawing a reaction from her, she asked with genuine puzzlement, "What people?"

The man who'd been involved in the brawl with Lee had left town after Lee's death was ruled accidental. Maud didn't doubt that the ruling was correct. Lee had fallen and hit his head against the sharp metal corner of a table, after alcohol had blurred judgment and fueled an argument to the point of violence. There had been several witnesses.

"As if you don't know," Robert snapped.

"The man who fought your father isn't even around here anymore," she said reasonably.

"I'm not talking about *him*."

She knew he wanted her to ask what man. She kept quiet, thinking. The conflict between Lee and the other man had arisen over who had the right to establish programs and receive federal funding for the True Echota Band—the band's elected officials or the Cherokee Nation of Oklahoma, which the TEB maintained had been abolished at the turn of the twentieth century, prior to statehood.

The TEB's claim had been the basis of a lawsuit filed against the U.S. Department of Interior, one of a number of lawsuits against state, federal, and tribal officials. The Cherokee Nation of Oklahoma had instigated lawsuits, too—against the TEB. In the cases already decided, the courts had ruled in favor of the Cherokee Nation.

Lee had served on the TEB council, and Maud knew that Robert had attended a few band meetings recently. There he'd evidently listened to the more radical members, whose claims went beyond those of the band's leaders. They wanted the government of the entire tribe turned over to the TEB. The radicals were a tiny minority, but so vocal that people sometimes assumed they spoke for the band.

Maud stayed out of tribal politics. She merely wanted to live her life in peace. She *had* voted for Wilma Mankiller for principal chief of the Nation in the last tribal election, but she had known better than to mention that to Robert. Mankiller hadn't needed her vote anyway; she'd won by a landslide.

Finally Robert couldn't stand her silence any longer. "Tom Battle is the traitor I'm talking about," he snarled, staring at her accusingly with his hot black eyes. Battle had represented the Cherokee Nation in most of the lawsuits involving the TEB. "You're going to be in that thing at the museum with him. How can you do that?"

"Tom Battle wasn't anywhere near your father the night he was killed."

He shoved back his chair. "He's going to court against his own people!"

Maud was tempted to remind him that the TEB had insti-gated its share of the lawsuits, forcing Cherokee Nation offi-cials to defend themselves. Not that she couldn't understand the band's position too. She'd listened to Lee's impassioned arguments often enough. It seemed there could be no compro-mise; the long-standing rivalry could only be settled in a court of law. The sad thing was that there could be only one winner.

Adopting a conciliatory tone, she said, "People can have different opinions, Robert, without being sworn enemies. Wolf and Josiah Kawaya are TEB members and they're taking part in the exhibit right alongside Tom Battle."

That seemed to throw him off balance for a moment. Then he shrugged, smiled a tight-lipped little smile, and said, "I guess they have their reasons," as though the Kawayas' partici-pation in the exhibition was part of some larger plan.

"Well..." Let it drop, she told herself. "If you'll finish get-ting dressed, you can carry those boxes out to the car and we'll go." He scowled and she added hastily, "You don't have to wait at the museum for me. After you help unload, you can take the car and come back in an hour or so." Robert's old Ford had two flat tires. It was out of commission most of the time, but she routinely turned down his requests to use her car. She was afraid he'd get drunk and have a wreck. But sure-ly he wouldn't drink in the middle of the afternoon, and she'd rather he take the car than stand around glowering and com-plaining while she worked on her exhibit.

Maud watched him slouch out of the kitchen and into the bedroom, nettled by his parting words. *I guess they have their reasons.* What reasons? She picked up his bowl and spoon, washed them, and set them in the rack.

The Kawayas were TEB activists, especially Wolf.

She drained the sink and wrung out the dish cloth, draping it over the faucet to dry. She had been looking forward to the arts-and-crafts exhibition. She liked talking to people, especially about weaving. But Robert's words continued to trouble her, one more worry added to an already ample supply.

Would the Kawayas use the exhibition to make some kind of political statement?

She frowned and shook her head. She couldn't believe even the quick-tempered Wolf would do a thing like that. And even if, by the remotest chance, Wolf was planning a demonstration of more than blowguns, he wouldn't confide in a hotheaded seventeen-year-old boy.

It was much more likely that Robert wanted her to think he had access to TEB members' secrets because he was Lee's son. Or he was merely blowing off steam.

She wasn't going to think about it anymore.

As Maud Wildcat and her grandson were loading her car for the drive to Park Hill, Tom Battle was getting out of his car at the Cherokee National Museum. He'd dropped by, hoping to find Daye there. He hadn't wanted to phone her house because he knew that if she wasn't at the museum she'd be working. She didn't like being interrupted when she was painting.

He didn't see her car but went inside anyway. Nobody was there but the receptionist. He left the museum and strolled across a paved courtyard to the ancient village, *Tsa-La-Gi*, which was closed now until next summer. He sat down on a bench near three tall pillars, all that remained of the old Cherokee Female Seminary which had burned to the ground more than a hundred years ago.

He leaned back, enjoying the warmth of the dappled sunlight. The wooded grounds of the Cherokee Heritage Center were prettier now than at any other time of the year. He watched a brown squirrel scurry up the trunk and out on a limb of an elm tree. The movement dislodged golden leaves, which drifted to the ground like gilded ornaments.

And he thought about Daye. He had believed himself in love before, had even been engaged once, but he'd broken it off a month before the wedding date. Now he knew he hadn't really loved a woman before Daye. Not with this all-consuming passion that was the first thing he felt when he awoke and the last before sleeping. He would marry her in a heartbeat if she would agree. As yet she hadn't, but he was counting on her coming around to it in time. He knew her well enough now to realize that pressuring her wouldn't work. So he had stopped mentioning marriage.

He turned his thoughts away from Daye and allowed his mind to drift. Closing his eyes, he relaxed and let the somnolent peace wrap itself around him.

He was half asleep when an approaching car roused him, but he couldn't see it from where he was sitting. The car stopped at the museum. Thinking that it might be Daye, he walked back across the courtyard and around to the front of the museum. It wasn't Daye, though.

The car's trunk was open, and Regina Shell was bent over it with her back to him. The trunk was packed full of cardboard boxes, and Regina was wrestling with one of them.

Tom came up behind her. "Let me help you with that."

She gave a start and jerked upright, banging her head on the trunk lid. "Good Lord, you scared me!"

Tom saw the box sliding from her arms, but before he could grab it, she lost her grip and it fell, strewing its contents on the ground. Regina knelt to gather tools and rags and pieces of wood that spilled from the box. He bent down to help her. "I'm sorry, Regina."

As usual, Regina's copper-colored face was devoid of make-up. At the moment, it was pinched as she struggled to recover from the fright he'd given her. It made him feel like a blundering fool.

She took a breath. "It's okay. I didn't know anyone else was around."

"I came out looking for Daye, but she's not here. I was taking a few minutes to enjoy the scenery before going back to town, and I heard your car."

She grabbed the last stick of wood, threw it in the box, and slapped the cardboard flaps shut.

"I'll take that inside for you," Tom said.

"No, not this one. I was just moving it so I could get to the baskets." Still a little shaken, she took hold of the bumper to steady herself as she stood.

"I really did frighten you, didn't I?" Tom said regretfully. "I'm so sorry."

"Honestly, it's okay." She gave him a tight smile. "I didn't have my mind on what I was doing. I was miles away—thinking about something else, a family problem. And all of a sudden, there you were right behind me."

He wondered if the family problem involved her brother, but he didn't know Regina well enough to ask. He was more familiar with Regina's work than with the woman herself. Her handwoven baskets were sold in Cherokee gift shops and in Native American art galleries around the country.

"Do you want all the rest of these inside?" he asked, indicating the boxes in the trunk.

"Yes."

He lifted one and she ran ahead of him to open the door of the museum, but she didn't follow him inside. He entered the reception area. On his right, artwork and books for sale were arranged on display counters and shelves. The receptionist's desk, an angled, waist-high counter, was on the left. Brenda Farley, the young Cherokee woman behind the desk, was eating a sandwich. "I thought you'd left, Tom," she greeted him.

"I intend to, as soon as I deliver some baskets for Regina Shell."

"You caught me having lunch. I'm the only one here right now, so I can't leave the desk."

"Where should I put these?"

"In there." The receptionist pointed at the open doorway leading into the exhibit area. "Anywhere. Regina can put them where she wants them when she gets here."

"She's right behind me," Tom said. He left the box in the exhibit area and went back outside. Regina had set the remaining boxes of baskets on the ground, returned the one she'd dropped to the trunk, and closed it. A red-and-blue fringed shawl was draped over her arm. As Tom came out of the museum, she bent and picked up a box.

"Looks like you'll be the first exhibitor to get set up," he said as he hefted another box and followed her into the museum.

The receptionist looked up and smiled. "Hi, Regina."

"Hello, Brenda. How are you?"

"Bored." Brenda tossed a paper napkin and plastic sandwich bag into the wastebasket. "I've been here alone all morning, and only three people have come through the museum."

"Enjoy it while you can," Tom advised. "Starting Saturday, you'll have plenty of business for a while."

In the exhibit area, Regina walked around with her thumbs hooked through the two front belt loops of her jeans, trying to decide where to display her baskets. A loom—Tom thought it probably belonged to Maud Wildcat—sat in one corner, a half-finished rug on it. Permanent exhibits behind glass lined both sides of the long room. Some of Daye's paintings covered the white spaces between the glass cases. She had hung them earlier in the week.

Several folding tables were stacked against a wall. Movable partitions created other exhibit "rooms" beyond the one where they stood. "Oh, well," Regina said. "I'll be selfish and take the center spot in front of the door."

"First come, first choice," Tom said. He put the box down and helped her unfold one of the tables and place it where she wanted it. She spread the shawl over it and began unpacking the baskets. The weaving was exquisite. Regina had turned a craft into an art form. Probably the best basket maker in the state, she managed to support herself from the sale of her handiwork, although it couldn't be easy.

Once, Tom had gone into the Cherokee Gift Shop, next door to the tribal office building, intending to buy a Regina Shell basket. He'd changed his mind when he saw the prices.

The baskets were made of cane, white oak, or honeysuckle, and only natural dyes were used. Judging from Regina's rough, stained hands and the wood and tools in the trunk of her car, she harvested the material herself. Her baskets were probably worth the price, but too rich for Tom's blood.

"I'll go get the rest," he said. When he came back, she was arranging some of the larger baskets on the floor around the table. He set the box down and went for another.

When he carried in the last box, she had stepped away from the table for a better view of the basket display.

"Looks great," Tom said, setting the box on the floor. "Here's the last one."

"I can't thank you enough."

"Glad to do it."

"Thanks, anyway."

He smiled. "It was the least I could do, after scaring the wits out of you. How's your head?"

She rubbed her crown where she'd bumped it when he startled her. "A little sore, but nothing serious." She smoothed her long hair back and refastened the barrette at the nape of her neck. "If Daye comes in, I'll tell her you were here looking for her." She seemed to want him to leave so that she could concentrate on her exhibit.

He nodded. "Thanks. I guess I'll see you at the reception tonight."

She had turned away. "Probably." The prospect didn't seem to cheer her. He suspected she was more comfortable roaming the woods, gathering the raw materials for her baskets, than in social situations. Maybe the family problem she'd mentioned was still bearing on her mind too.

"You sure you're okay?"

She looked around at him as though surprised to find him still there. "Oh, yes."

He said good-bye to Brenda at the reception desk and drove back to Tahlequah. He'd started a week's vacation today and felt at loose ends. Since Daye was unavailable, he might as well put in a few hours on the brief he'd been working on at home.

# 3

Park Hill was once a real town, but it hadn't been worthy of the name for years. It had a post office, two or three churches, a few dozen houses, and the Cherokee Heritage Center, consisting of: a museum; an open-air amphitheater used during the summer months for the Trail of Tears drama; an ancient village where modern-day Cherokees portrayed the way their ancestors lived and dressed in 1700; and Adams Corner, a rural village typical of small settlements in Indian Territory at the turn of the twentieth century.

Friday afternoon, Molly Bearpaw locked her office in Tahlequah and drove to Park Hill to visit her grandmother, Eva Adair. Molly had grown up in Park Hill, except for her high-school years when Eva had rented out the house and moved to Tahlequah. Eva had returned to Park Hill when Molly moved into a dorm on the NSU campus.

Although Molly hadn't lived there since she was fourteen, it still felt as though she were coming home. For the last two years, after three years in Tulsa, she had lived in Tahlequah, in a garage apartment behind the home of retired university professor Conrad Swope.

She was fond of her landlord, and on occasion he took a paternal interest in her, particularly when it came to men. When she wasn't dating anyone—which had been most of the time since she'd moved into Conrad's garage apartment—he worried that she was too much alone, frittering away her youth without having any fun. Recently she'd been seeing D. J. Kennedy, a Cherokee County sheriff's deputy, and Conrad approved.

Molly hadn't seen much of Conrad the last few days, though. Since his retirement from her alma mater, Northeastern Oklahoma State University, he occasionally took freelance research jobs. Recently he'd been gathering information for a writer who planned a book on early oil-boom towns. But he had finished that job, he'd told her, and he planned to spend Saturday morning at the Cherokee Arts and Crafts Exhibition. One of Conrad's many hobbies was collecting books on the Cherokees.

Conrad took up hobbies, abandoning most of them when the first flush of interest waned, but Cherokee history and culture was a perennial passion.

"Florina has been dropping hints that she wants to ride out with me," he'd added, looking as though he'd swallowed something that tasted bad. "I made the mistake of mentioning to her that I was going." The widowed Florina Fenston was Conrad's next-door neighbor. She'd taken a proprietary interest in Conrad since his wife died. "When will I learn to keep my mouth shut?"

"You?" Molly chuckled. "Maybe it was a Freudian slip."

Conrad looked at her disgustedly. "Hah."

"I saw Florina bringing you something on a plate yesterday," Molly informed him. Florina had once told Molly that the way to a man's heart was still through his stomach, no matter what those women's libbers said.

"Half of a fresh-baked cake," Conrad said. "She said it would get stale before she could eat it all. Could I say no?"

"Of course not."

His blue eyes twinkled. "I have to admit, nobody can match Florina's cakes. This one's chocolate."

Molly grinned. "Your favorite. How sweet of Florina."

Conrad had looked gloomy then and brushed that aside with a wave of his hand.

Florina wasn't the only neighborhood widow who carried food to Conrad. Molly didn't think he disliked the attention as much as he let on.

"So, you're taking Florina to the exhibit?" Molly had asked.

He'd shaken his head. "If I do, she'll have it all over town that we had a date. No, thank you. I'll think of some excuse."

In Park Hill, Molly parked in front of her grandmother's two-story white house. It sat in a big yard shaded by venerable oak and hackberry trees, with a wide front porch and a line of sandstones from the road to the steps. Eva was walking across the backyard toward the woods, carrying a shovel.

Molly jumped out and called, "Grandmother!" Eva turned around and her wrinkled brown face broke into a wide smile when she saw Molly loping across the yard.

"You almost missed me," Eva said as they embraced. "I'm so glad you didn't." She was dressed in faded overalls, an old denim jacket, and thick-soled boots that laced up her ankles. "Seems like a coon's age since I saw you."

Eva always said that. "It's only been a few days, Grand-mother."

"Seems longer." From her height of barely five feet, Eva peered up into Molly's face. "You look tired. Are you getting enough rest?"

Eva always said that too. "Plenty. Where are you off to?"

"Going to dig some sassafras roots. My supply is getting low and I want to stock up before cold weather." She scanned

Molly's sweater, jeans, and Nikes. "Come with me. There's a grove of saplings not far into the woods."

Eva boiled the roots to make tea, which she used to doctor coughs and to wash down aspirin when she had a fever. As a child, Molly had been liberally dosed with the not-unpleasant-tasting tea at the first sign of a cough. Now she used over-the-counter cough syrups, which didn't work noticeably better than sassafras teas.

Molly took the shovel and they walked into the woods among cedar trees and scrub oak. Within five minutes they reached the sassafras trees, several tall ones surrounded by new saplings. Some of their gold leaves had already fallen, cushioning the ground around the trunks. It felt to Molly as though she were walking on a thin mattress.

Molly turned over a few shovelfuls of dirt, exposing the roots of two saplings. Eva pulled a knife and a plastic grocery bag from her pocket and began to hack off sections of root and drop them into the bag.

"I can do that," Molly offered.

"Not as fast as I can," Eva told her. "I've had more practice."

Molly dropped the shovel and sat on fallen leaves, drawing her knees up. The woods had a pleasantly musty smell, the scent of autumn. "It's so beautiful here in the fall," she said.

Eva shook dirt off a root ball. "Used to be my favorite time of the year," she said. "But the older I get, the more I prefer spring."

In the springs of her childhood, Molly had roamed all over these woods and nearby meadows. In spring, the hills were trapuntoed quilts of green stitched with redbuds and white-blossomed wild plum trees, and the lushly blanketed meadows were spangled with white wind flowers and buttercups and deep orange wildflowers that Eva had always called Indian paintbrush. Beautiful but, in northeast Oklahoma, unhappily brief.

"Fall's a sad time," Eva said. "You don't notice that when you're young." She dropped a handful of roots into her bag and stared off into the trees. "You don't dread winter like old folks do. The days get short and dreary. The world is dark too much of the time. And the cold gets in old bones. I swear the last few years my feet get cold in December and don't warm up till April."

Molly shivered. She didn't like being reminded that Eva was seventy-five years old. She could not imagine an existence without the woman who had anchored her life in love and security since she was a small child. Without Eva she would be cast adrift.

"Are you feeling all right, Grandmother?"

Eva looked around at her sharply. "Feeling fine. Just haven't been sleeping too well lately. That's another thing that happens to you when you get old. You wake up in the middle of the night and the God-awfullest things run through your mind."

"What things?"

"Confusion, mostly. Things that don't hang together, like half dreams."

Molly wondered if this was a sign of hardening of the arteries. Or just a case of the blues. Eva did seem to be down in the dumps.

"Take last night," Eva said as she pocketed the sack of roots. She picked up the shovel and grasped the handle, leaning on it. "I dreamed about you—you were running away from something, that's all I remember. Later I woke up with pictures in my head of the stomp dances Mama and Papa used to take me to when I was a child. People dancing. Fires. Reminded me of the time I saw a young man drop dead in the middle of a dance. Fell like a rock and stopped breathing. I don't remember ever hearing what killed him." She sighed and dropped the knife into her pocket, frowning a little. "Hadn't thought of that in years. Now why would I wake up thinking about it, all of a sudden? Like to never got back to sleep again."

Molly stood up. "You sound depressed, Grandmother. It's not like you."

Eva handed her the shovel. "It's winter coming on that has me down. It's coming early this year. We'll have a hard freeze before Thanksgiving, mark my words." She shrugged. "I'll get over this gloomy spell. As you say, it's not my nature to mope around like dead flies are falling off me. Now, let's go to the house and I'll fix us some hot cider."

She held on to Molly's arm and they walked back in companionable silence. As they reached the back steps, Molly said, "Grandmother, why don't you think about selling this place and moving in with me. I could rent a house in Tahlequah."

"Now, don't you start that again," Eva said in the voice she'd used for reprimands when Molly was a child. "I'll be right here until they carry me out feet first."

Molly stared at her grandmother's lined face, wondering if Eva's oblique reference to her own death was meant as a gentle reminder that she wasn't afraid of it and didn't want Molly to be. But Molly was.

Before she left, Eva went to her bedroom and returned with something, which she thrust into Molly's hand. "You keep this. Carry it with you."

"What is it?"

"*Yu:gwila'*, Venus's-flytrap root."

Some of the older Cherokees put great store by Venus's-flytrap root as a good-luck charm, but Molly hadn't known Eva was among them. It appeared that Molly's appearance in Eva's dream still troubled her.

"I don't want to take this," Molly said. She held out the dried piece of root, but Eva shook her head.

"Don't argue, girl. I'll feel better if you keep it."

Molly wondered suddenly if Eva knew something she wasn't telling. People contemplating their own death sometimes gave away prized possessions. But she pocketed the root and said nothing.

Molly remembered Eva's gift that evening as she again drove to Park Hill through a purple dusk. She'd put the root in her kitchen cabinet and forgotten about it until then. She'd retrieve it later and put it in her car.

She tried to shake off the apprehension that something was wrong with her grandmother. Eva was in good health for a woman of her advanced years, Molly assured herself, and she had good genes. Eva's parents had lived into their nineties.

Molly was on the way to the reception at the museum, but perhaps she'd look in on Eva again before driving back to Tahlequah.

Night was blotting out the plum-colored sky as Molly made a left off Highway 62 on Willis Road. Rural mailboxes stood like sentries along both sides of the two-lane country blacktop. A mile farther along, she made another left off Willis Road and followed a narrow graveled lane that wound through the wooded grounds of the Heritage Center and ended at the museum. Thirty or forty cars were parked near the building.

4

Regina Shell, a friend since high-school days, was getting out of her car as Molly drove up. She and Molly had been in the same graduating class at Tahlequah High. Regina spotted Molly's Civic and walked over.

"I hoped you'd come," Regina said. Wearing a red-silk dress and high-heeled pumps, she looked about as comfortable as a field hand in tails. It was one of a handful of times Molly had seen Regina dressed up, in all the years she'd known her.

"I'm expected to put in an appearance," Molly said.

Regina nodded. "I keep forgetting you work for the tribe now."

"I'd have come, anyway," Molly said. "I haven't seen you in a while." They embraced and Molly added, "You've been traveling lately, I hear."

"I took my baskets to Albuquerque and Santa Fe last month," Regina told her. "They were having arts-and-crafts shows in that whole area. Collectors everywhere. Lord, some of them have more money than brains. I mark everything up twenty percent when I go to Santa Fe."

Molly had visited Santa Fe for a week once. Except for that, she'd never been away from northeastern Oklahoma. "That's a beautiful part of the country."

"Yes, but after a few days I start feeling antsy. I get lonely for Oklahoma trees and lakes. I would never want to live out there. Half the population are artists and craftsmen. Too much competition."

"Not for you," Molly said. Regina shrugged modestly and Molly asked, "New dress?"

Regina smoothed the silk fabric over her lean hips. "Yeah. I didn't have anything decent for tonight."

"Very pretty."

Regina eyed Molly's cotton blouse and skirt. "Next to you, I'm horribly overdressed. Makes me feel like I'm going to a costume party."

"You know me." Clothes were about as much of a priority for Molly as for Regina.

"Where's D.J.?" Regina asked. Molly and D. J. Kennedy had been seeing each other on a fairly regular basis since the end of summer. As often as Molly would allow, anyway. After her one serious relationship with a man had ended so painfully, she was leery of getting too deeply involved again.

"Working. He had to cover for another deputy who called in sick."

"Too bad," Regina commiserated. "You'll have to make do with me." One corner of her mouth lifted wryly. "I know it's not the same." She glanced toward the museum. "I hope I'm not supposed to stay long. You know how I hate these little tea parties. I was really tempted not to come at all."

"That would've been tacky," Molly told her. The reception was to honor the artists and craftsmen who were taking part in the exhibition which opened the next day. The other guests would be tribal employees and tribal council members, getting a pre-opening look at the exhibits. All except Principal

Chief Wilma Mankiller, who was speaking at a Native American symposium in Chicago this weekend. Next week she was scheduled to receive an award in Washington, recognizing her as a positive role model for Native American women.

"I thought of that," Regina admitted. "It's the only reason I'm here."

"I have to leave early too," Molly said. "I want to drop by Grandmother's house before I go home."

As they neared the lighted museum, Molly got a good look at Regina's face for the first time. It was drawn, her eyes dull. This was more than a dislike for parties. "Hey." Molly stopped and pulled Regina around to face her. "What's wrong?"

Regina's shoulders sagged. She sighed and looked away. "Is it that obvious?"

"Are you sick?" Molly asked.

Regina's eyes settled on Molly and she nodded heavily. "Yeah, I'm sick. In here." She laid a palm over her heart. "I brought Steven home this week. He was in Eastern State again. Four months this time."

"Oh, Regina, I'm sorry." Regina's twin brother was a paranoid schizophrenic, diagnosed when they were eighteen. In the ten years since, he'd been in and out of the state mental hospital in Vinita half-a-dozen times. Molly assumed that all twins were close, but Regina and Steven were like two parts of the same person. Growing up, they'd been practically inseparable. Even more so after their father died when they were thirteen. Instinctively, they'd turned to each other for comfort, and Molly had often wondered who had comforted their mother. For a while there, the twins had shut out everybody else.

During their last year in high school, Steven, always more reserved than Regina, began to withdraw even from his twin. Their mother had said it was a phase, that they were growing up and it was natural for Steven to want his privacy. But Regina had been frantic, sensing it was more than that, trying to find out what was wrong and fix it, trying to make things be the way they'd always been.

Gradually even their mother had realized that Steven's problem was more serious than a desire for privacy. He began to wander through the house at night, talking, answering voices issuing from the cradled phone or from the TV set that was turned off, voices that no one else could hear. Many of those nights, Regina had walked with him, talked to him, trying to hang on to him and keep him from going deeper into the twisted maze of his mind. But, eventually, Steven slipped away from her. When their mother died a couple of years ago, it had left the burden of Steven's care completely on Regina's shoulders.

"Is he staying with you?" Molly asked.

Regina nodded. "I want him there where I can keep an eye on him. He can't live alone, anyway, because he can't hold a job."

"How is he?" Molly asked.

Regina's lips trembled. She covered her face and began to cry. Molly gave her a hug. She couldn't think of anything to say that didn't sound trite.

"Every time he comes out of the hospital, he seems worse than the last time," Regina choked out. "He won't talk to me. He just sits and stares at nothing. And he gets this silly grin on his face for no reason. They turn him into a zombie with those drugs."

"He'll get better," Molly said, mouthing the words with no real confidence. Usually by the time Steven was forced into the hospital, he was raving. He had been off his medication awhile and was driven to madness by delusions. The psychiatrists dealt with it by giving him massive doses of antipsychotic drugs and tranquilizers. Then they reduced the dosages gradually until they judged they'd reached maintenance level. At that point, Steven was released and cautioned to stay on his medication. Which he would do for a while, until he decided he didn't need the medicine any longer. Then another downward spiral in his illness would begin. The streets of cities were full of people like Steven, homeless because they weren't fortunate enough to have somebody like Regina to look after them.

Regina dropped her hands and lifted her head. Tears streaked her face. "The drugs stop the delusions, but they take away whatever's left of the old Steven too. It's like he's sleepwalking."

"I know," Molly murmured, although she didn't really. She hadn't seen a lot of Steven since the onset of his illness. She found a tissue in her purse and handed it to Regina.

Regina wiped her eyes and blew her nose. "It's weird," she said, "but when he's off his medication, even when he's wildly delusional, I still get an occasional glimmer of my brother, the way he used to be."

"Maybe they can reduce the medication even more, in time," Molly said.

"Yeah, right." Regina wadded the tissue and clenched it in her fist. "I hate that hospital!" she said with sudden vehemence. "It's nothing but a warehouse. I'd as soon see Steven in jail."

"No, you wouldn't."

A hoot owl called from the woods, a lonely sound, and Regina turned to stare mournfully into the dark trees. Then she straightened her dress and said, "You're right, jail would kill him. Can I borrow your lipstick?" She made a couple of inexpert passes at her mouth and handed the tube back. "How do I look?"

Worn out, Molly thought. "Perfect."

Regina smiled feebly. "You never could lie worth a damn, Molly." She tilted her head and gazed up at the stars for a moment. Perhaps wishing she could escape to one of them. The owl hooted again, and she drew air into her lungs and let it out slowly. "Remember that old man who lived near your grandmother when we were kids?" she asked. "We were all half afraid of him."

"You mean Sedge Fourkiller?" Fourkiller had been dead for years.

"Yeah. The other kids said he was a witch."

"I heard that too," Molly said.

"Steven and I used to follow him," Regina told her, "hoping we'd catch him changing himself into an owl or maybe a deer. That always seemed like a neat trick to have at your disposal."

Inexplicably, Molly felt chilled, and the light from the museum was warm and inviting.

"Well—" Regina took Molly's arm. "Let's get this over with."

It occurred to Molly that taking care of Steven must have virtually destroyed Regina's private life. She hadn't had a romantic relationship for a long time, as far as Molly knew. How could she help resenting Steven sometimes?

Regina would be all right, Molly assured herself. She was at a low point now, but, on the whole, Steven's illness seemed to have made her stronger, as if she'd absorbed the sanity he'd lost. She was tall, lanky, and loose-limbed, and she had a way of walking that exuded confidence, even in the unaccustomed high heels. She was a woman who coped and did whatever had to be done. It was rare for her to break down. But Steven's illness was grinding away at her, and it wasn't going to go away. Regina would have to deal with that, possibly for the rest of her life.

## 5

When Molly and Regina stepped into the museum, they were greeted by one of the council members and directed to the refreshment table. En route, a woman stopped Regina to ask when she would next be teaching a basket-weaving class. Molly listened for a minute. She had often thought of taking craft classes herself. The woman was asking Regina about various weaves. When it got too technical for Molly to follow, she said she'd see Regina later and headed toward the refreshments. Her progress was slow because she knew most of the guests and she kept stopping to say hello.

The tribe did not serve alcoholic beverages at its functions. Molly helped herself to fruit punch and a chocolate-chip cookie, which she ate standing beside the table while she chatted with Maud Wildcat, another of the exhibitors.

Maud's braided black hair was shot through with silver. Molly had known Maud most of her life, but she hadn't noticed before how gray Maud was getting. It surprised Molly how much she'd aged in the past year. She must be well into her sixties now, Molly thought.

"I'd like to learn finger weaving," Molly told her. "Do you ever take students?"

"Not anymore, but I can recommend somebody. Let me think about it."

"I'll check with you after the exhibition."

"Good. Now I'd better go to my table."

Disposing of her cup and paper napkin, Molly followed Maud into the exhibit area where guests were examining the arts and crafts. Beyond the tables, at the back of the room, several people were gathered around an exhibit case on the wall.

Herb Cochran, who worked in the tribal offices, stood near the group. He saw Molly and motioned her over. Herb was in his late forties, the father of six children. His avocation was cooking and he prepared many of his family's meals. Lately he'd discovered Cajun dishes. Unfortunately, he liked to eat his own cooking too much, and his girth had increased steadily since Molly had known him. His paunch hung out over his brown trousers and hid his belt, his white shirt gaping open between the buttons, exposing the ribbing of a white undershirt.

Molly eyed the paunch. "You'll have to buy a new wardrobe if you don't watch it, Herb."

He patted his stomach. "That's what I'm doing, getting it out there where I can watch it."

Molly chuckled. "You need a new hobby. Cooking is detrimental to your health."

"Yeah, well, all the great chefs are big," he said. "It's an occupational hazard." His gaze wandered over the milling guests. "Have you been out to the complex today?"

"No," Molly replied.

He looked over his shoulder, as though to see who stood nearby. He waved at a man who was passing. "Hey, Dale.

How's it going?" He swung back to Molly. "Then you haven't seen our new sign."

"What sign?" Molly asked, thinking that Herb, who liked jokes, was setting her up for a punch line.

He eyed her suspiciously and hitched up his sagging trousers. "You really haven't heard?"

"I've been home all day. Haven't talked to anybody but my landlord."

He pulled Molly farther away from the group and lowered his voice. "Somebody spray-painted the south side of the office building with big black letters."

"You mean obscenities?"

He smiled. "Some people might think so."

"What exactly does it say?"

" 'Property of True Echota Band. Trespassers Beware!' "

"You're kidding!"

"Would I kid you, Molly?" She lifted a brow. "Okay, scratch the question. But I'm not kidding this time."

"What did they hope to gain by that?"

"They? You mean the TEB?"

Molly nodded.

"It wasn't the TEB," Herb said. "One of their council members called the complex today and swore they had no prior knowledge. Denied all responsibility."

"Who did it then?"

"A loose cannon." He winked, his glance flicking to one of the exhibit tables behind Molly. "I'll bet we could come up with a shortlist of likely suspects." Molly turned her head and followed his gaze to the blowguns-and-darts exhibit. Josiah Kawaya lifted a long, hollowed-out cane stalk to his mouth and blew, demonstrating the Cherokee blowgun used, in ancient times, to down small game. Josiah's son, Wolf, was whittling a dart from a piece of wood. TEB members, the Kawayas were among those who were convinced the band had a historical and legal right to govern the entire tribe, which included control of tribal land and buildings.

Herb was right. The shortlist would definitely include the Kawayas.

"The council decided to cover the letters with paint the color of the brick until they can have the wall sandblasted," Herb said. "They'll get somebody on it Monday. Hey, you're an investigator. Find out who did it." Molly was employed by the tribe as an investigator for the Native American Advocacy League, officially to inquire into alleged violations of the civil rights of tribal members. In practice, the official guidelines were broadly interpreted. She'd undertaken cases based on some pretty strange requests, including witnessing an autopsy and, subsequently, investigating a murder.

"Sure. I'll disguise myself and hang out in TEB smoke shops."

Herb laughed. "You can get trampled that way. The Oklahoma Tax Commission raided another one of those shops yesterday and confiscated all the tobacco products."

"I thought they could continue selling tax-exempt tobacco while they appealed the court's ruling," Molly said. The TEB smoke shops were on land owned or leased by the TEB, which they said fit the legal definition of tribal land, and made the shops exempt from state tax laws. One judge had ruled against them, but they were appealing.

"The judge refused to block the commission raids until the band posts bond in the amount of taxes the state says it owes."

"How much is that?"

"A bunch. State tax on one carton of cigarettes is more than two dollars."

"I don't think they can come up with that kind of money," Molly said. "Especially if they can't sell tobacco." The smoke shops provided a substantial portion of the band's operating income. "Won't they have to shut the shops down?"

"Your guess is as good as mine." Herb sucked in his gut so he could find his beaded belt and loosen it a notch. "Hey, have you heard the one about the white man who lived next door to an old Cherokee?" He didn't wait for Molly's reply. "One day the white man said to the Cherokee, 'It's so dry. When do you think it will rain?' The Cherokee said, 'It'll rain today because I heard a hoot owl,' which made the white man think the Cherokee was very wise. A few days later, the white man met the Cherokee again and asked him why it hadn't rained when he said it would. The Cherokee said, 'The hoot owl said it was going to rain, and when he says it's going to rain, it usually does. But I guess this one was too young to know anything yet.' "

Molly laughed, even though she'd heard the story before. It was one of Herb's favorites, and he laughed even harder than Molly. He got such a kick out of telling it that she could never bring herself to stop him when he got started.

The exhibit that had drawn the small crowd was still hidden from Molly's view by people's heads. "What's the attraction?" she asked, waving her arm toward the crowd.

"The wampums," Herb said. "The Nighthawk Keetoowahs let the museum display them during the exhibition." Molly had a vague recollection of reading something about that in the tribal newspaper. "Have you ever seen them?" Herb asked.

"No." Few people outside the Nighthawks had. Their leader had had possession of the ancient wampum belts for many years. He brought them out only on ceremonial occasions. To Molly's knowledge, they'd never been on public display before.

"They just put 'em up today," Herb said.

The Nighthawk Keetoowahs were one of several organizations presently using the Keetoowah name, which, like Echota, came from the name of an ancient tribal town, *Kituwah*. It was very confusing to outsiders, who sometimes thought they were dealing with one group, only to learn they were dealing with another.

Two of the organizations, the Nighthawk Keetoowahs, keepers of the wampums, and the Keetoowah Society, were grass-roots movements organized to preserve the old cultural, spiritual, and traditional beliefs of the Cherokee people.

"Come on," Herb said. "Let's see if we can get a look."

Leading the way, he squeezed through the crowd with Molly following in his wake. The seven beaded wampums behind the glass were dim with age and frayed in places. Most of the beads used in the largest belt and four of the smaller belts had been white when they were new and had grayed with time. On the white belts were sacred symbols, worked with darker beads, which Molly could not interpret—stick figures, a series of X's, and short, straight lines, and one that looked like the letter W turned upside down.

Molly leaned closer and touched the glass. Herb winced, and she looked at him questioningly. "What?"

He stuffed his hands into his trouser pockets. "My grand-dad used to say it was dangerous to touch the wampums."

"I didn't touch them," Molly pointed out. "I touched the glass."

"I wouldn't do it. Maybe it's silly, but I feel kind of funny about them being on public display."

Molly turned back to the wampums. "Do you know what the symbols mean?"

"Nobody does for sure," Herb told her. "Back in the early 1900s when old Redbird Smith first brought them to a Nighthawk meeting, the oldest people there didn't know what they meant." Redbird Smith had led the secret society early in the century and had revitalized the movement to preserve the old ways. "Redbird reconstructed the interpretation as best he could from what he learned about the old ways from medicine prayers and things told to him by the older members of the tribe. The white beading represents the White Path."

"The way of peace," Molly murmured. Two of the smaller belts were worked with dark-red beads. One showed a wavy line of lighter beads, perhaps representing smoke. In the center of the other were what appeared to be three white crosses.

"Those crosses almost look like Christian symbols," Molly observed.

"Can't be, though," Herb said. "These things were made before the Cherokees had contact with Christian missionaries."

That was debatable. Contemporary Cherokees had different ideas as to the origin of the wampum belts. Many thought they were made by ancient Keetoowahs, before that movement had split into factions, to pass their beliefs along to succeeding generations. Another prevalent opinion was that these were the wampums presented to the tribe by the Iroquois to seal a peace treaty made in the 1760s between the two tribes.

Principal Chief John Ross had carried these wampums with him over the Trail of Tears to Indian Territory. Sometime between the removal of the tribe to the west and the turn of the twentieth century, the Nighthawks had come into possession of them.

Everyone agreed on one thing, however. The wampums were at least two hundred and thirty years old and possibly much older. How many long-dead principal chiefs had held the wampums in their hands? Molly wondered. Standing there, she felt a mystical connection to generations of her people. If only it were possible to pierce the murkiness of time and know the original meaning of the symbols.

She became aware that she was being squashed between a tall woman and a young man, who were trying to get closer to the wampums. "I'm going to say hello to the exhibitors," she told Herb, "and let somebody else have my place."

He nodded, still engrossed in the wampums. Molly squeezed back through the crowd. She saw Regina standing before one of the paintings on display, talking to the artist, Daye Hummingbird, and Tom Battle. The fourth person in the little group was Lily Roach, the museum director and president of the Cherokee Historical Society, whose members volunteered at the museum. Tom was talking about having unwittingly frightened Regina earlier in the day.

"She was unloading her trunk and didn't hear me come up behind her until I spoke," he was saying. "I made her drop a box and spill her tools and supplies all over the parking lot."

"And bang my head on the trunk lid," Regina put in. "Don't forget that."

"I never saw anybody jump so high in my life," Tom said.

"I thought he was a night walker," Regina joked, and the others laughed. Regina seemed to have witches on her mind tonight.

And Lily's laugh sounded a bit forced, Molly thought. Although the Cherokees were among the most assimilated of Native Americans, belief in night walkers, Cherokee witches who could change themselves into animals or birds at will, still existed in Cherokee County.

Molly joined the group and said hello all around.

"I wondered where you'd run off to," Regina greeted her.

"I was looking at the wampums." Molly turned to glance toward the exhibit. "Back there where's the crowd's gathered."

Regina stared at the crowd blankly. "You mean the ancient wampum belts?" Molly nodded and Regina turned to Lily, a small, energetic woman in her mid-fifties. "How did the museum manage to get them?"

"We only have them on loan for a week," Lily told her. "Then they go back to the Nighthawks. There was an announcement in the *Cherokee Advocate*."

"I haven't read the *Advocate* much lately," Regina said. "It's too depressing, reading about all the lawsuits."

"The Tahlequah paper ran an article yesterday about a decision in one of those lawsuits," Lily said, glancing at Tom. "It mentioned your name, Tom."

Tom Battle admitted that he had represented the tribe in the suit and added, "The judge ruled that the Cherokee Nation does indeed exist and has jurisdiction over the tribe."

"Another defeat for the TEB," Regina murmured.

Tom nodded. "I keep hoping they'll run out of claims to base legal actions on."

Something flared briefly in Lily's dark eyes, reminding Molly that Lily and her husband were band members. "Don't count on it," Lily said curtly.

"That decision may be what's behind the sign somebody painted on the tribal office building," Daye put in. "Have you all heard about it?"

Everybody had. "Don't blame the TEB for that," Lily said a bit combatively. "The council denies any knowledge of it, though they feel very strongly that they've been unjustly excluded from tribal government."

Molly hoped the discussion wouldn't deteriorate into an argument. "Both sides feel strongly," she said placatingly. "That's why we can't heal the division in the tribe."

"Tribal factions have existed for hundreds of years," Lily observed sadly. "Forever, I sometimes think."

"True," Tom agreed. "I wonder what we'd fight about if the conflict between the Nation and the TEB were resolved to everyone's satisfaction."

"That," Regina said, "would be a miracle."

Suddenly the conversation seemed to be making Daye Hummingbird uncomfortable.

"You're right," Lily said, "and if the miracle happened we'd find something else to disagree about." She made a face. "This conversation is making me sad. Let's talk about something else."

"Yes, let's," Daye said fervently, glancing over Molly's shoulder and away quickly. Molly turned around and realized why Daye was so uneasy. Wolf Kawaya stood alone a few feet away, looking mutinous. Clearly, he had overheard the conversation.

"The band will never give up their rightful claims, Battle," Wolf snapped.

Tom, who had seemed unaware of Wolf's presence before he spoke, studied him speculatively. "Don't you mean the band's leaders?" he asked. "Some of my best friends are TEB members, and I don't think you speak for the majority of the band."

Daye tugged on Tom's arm. "Don't argue with him, Tom," she pleaded. "Come on. Let's go get some punch."

"You don't know a damned thing about it!" Wolf's voice had risen, drawing the attention of other guests. "You're so white your blood's not even red."

"Come *on*, Tom," Daye hissed, tugging frantically on Tom's arm.

"What's it like, screwing a white man, Daye?" Wolf demanded.

Daye looked as if Wolf had slapped her across the face. She swallowed hard and glanced from Regina to Lily to Molly, her expression pleading sympathy. "I can't believe this," she whispered. "I didn't think he'd make a scene in public. He'll never stop tormenting me!" Tears welled up in her eyes and she dipped her head and hurried away.

Tom went after her, leaving Wolf standing there, his hands clenched, his shoulders bunched up around his neck. For an instant, Wolf seemed frozen in the center of the room and all around heads were turned in his direction, as if they were all part of a dramatic photograph. Then, Wolf cursed and brushed rudely past several people en route to his exhibit table, from where his father had watched the interchange with hard, narrowed eyes.

There was a tense silence. "Poor Daye," Regina murmured finally. "That man is crazy."

"He can't seem to accept that he's lost Daye," Lily said, looking unhappy. "I feel sorry for him, but if he causes any more trouble, we'll have to ask him to leave." As director of the museum, she would get the job of telling Wolf Kawaya that he was no longer welcome. Not a pleasant prospect. "Well—" It was a moment before Lily added briskly, "Molly, I've scheduled you to be here tomorrow from nine to one."

Josiah Kawaya had taken his son aside and was talking to him earnestly. Molly transferred her attention from them to Lily. "Pardon?"

"You signed up to help during the exhibition," Lily reminded her. Molly was a member of the historical society, but it had been so long since Lily had asked for volunteers to help at the museum during the exhibition that she'd forgotten about it. "I know you're busy during the week," Lily was saying, "so I thought Saturday..."

Molly scanned her memory and could recall nothing that she had to do the next morning. "Saturday's fine." D.J. was coming over tomorrow, but not until later in the afternoon. He was cooking Mexican. D.J. was a better cook than Molly, or possibly it was only that he enjoyed it more. She had promised to make dessert, but she'd be home by one-thirty, so there would be plenty of time.

"I'd better spend a while at my table before I leave," Regina said, but she made no move to go.

Molly's eyes skimmed the exhibits. Wolf Kawaya was now seated at his table, but he still looked thunderous. Daye and Tom were nowhere to be seen. They must be in the reception room at the refreshment table. Molly thought it would be a good idea if they left the museum and gave Wolf time to cool off.

Wolf was talking to a guest now, answering questions about the blowguns and darts. The next week would be tense for everybody at the museum, especially if Wolf didn't stay away from Tom and Daye. Molly hoped his father would keep him in line.

"A lot of people seem to be looking your baskets over, Regina," Molly said. "You'll probably sell most of them before the week's out."

"I hope so. Steven gets bored and eats. My grocery bill has tripled since he moved in. Speaking of which, I'd better go push my wares."

"Say hello to Steven for me."

"I will."

"And try not to worry too much."

"Sure. See you later, Molly."

Regina went to her table, which was next to Maud Wildcat's. Maud had turned half around in her chair and was eyeing the circle of people around the wampum belts.

As Molly watched, Maud closed her eyes and seemed to be trying to calm the noticeable rise and fall of her breasts. She pressed a hand against her brow and her lips moved, as if she were arguing with herself. When she opened her eyes, she looked frightened.

Maud hadn't known the wampum belts were on display until she'd arrived at the reception. They had not been there that afternoon when she brought her things in. In fact, she hadn't believed it when she was told. Not until she'd seen them with her own eyes.

Knowing that the wampums were there, behind her, made her so nervous that her scalp prickled and she kept looking compulsively over her shoulder. Right now she couldn't see the wampums for the people, but she felt their presence, like an ominous humming in the air.

Who had brought them to the museum? Probably the leader of the Nighthawk Keetoowahs, who knew how to handle them with reverence. But how many others had touched them in the process of transferring them to the glass case? Handling them could be dangerous. The power of the wampums could turn against the one who touched them. Maud hadn't even felt safe standing close to the wampums, with the glass separating her from them.

If the power of the wampums had been stirred up by this unprecedented display, it could spill over on whoever was around. Where might it strike? Was it safe even to be in the same building with them? She wanted nothing so much as to be somewhere else. Anywhere else.

She thought briefly of bowing out of the exhibition before it started. But they probably couldn't get another weaver to take her place at the last minute. Lily Roach would never forgive her. Maud gave up the idea, knowing she couldn't be so irresponsible.

She turned back around, swallowed, and ran her tongue over her lips as she stared at her lap. Since she had to be in the museum for the next week, she wished the Nighthawk Keetoowahs would take the wampums out of there. She tried to think of a way to make them do it, but nothing occurred to her.

After a bit, she composed herself and looked up to answer a question about the yarns she used in her weaving.

# 6

The beautiful face was contorted by contempt, spittle forming at the corners of soft lips, hatred spewing out. *I don't want to see you, I don't want to talk to you! Stay away from me or I'll go to the police, I swear I will! I hate you! I wish you were dead! Dead.* Daye's face, Daye's words, in his dream.

Wolf came to, the whiskey bottle still clutched in the hand resting on his chest. His head throbbed. Lamplight hurt his eyes. He was still fully dressed, sprawled on the couch. He'd fallen asleep with his head propped against the couch arm at an unnatural angle. He moved it and pain shot down the back of his neck. He groaned and sat up slowly. He moved his head gingerly back and forth until finally the pain became bearable.

He looked at his watch, dismayed to find he had slept for three hours and that the bottle was empty. He could not remember draining it. How much had been in the bottle when he came home from the reception and started drinking? It hadn't been more than half full, maybe one-third full, but he shouldn't have had any on an empty stomach. He was drinking too much lately. Had to stop.

Three-quarters awake now, he longed for a taste to dull the throbbing in his head. Only a taste. But there wasn't even a can of beer in the house. Trying to shake away the dream, he stumbled to the bathroom and saw his own image in the mirror. He was a mess, his hair standing on end and in need of shampooing, his face cadaverous. He had forgotten to eat dinner again. He looked closer to forty-nine than the thirty-nine he was. He touched black chin stubble and was disheartened to see the unsteadiness of his hand. Was it any wonder she didn't want him? Young, beautiful Daye.

He splashed cool water over his face and combed his hair, swallowed four aspirin tablets. Back in the living room, he dialed Daye's number, immediately remembered the dream that had wakened him, Daye's face hideously transformed by rage, and hung up after a single ring. It was 3:00 A.M. What was wrong with him? Was he trying to alienate her even more?

He turned on additional lights and wandered through the rented house where he'd moved when Daye kicked him out of their home. She'd received the equity in that house in the divorce settlement, and he'd agreed to keep up the mortgage payments until her income increased to a certain level.

Or until she remarried.

He could not bear to think of Daye married to somebody else. Tom Battle's image floated in front of his eyes and he cursed. Battle was the cause of all his trouble. If he'd leave Daye alone, she'd come back to Wolf. He believed that. Had to, dammit, or why go on living?

*I don't think you speak for the band.*

Damn the man's calm arrogance! Rage welled up in Wolf. He grabbed a lamp and threw it against the wall. The ceramic base shattered. He stared at the pieces for an instant, then left it and went to the kitchen. Dirty dishes and carry-out food containers were scattered over the counter. Streaks and puddles of ketchup and mustard had hardened on the tabletop. His shoe soles stuck to the filthy linoleum with every step. Daye's house was spotless, she had always kept it so clean. He had loved going home to that house, and here he was, living like an animal. His whole life was falling apart. Had to get a grip on himself, clean up around here.

But he couldn't bring himself to start on it now. The place smelled of stale, greasy food. Craving fresh air, he went out the backdoor and stood in the weedy yard. The aspirin had taken the edge off the pain in his head. He walked around to the driveway and got in his car with the bent fender and used plastic foam cups littering the back floorboard. He rolled down the front windows and backed out of the driveway, engine roaring.

With no thought of where he was going, he drove with the cool night air whistling past his face. His life was hell and he didn't know how to make it better. Any life without Daye would be hell, and Daye would not have him back. She had even refused to keep his name.

Muskogee Avenue, Tahlequah's main street, was deserted. He drove it, doing sixty, all the way to the highway and then accelerated to eighty, ninety, ninety-five. If he missed a curve, hit an embankment, the pain would end permanently. He drove out Highway 51 for ten miles without meeting a single car, squealing around curves, the wind whining and shrieking through the car. How easy it would be to release the steering wheel and let the car go, but he couldn't do it. God took care of children and idiots.

He turned around and drove back to town, doing fifty-five. The car seemed to turn automatically down Daye's street. He killed the motor and coasted to a stop in front of her dark house.

Tom Battle's car was parked in the driveway.

Wolf's heart contracted and a vision of his wife in the arms of another man rose up to mock him. Only, now, she was his ex-wife. No, she wasn't *his* anything any longer. He wanted to break down the door or ram his car through the bedroom wall. Smash things.

Well-meaning advice from family and friends echoed through his mind.

*You keep bugging her, you'll make it worse.*

*Make yourself scarce. Give her a chance to see what it's like, not having you around.*

*When a woman's gone, man, she's gone.*

He knew he was making it worse, knew he should leave Daye alone. But he couldn't, and he couldn't let go of the thought that, if Tom Battle were out of the picture, he could win Daye back.

He had never hated anyone the way he hated Battle. If only he could snap his fingers and make him disappear. Forget her, his father said, find another woman.

Good advice, but there was no other woman for him.

Heavy with weariness, he let his head drop to the steering wheel. Pain clutched his neck as the muscles tightened into a knot that felt as big as a balled fist.

Sorrow was a lump in this throat. He felt utterly hopeless. Sobs racked him, the sound tortured and harsh in the silence.

## 7

From her kitchen window Saturday morning, Molly watched robins and blue jays fighting over the bird feeder in Conrad's backyard. The feeder hung from the yellowish-orange branch of a large red maple tree. The robins made repeated landings on the edge of the feeder, only to be driven off by the bullying blue jays. Molly was rooting for the robins, but they finally withdrew from the battle and flew away in search of a more hospitable feeding ground.

As Molly watched, Florina Fenston came out in her backyard and pretended to be checking her chrysanthemums. What she was really doing was watching Conrad's house. It wouldn't be easy for Conrad to get off to the exhibition without her. After a while, Florina went back inside to continue her watch from there.

After leaving the reception last night, Molly had driven to Eva's, but the house had been dark, so she hadn't stopped. She would run by there that afternoon, after her stint at the museum.

Four blue jays were perched on the feeder now. Watching the birds brought back old memories. Like Conrad, Eva fed the birds, even though the greedy blue jays and grackles ate most of the seed she scattered in her backyard. As a child, Molly had spent many cold winter hours naming and count-ing the birds in the backyard from her bedroom window.

Sitting at her kitchen table, she sipped on a second cup of fresh-brewed Dutch-chocolate coffee and ate an orange and toasted raisin bread soaked with melted butter. She'd baked the bread herself. Bread and coffee were the two foods that she took pride in making properly. Eva had spoiled her for store-bought bread, and making her own served a dual purpose. Kneading bread dough was a great tension reliever.

As for coffee, she was nearly fanatic about making it right. Her mornings always started with two or three cups of coffee, fresh-ground and brewed in her Krups. She kept the beans in the freezer and ground only enough for three or four cups at a time. Gourmet coffees, purchased in specialty shops in Tulsa or Muskogee, were one of the few luxuries she indulged in.

Her apartment, one room and a bath over Conrad Swope's garage, was certainly not luxurious, but the modest rent fit her budget. The kitchen consisted of an oak table and chairs and one wall of cabinets and appliances that could be hidden by louvered wooden doors. She slept on the sofa bed which sat against the wall facing the door, at right angles to a matching armchair.

A personal computer and printer took up the remainder of the sofa wall. She had an office in the old Cherokee Capitol Building in Cherokee Square in Tahlequah's business district, where she scheduled meetings and picked up her messages, but she used the PC at home for correspondence and inves-tigative reports.

Molly got up to put another piece of raisin bread in the toaster. At the movement, Homer, her golden retriever, who was sacked out in front of the sofa, lifted his head and whined and looked pitiful.

"Okay, I'll fix you a piece," Molly said. Homer flopped his plumy tail in thanks, got up, ambled over, and jumped up on Molly.

"Down, boy."

He obeyed, which pleased Molly. Florina Fenston dropped a remark now and then about Homer's lack of good manners. Maybe he was learning.

"Good boy." Homer jumped up on her again.

Maybe not. She shifted her leg and he got down and stayed down.

The dog had been a bag of bones covered with matted fur when he'd appeared beneath the apartment stairs one day last summer. She'd run a "found dog" ad in the local newspaper, but no one had answered it. He'd probably been dumped from a passing car on the highway near town.

Conrad had not been particularly pleased when she'd decided to keep Homer, or had pretended not to be, claiming he was not a pet person. With good reason. Conrad's late wife's Chihuahua had lived to take nips out of Conrad's ankles. But Homer wasn't a biter. He loved everybody.

The dog had won Conrad over quickly and now Conrad considered Homer as much his dog as Molly's. He took Homer along on his daily walks and had recently built a doghouse in the backyard. Homer stayed in the fenced yard at night, usually beneath the stairs, but he'd need the warmth of the snug doghouse as the nights grew colder.

Molly tossed Homer his toast. He caught it in midair, his teeth snapping together, and gulped it down. As she buttered her own piece, Homer tried to wag his rear end off. When that didn't work, he went back to looking pitiful. "Forget it," she told him. He tilted his head and cocked his ears. "You heard me," Molly said. He'd already eaten a bowl of dry dog food that morning. "You're getting fat."

Homer stuck his nose against her leg and snuffled loudly. Then he sighed and went back to the sofa to lie down, his head resting on his outstretched paws. He watched her intently as she ate her toast, his eyes following her hand to her mouth and back to her plate, in case his charms overcame her and she changed her mind and tossed him a crust. She didn't.

The phone rang as she was setting her breakfast dishes in the sink. It was D.J.

"*Good* morning," he greeted her.

"Hi." Another deputy had called her yesterday to say that D.J. had to work and couldn't go to the exposition with her. She hadn't talked to D.J. himself since Tuesday, and she'd begun to miss him. Somehow, when she wasn't looking, D.J. had become an important part of her life. She imagined him having his morning coffee. He'd probably just stepped out of the shower and was using the kitchen phone while sipping his first cup, his brown hair still wet and tangled. Her wayward imagination pictured him wearing nothing but a towel, every lean, muscular inch of him.

To distract herself, she sat down and made a face at Homer. Encouraged, he came over and leaned against her leg. She scratched behind his silky ears, and he laid his head in her lap and gave a contented grunt. Getting scratched behind the ears was the next best thing to food.

"Are you going to work today?" Molly asked.

"I've been working since six forty-five," D.J. said. It was ten after eight now. His words shattered the towel-wrapped image and replaced it with a rumpled khaki-clad one. D.J. could manage to look rumpled five minutes after putting on a fresh uniform. Actually, Molly thought that D.J.'s clothes somehow wrinkled in the closet before he put them on.

"A house north of town was vandalized last night," D.J. went on. "The other deputies were busy. I was scheduled to work this morning, anyway, so I got the call. I didn't even have time for a cup of coffee until I got to the station."

"Poor baby," Molly chided. "Working for a living is the pits, isn't it?" She noticed that the blue jays had abandoned the feeder and the robins were back.

"Sad but true."

"Whose house was it?"

"Tom Battle's. The place was trashed. He found it when he came home this morning."

Molly's hand on Homer's head grew still. "Did you say Tom Battle?"

"That's right. He went by the house to shower and change clothes after spending last night with a woman, at her place."

"Daye Hummingbird," Molly said. Homer whined and pushed his nose under her hand. He licked her fingers. She scratched behind his ears some more.

"He didn't want to give me her name, but I figured that's who it was." Tahlequah was too small for secret lives. "I asked him if he had any idea who might have a score to settle. He said he'd had problems with a couple of TEB members. I gather there was some kind of altercation last night at the museum reception."

"Uh-huh. Tom got into it with Wolf Kawaya, Daye's ex-husband. Wolf started it after he overheard Tom say something he didn't like."

"Did they get physical?"

"No, it was just words. Mostly Wolf's. The TEB lost another court case this week in which Tom represented the Cherokee Nation."

"I read about it."

Molly lifted Homer's head off her lap and rose to pour more coffee. "Wolf called Tom a white man and announced to the crowd that Daye was sleeping with him."

"Ouch. Sounds like a real prince."

Homer came over and leaned against her leg some more. Molly took a cautious sip of coffee, frowning. "Well, he's hurting. He still loves Daye. I felt kind of sorry for him. Daye too. She was mortified, naturally. She was crying when Tom took her out to the reception room. They left the museum not long after that."

"You think Wolf Kawaya would break in and trash Battle's house?"

Wolf's was the first—the only—name Molly had thought of when she heard Tom Battle's house had been vandalized. But she said judiciously, "He was mad enough at Tom last night to physically attack him if Tom had given him half an excuse. But Wolf's father seemed to be talking sense to him." She mentioned the message painted on the tribal office building Friday night.

"I saw it," D.J. said. "You think Wolf Kawaya was behind that?"

"It wouldn't surprise me, but breaking into Tom's house—I really don't know."

"Well, it wasn't a burglary. They ripped open the sofa and chair cushions, pulled the curtains off the windows, threw dishes out of the cabinets, and destroyed some legal files he'd been working on at home. The files are on his office computer, so they can be replaced. The rest of the damage will come to two or three thousand dollars, but, as far as Battle could tell, nothing was taken."

Molly put the mug down and stared out the window at the bird feeder, which was now abandoned by both robins and blue jays. "Sounds like somebody with a personal score to settle."

"Uh-huh," D.J. agreed.

"Have you learned where Wolf Kawaya was last night? I left the reception before he did, so I don't even know what time he left the museum."

"I'll get to work on that as soon as I report to Claude."
Claude Hobart was the county sheriff, D.J.'s boss. "He just
came in."

Homer looked up at Molly wistfully, decided against pushing his luck by jumping on her again, went back to the spot
in front of the sofa and lay down. "I'm going out to the museum this morning," Molly said. "The exhibition opens at nine.
In a moment of insanity I volunteered to help."

"Maybe you can find out what time Wolf left last night and
if anybody knows where he went from there."

"I'll try."

"I don't relish getting into that whole TEB–Cherokee
Nation mess," D.J. muttered.

"I don't blame you. Ever since last night, I've been worried
about Tom and Wolf both being involved in the exhibition.
The only thing that kept the argument from escalating then
was that Tom kept his head. But if he thinks Wolf vandalized
his house . . . "

"I definitely got the idea that's what he thinks."

"Oh, Lord. Maybe I'd better get on out there."

"Let me know if they get into it. In the meantime, I'll contact the tribal police and tell them I may need to question
Kawaya at the museum." County law-enforcement officials
were cross-deputized to enter tribal land to investigate certain
crimes, but when all parties involved were Indian they
informed the tribe's law-enforcement officers first, as a cour-
tesy.

"If I don't see you out there," D.J. continued, "I'll be at
your place by six. Don't forget dessert." She was sure he was
grinning now. D.J. was well aware of Molly's general disinterest in cooking. He accused her of being disinterested in food
too, but he was wrong. She was as thin as a reed, but that was
genetic. It was true she was no gourmet, but she didn't miss
many meals.

"I won't forget," she promised.

"Bye, sweet."

Molly was smiling as she hung up, but the smile faded quickly as her mind returned to the vandalism of Tom Battle's house.

She could easily imagine Wolf Kawaya driving by Daye Hummingbird's place late last night, seeing Tom's car and going into a rage, then breaking into Tom's house to vent his fury. Wolf was the sort who reacted first and got around to thinking about possible consequences later—if at all.

# 8

Molly arrived at the museum a few minutes before nine. A long line of people waited in front. Lily Roach answered Molly's knock, let her in, then locked the door behind her.

"Thanks for coming, Molly," she said. "From the looks of that bunch outside, we're going to need you." Lily appeared a little frazzled already, and the exhibition hadn't even opened yet.

From the reception area, Molly could see two of the exhibitors and their tables—Maud Wildcat and Regina Shell—and she waved at them. She was surprised to see Steven seated behind Regina's table too. It appeared Regina had been serious about keeping an eye on him. Leaning back in his chair with his arms folded, he looked bored, his gaze wandering. Molly smiled at him and mouthed hello, but he didn't seem to notice.

One end of the blowguns-and-darts exhibit was visible from where she stood too. Josiah Kawaya, wearing a traditional Cherokee ribbon shirt, was standing next to it, his hands clasped behind him. His attention was on something or someone whom Molly couldn't see from where she stood.

Molly spoke to Brenda, the receptionist, and turned back to Lily. "Everything okay?"

"So far."

"Are all the exhibitors here?"

"You mean Tom and Wolf? Oh, yes." Lily's gaze slid toward the exhibit area. "Did you know somebody broke into Tom's house last night?"

"I just heard. Did Tom tell you?"

"No. Daye did. Tom seems pretty shaken up and Daye's awfully upset too. After what happened at the reception, who can blame her. She's ready to take to the woods at the first sign of trouble. She thinks it was Wolf who broke into Tom's house."

"Did she tell you that?"

"Not in so many words."

"Has either of them talked to Wolf?"

"No. Daye and Tom are keeping their distance, thank goodness. Wolf hasn't said much to anybody, either, but he must have heard about the break-in by now. I can't believe he did it, Molly. But he'll know that Daye and Tom blame him."

"Why don't you think he did it?" Molly asked.

"Because it would be stupid after making that scene over Tom and Daye at the reception in front of seventy or eighty witnesses. Wolf's not stupid."

"Maybe he could be," Molly said, "if he got mad enough." She had seen ample evidence of Wolf's explosive temper.

"Well, he's in a black mood this morning," Lily muttered. "Keeps staring at Tom and Daye like he's daring them to accuse him. There's so much tension in the exhibit area you can hardly breathe."

"Wonderful," Molly murmured. "Do you remember what time Wolf left here last night?"

Lily shook her head and her eyes swept the portion of the exhibition area that was visible from where they stood. She turned back to Molly unsmilingly. "Not exactly. He was one of the last to leave, so it was fairly late. Ten-thirty, maybe."

"Was Josiah with him?"

"No. Josiah went home earlier."

"I don't suppose you heard Wolf say where he was going."

"No." Lily was looking a little uneasy now. "Do *you* think it was Wolf who broke into Tom's house?"

"I don't know enough about the break-in to have an opinion one way or the other." That wasn't true. She had an opinion, but it wasn't based on what she knew about the break-in.

Molly checked her watch. "We've got three minutes before we open for business. What do you want me to do?"

Lily seemed to relax a little. "You can start by helping Brenda sell tickets. Whenever there's a lull at the reception desk, stay in the exhibit area. You can help answer questions."

"And try to head off any trouble I see brewing?"

"Please," Lily replied glumly. "Beginning at nine-thirty, Tom will start a story every half hour, so direct the crowd over to him a couple of minutes before that."

"Got it," Molly said.

"I'm going to stay out here and keep an eye on browsers, to cut down on theft. We lost some books and small prints the last time we had a big group of people in here." She turned to the receptionist. "Ready, Brenda?"

"Ready as I'll ever be."

Molly hurried behind the desk as Lily unlocked the door and swung it back. Two teenage boys jostled each other as they pushed inside and ran to the desk to be first in line for admission tickets.

"Hey, man, watch it."

"Get outa my way, then, bumble foot."

"Who you calling bumble foot?"

"Ain't nobody else here but you, that I can see."

Molly feared she would have to break up a fight first thing, but it turned out to be good-natured bantering. The boys laughed as Brenda took their money and Molly stamped the backs of their hands, in case they wanted to leave and come back again.

As the boys went into the exhibit area, Brenda muttered, "There go two wild Indians."

The taller of the two seemed familiar to Molly, but she couldn't place him. "Who are they?"

"The skinny one is Robert Wildcat, Maud's grandson. I heard he's staying with her now." Molly hadn't seen the boy for a couple of years. He must have grown a foot in that time. "The shorter one is Victor Halland," Brenda continued. "My niece goes to Tahlequah High with them. She says whenever there's trouble at school, those two are usually at the bottom of it."

"That's what we need around here, a couple more trouble-makers."

"Tell me about it," Brenda agreed.

As soon as Molly could get away from the desk, she went into the exhibit area. The two boys were standing in front of the wampum belts, their heads together. The other visitors were clustered at the exhibit tables. Daye Hummingbird had set up an easel at one end with a canvas propped on it. She was sketching in the outlines of a painting as several people gathered around to watch.

Wolf and Josiah Kawaya were answering questions from several men about their blowguns and darts. Molly couldn't understand the Kawayas' words, but she caught some of what Regina was saying to the two women who were looking over her wares. "The earliest evidence of basket making dates back more than seven thousand years. Native peoples used them for carrying and storing and even for game traps."

One of the women asked a question and Regina replied, "All Cherokee basketry can be classified as one of three types—checkerboard, diagonal, or wickerwork. I used checkerboard in that one." Her gaze kept straying anxiously to Steven, who sat beside her. But Regina had answered the same questions so many times, she had the words down pat. Steven observed the exchange with disinterest, a faint smile on his face, as though he had an amusing secret.

Maud Wildcat left her table to walk toward her grandson and Victor Halland. She said something to them. The boys laughed and Robert shook his head. Then, ignoring his grandmother, Robert took a playful punch at Victor's arm. Maud hesitated as three other people approached the wampums. Turning away, she retreated to her table.

Tom Battle leaned against an exhibit case in the area where chairs had been arranged in a semicircle. He was studying Wolf Kawaya, who was holding a blowgun and explaining its use to a group of elderly people. From where Molly stood, she could see Wolf's face. It seemed unnaturally rigid, as though it might crack if he kept moving his mouth.

She turned her attention back to Tom Battle, who wore a ribbon shirt, jeans, and a beaded headband to keep his collar-length hair in place, but he didn't wear his usual unruffled demeanor. He kept watching Wolf and mopping his face with a white handkerchief, an oddly agitated action for someone who was ordinarily so self-controlled. Was he afraid of Wolf? Worried that Wolf might come after him next time, instead of his house?

Molly was distracted by Robert Wildcat and Victor Halland, who had gotten into a scuffle at the back of the hall. The two men and woman who were viewing the wampums jumped back to keep the boys from stumbling against them. Molly sighed. It was going to be a long morning.

She walked over to Robert and Victor. Robert was about five-ten, his hands and feet too big for the rest of him, but he would grow into them eventually. His friend was shorter and stockier. Victor appeared to be a mixed blood, his skin lighter than Robert's.

"You boys will have to go outside if you want to rough-house," Molly said.

Robert glanced around at her in surprise, as though he hadn't expected anyone to have the audacity to reprimand him. Then he looked sullen. "Who're you?"

"Molly Bearpaw."

"You in charge here or something?"

"At the moment," Molly said. She didn't think she was going to like this kid. "You're welcome to stay, but you'll have to save the tough stuff for another place."

Robert's black eyebrows drew together in a fierce V, as though he were wondering who died and made Molly boss. "You can't tell us what to do."

"Actually, I can—when you disrupt the exhibition," Molly contradicted. "I can get reinforcements if I need them too. It's your call."

Victor clapped his friend on the shoulder. "Aw, forget it, man. Let's go talk to Wolf."

Robert indulged in a little more macho posturing. "Whoo-oo, ain't she bad?"

Molly held his gaze until he looked away. "I'm shakin' in my boots," he sneered. "Come on, Victor," he added and walked away with his friend.

"Thank you," said the woman who was still standing there with the two men. "What ill-mannered boys." She was short and blond and forty-fivish. Her polyester slacks were stretched to the limit by a fat rear end. The bald man with her was about the same age. He was wearing a Western-style suit and lizard boots. The second man was slender and much younger.

The woman's husband and son, Molly guessed. The woman stepped up to the glass and read the sign beside the case. "This says they're wampum belts. I thought wampum was Indian money."

"The word refers to beads made from shells, like the ones in those belts," Molly explained. "They were used by many North American tribes for jewelry and other decorative pieces and also as currency."

The woman read the sign again. "This calls them sacred. Do the Cherokees worship them or what?"

"We treat them with reverence," Molly said, "because they were brought here from the old Cherokee country on the Trail of Tears. They help us preserve our culture."

"But it says they're sacred," the woman repeated argumentatively. "I don't get it. They're just some old pieces of beadwork. I thought the Cherokees were supposed to be civilized Indians." Her son looked pained and edged away, as though to disassociate himself from his mother.

"That was later, Sue," the bald man said. "After the white man taught them better. All Indians were savages back when those things were made."

Ignorant red-neck. Molly pressed her lips together to keep from saying it.

"It must have taken a long time to make these," the woman named Sue observed. "I mean they'd have to gather the shells before they could even start. But then I guess they had plenty of time on their hands." Molly wondered if she was actually puzzling over how people managed to occupy themselves before automobiles and television were invented.

"Not as much as you might think. They spent a great deal of time harvesting and hunting for food."

The woman cocked her head, thinking. How long could that take, right? She probably accepted the stereotype of Indians as basically lazy. "What else did they do?"

"Made pots and baskets and clothing," Molly said. "Raised children—listened to the earth spirit."

"What?"

"Nothing. I have to get to work. The storyteller will start a story at nine-thirty. Over there where the chairs are. You may want to grab a seat before the crowd gathers."

"Look, Delbert," the woman said as Molly walked away. "Here are some kind of weird symbols on these. What do you suppose they mean?"

"Indian superstition," Delbert replied as though he knew what he was talking about.

Molly noticed Conrad coming into the exhibit area. He looked sporty in a yellow cardigan sweater, khaki trousers, and white walking shoes. He'd even brushed and sprayed his unruly shock of silver hair into place. Molly started toward him but was detained by somebody with a question.

By the time she finished with that and made her way toward Conrad, Florina Fenston, in a red-print dress that did nothing for her plump figure, had appeared in the doorway. Her face was rosy, either from exertion or anger.

Florina headed straight for Conrad, reaching him seconds before Molly did, and tapped his shoulder.

Conrad's face reddened. "Oh, hello, Florina."

"Looks like you decided to postpone your errands till later," Florina snapped.

Surely Conrad could have come up with a better excuse than that, Molly thought. He must have assumed that Florina wouldn't come to the exhibition alone.

"Er-uh, well—" Conrad stammered. "They didn't take as long as I expected."

"Obviously," Florina shot back, "since I left the house five minutes after you did."

"Hi, you two," Molly said cheerily, earning a grateful glance from Conrad. Florina continued to look irritated.

"Conrad," Molly went on quickly, "I know you'll want to see the wampums, and now would be a good time. Tom Battle will be telling a story in about fifteen minutes."

"Yes, I definitely want to look at the wampums," Conrad said. "Excuse me." He hurried away.

"Florina," Molly said, "is there anything in particular you'd like to see?"

"Can you believe that man?" Florina demanded. "He told me an out-and-out lie to keep me from riding out here with him. Does he think I'm *interested* in him? Huh! What an ego!"

"Let me introduce you to the craftspeople," Molly suggested.

"Well...I do want to see the finger-weaving exhibition," Florina said grudgingly.

"Come with me, then. Maud's working on something now."

Florina sniffed and tossed her head in the direction of Conrad before following Molly.

"Oh, good, there's a space for you right in front of Maud," Molly told her.

She left Florina watching Maud weave a belt and made her way around the exhibit area, alerting visitors that the storyteller would soon perform. Shortly, people began closing in around Tom Battle. Molly noticed that Robert Wildcat and Victor Halland, however, stayed at the Kawayas' table, apparently more interested in the blowguns and darts than in the old stories. Steven Shell left his chair and sauntered over to join them. But he didn't speak to the others, and nobody took any notice of him. Steven merely stood there and continued to look alternately bored and faintly amused. He gave Molly a creepy feeling.

# 9

Standing at the back of the listeners, Molly watched Tom Battle mop his face with his handkerchief. Was it really that warm in here? With the handkerchief still crushed in his hand, Tom began.

This is what the old men told me when I was a boy. The Sun lived on the other side of the sky, but her daughter lived in the middle of the sky. Every day, as the Sun was climbing across the sky to the west, she used to stop at her daughter's house for dinner.

Molly recognized the beginning of the Cherokee origin-of-death myth. She moved a little closer.

Now, the Sun hated the people on earth because they could never look at her without screwing up their faces. But the Moon loved them because they always smiled pleasantly when they saw him in the sky at night. This made the Sun jealous. So she sent down such hot rays that a great fever came upon people and they died by the hundreds. Before that nobody had ever died, you see.

Tom paused to wipe his face again. Molly decided to find Lily in a little while and ask her to turn on the air conditioning. Tom took up the story.

When only a few people were left, they asked for help from the Little People who lived in caves and at the bottom of streams. The Little People made medicine and changed one of the men into a rattlesnake. They told him to hide near the house of the Sun's daughter and when the Sun came out, bite her and kill her. The rattlesnake waited, as the Little People told him, but when the door opened, it was the Sun's daughter who came out. The rattlesnake sprang up and bit her and she died. When the Sun found her daughter dead, she went back into the house and grieved, and people did not die of the fever anymore, but now the world was dark all the time because the Sun would not come out of the house.

Molly glanced over the crowd of rapt faces. Conrad joined the listeners not far from Molly, and Florina drifted over to stand a few feet away and glare at him. For the first time, Molly noticed Daye Hummingbird standing next to the front row of chairs. She looked tense and unhappy, and her eyes remained unwaveringly on Tom. The woman had to be under tremendous pressure, caught between Tom and Wolf.

Tom's eyes settled on Daye and he smiled, but when his gaze drifted over the crowd to the exhibits where Wolf Kawaya stared back at him, sweat popped out on his forehead. He wiped it away and looked over the listeners. For a moment he appeared confused, as though he'd lost the thread of the story. Then he seemed to shake himself and he went on.

The people went back to the Little People for help. The Little People told them if they wanted the Sun to come out again, they must bring back her daughter from the ghost country in *Usunhi'yi*, the dark land to the west. They chose seven men to go and gave them sourwood rods and a box. They must find the Sun's daughter, strike her with the rods, imprison her in the box, and bring her back to her mother. The Little People warned them they must be very sure not to open the box, even a crack, until they were home again.

The seven men did as they were told. When they got to *Tsusgina'i*, the ghost country, they found all the ghosts at a dance. The young woman was in the outside circle, and as she swung around to where the seven men were standing, they struck her with their rods and she fell down. They put her in the box and closed the lid. Then they started home.

Somebody brushed Molly's arm, and she turned to see Steven Shell beside her. She smiled and his mouth curved in response, but it was a reflex action, not a smile. Standing next to him, Molly realized that his manner couldn't be explained as mere boredom. It was more as if he were numb. A zombie, Regina had said.

"Hi, Steven," she whispered. "How are you?"

"Okay." He had always been lanky, like his twin, but recently he'd gained weight and his face looked puffy and stiff somehow. His dark eyes appeared blurred, perhaps the result of the medications he took. Molly could see what Regina had meant. The Steven she'd grown up with seemed to have gone away. She turned her attention back to Tom Battle.

In a little while, the girl woke up and begged to be let out of the box. The men didn't answer. Soon she called again and said she was hungry. Still they didn't answer. After a while, she called for a drink and pleaded so that it was hard to listen to her, but the men said nothing and continued their journey.

Beside Molly, Steven shuffled restlessly. He didn't seem interested in the story or anything else. Molly searched for something to say to this stranger who had once been her friend.

"Are you keeping busy, Steven?"

"Not really."

"Doing any running?" Steven had been a long-distance runner in high school, had set a couple of school records.

"No," he mumbled as his gaze wandered over the crowd. Conversation with Steven was tough going. Living with him wouldn't be easy. It had to be stressful for Regina. Molly gave up trying to talk to him.

When the men were near home, the Sun's daughter called again and begged them to raise the lid just a little because she was smothering. They were afraid she was really dying, so they lifted the lid only enough to give her air. But as they did so there was a fluttering sound inside and something flew past them into the thicket and they heard a redbird cry, "Kwish! kwish! kwish!" So we know the redbird is the daughter of the Sun, and if the men had kept the box closed as the Little People told them to do, they would have brought her home safely and they could have brought back their friends from the ghost country. But now no one can ever be brought back.

A baby cried in the crowd, briefly diverting the attention of those nearby, including Molly. The young mother tried to shush the child, without success, and finally pushed through those standing behind the seated listeners and took the baby out.

Tom had paused when the baby started to cry. He watched the mother leave with the baby, frowning slightly, and then he said:

> When the men returned without the Sun's daughter, she grieved and cried until her tears made a flood and people were afraid they would all drown. The people had to send their handsomest young men and women to amuse the Sun so that she would stop crying and smile again. But people still die and no one can ever return from the ghost country.

As Tom finished the story, the audience applauded and began to disperse. Molly looked around, surprised to discover that Steven was gone. He'd wandered back to the Kawayas' exhibit without a word. Steven seemed drawn to that particular exhibit; in fact, it was the only thing he'd shown any interest in at all.

Then Molly saw Daye hurry to Tom's side and speak to him. He placed his hand on her shoulder, as though to reassure her, and bent close to her as they talked. Anyone who noticed them would know immediately that they were deeply in love.

Merely watching them seemed an intrusion, and Molly turned away and saw Wolf Kawaya. He was standing up behind his table, observing Tom and Daye with a piercing stare, his jaw locked, seething. He'd like to kill Tom, Molly thought suddenly and looked for Wolf's father, who might be needed to restrain Wolf. Josiah was standing some distance away from Wolf, his attention diverted by the woman he was talking to. A man walked up to Wolf and said something. Wolf tore his eyes away from Tom and Daye, and Molly relaxed a little.

Robert Wildcat and Victor Halland were at the end of the Kawayas' table, handling the merchandise. Victor inspected a dart, put it back down, and picked up another. Robert was peering through the hollowed-out cane shaft of a blowgun. Victor nudged him and handed him a dart. Robert grinned as he inserted it into the blowgun he held.

For an instant, Molly watched the boys, unable to accept the evidence of her own eyes. Robert couldn't possibly be thinking of using the blowgun. Not in this crowd! Surely he was only making a show of it for his friend's benefit. She realized, as Robert brought the gun to his mouth, that he wasn't pretending. He was actually going to do it.

"No!" She started toward the boys.

They didn't hear her. Robert drew air into his mouth. Then he blew it out, and the dart left the blowgun with amazing speed.

"Watch out!" Molly yelled.

People, unaware of what was going on, turned around to stare at her. Robert heard her too. He looked dazed, like someone waking up from a bad dream, and his face was distorted by amazement or fear. Possibly both. He dropped the blowgun, as though he hadn't realized what he was doing until it was too late. Maud Wildcat stood up behind her table. She stared at her grandson with wide, fearful eyes. She looked ready to faint. The hall had gone absolutely still.

Then Daye Hummingbird screamed. As Molly spun back around, she saw Tom grab the side of his neck and Daye reach out to him with both hands.

Forgetting Robert, Molly ran toward Tom and Daye. With one hand pressed to his neck, Tom grabbed for the back of a folding chair with his other hand. The chair tipped over and clattered to the floor. Tom appeared to have lost his equilibrium.

As Molly got within a few feet of Tom, strength seemed to drain from his body and he crumpled. Daye tried to hold him upright, but he was too heavy for her. Slowly, like a rag doll sliding off a shelf, he sank to the floor with a thud.

# 10

Molly and Daye bent over Tom's sprawled body. A trickle of blood ran down the side of his neck where the dart had struck him.

"Tom? Tom!" Daye cried. He didn't respond. He lay where he'd fallen, breathing shallowly, and he appeared to be unconscious.

Molly looked up frantically to find a dozen people in a ring around them, and others converging on the spot. "Get back," she said. "Give him room to breathe." She noticed Lily Roach in the circle. "Lily, call nine-one-one." Lily hurried away.

Molly touched two fingers to the side of Tom's neck. His pulse was quick but faint. She wiped his damp forehead with her hand. "Tom, can you hear me?" There was no response.

She didn't like the looks of this at all. She scanned the crowd, vowing to take a CPR course at the first opportunity. "We may need somebody who knows CPR."

"He stopped breathing!" Daye's anguished words rose shrilly in the hushed silence. "Somebody help him!"

A man stepped from among the spectators and knelt over Tom. "I know CPR," he said.

Molly gave him room. Daye stayed, kneeling beside Tom, clinging for dear life—Tom's life—to his outstretched hand. As Molly straightened up, she started to shake. She felt cold and hugged herself. Was Tom dead?

He had stopped breathing, but how could that be? He hadn't lost much blood and, besides, the dart was made of wood. *Wood.* Sufficient to stun, maybe even kill, a small animal. But not a man.

People did not die from blowgun-dart wounds. This was insanity. Her mind raced back over the events of the past twelve hours. First, Tom's house is vandalized. Then, two rowdy boys are horsing around with blowguns and darts made by the chief suspect in the vandalism, and they accidentally shoot Tom. Accidentally? Yes, Molly told herself. She would almost swear that Robert hadn't been aiming at anyone in particular. But he couldn't have made a better hit if he'd been trying. Then Tom dropped to the floor and stopped breathing.

This scenario seemed to be missing a few cause-and-effect links. A man could not die as a result of this chain of events. But she'd seen it.

Molly stood beside Daye as the man who had come forward administered CPR. When he stopped to see if Tom was breathing on his own, he got no response and continued the life-sustaining measures.

Daye had begun to moan softly and rock back and forth on her knees, still clutching Tom's hand.

"This is crazy," Molly said, half to herself. "A blowgun dart can't kill a man." She looked around to find Conrad and Florina at her elbow, the others having heeded Molly's command to stay back. Florina's face was flushed, and her fingers made little fluttering movements at the bodice of her bright dress. She seemed to have forgotten for the moment that she was mad at Conrad, who had turned pale, his shrewd blue eyes sharp with concern.

"I know," Conrad said grimly. "One of those darts couldn't even kill a baby, but Tom Battle is a young man, and he looks strong."

He exchanged a confused glance with Molly. "I did think," Conrad said, "that he seemed nervous while he was telling the story."

"I noticed that too," Molly said.

"Does he have a history of anxiety attacks or heart problems?" Conrad asked.

"I don't know," Molly said. "I haven't heard of it, if he has." She could not believe that calm Tom Battle had ever had an anxiety attack in his life. And it would be unusual for such a young, healthy man to suffer a fatal coronary. Not impossible, though.

Lily had come back and was herding everybody to the other side of the exhibit area. Daye was weeping uncontrollably now, her ragged sobs filling the hushed museum. Molly knelt and put her arm around Daye's shoulders. "They're doing all that can be done until the ambulance gets here," she murmured. "Come and sit down. Can I get you a drink of water?"

"No!" Daye cried brokenly. "I can't leave him."

Lily came back with another visitor who knew CPR. He relieved the first man, who had begun to sweat profusely. "Am I glad to see you," he said, wiping his brow with the back of his hand as the second man took over. Then the first man sank into a folding chair to watch silently, along with Florina and Conrad, and the crowd from a greater distance. Molly stayed beside Daye, hoping her mere presence might be a small comfort.

They remained like that for what seemed hours before they heard the ambulance siren.

The medics took over and rushed Tom to the ambulance on a litter. Molly walked with Daye toward the door. Daye stayed on the medics' heels until she reached Wolf Kawaya. She whirled on him.

"You did this!" she cried and without any other warning went for his face with her fingernails. Wolf uttered a surprised curse and grabbed her wrists, holding her away from him. Daye sobbed and struggled to free herself. Then suddenly she went limp and Wolf released her and stepped back.

"Have you lost your mind?" His eyes blazed, his face looked like thunder.

"You'll pay for this," Daye said in a low voice. "I swear you will."

The crowd had watched all this, stunned into paralysis. Molly was the first to move. She took Daye's arm and led her, unresisting, out to the ambulance, where Daye climbed into the back with Tom. The ambulance sped away, siren blaring.

Molly returned to the museum. In the exhibit area, a hush still gripped the crowd. With Molly's return, they began to stir and murmur quietly to each other. Wolf Kawaya had disappeared, probably into the rest room at the back of the museum.

"Why did she attack that guy?" a woman asked. "Is he the one who shot the dart?"

"No, it was a kid," a man answered.

"The storyteller dropped like he'd taken a bullet in the heart," another man said.

A woman's voice edged upward with panic. "Did somebody say he was shot? I didn't hear a shot. Where's the gun now?"

"That's not what he said," the first man corrected. "The storyteller was hit with one of those blowgun darts. I saw the whole thing."

Conrad touched Molly's arm. "We should find that dart."

Of course. Molly must be in a state of shock not to have thought of it herself. If they couldn't revive Tom, this could be manslaughter. "It has to be around here somewhere," she said.

She and Conrad scanned the floor near when Tom had been standing when the dart struck him. After a few minutes of searching, Conrad found it lying behind one of the folding chairs about twenty-five feet from where Tom had fallen. Somebody must have kicked it there from where it fell.

"Maybe we shouldn't touch it," Conrad said.

"Good idea," Molly agreed, although if any clear finger-prints could be lifted from the wood, she knew whose they would be. She'd watched Robert and Victor handling the dart.

"You stay here," Conrad said, "and I'll go find a container."

Florina, who had trailed behind Molly as she searched for the dart, wailed, "This is just dreadful," her green eyes wide. "Dreadful, dreadful, dreadful."

Florina's face was so pink that Molly was concerned about her. "You'd better sit down, Florina."

"No, dear, I'm fine. Really."

Molly let it go, but she hoped Florina would go home soon.

Florina asked, "Where did the dart come from? Did you see?"

Molly hesitated. "I don't have time to discuss it now, Florina." Unfortunately, Florina had a tendency to embellish a simple set of facts and spread the expanded version among her friends. She would find out who shot the dart eventually. Everybody would. But Molly wasn't going to be the one to tell her.

Florina sniffed. "Well, pardon me. I won't take up any more of your precious time. You and your professor friend just go on about your business." She stalked off.

"Florina . . ." Molly sighed but didn't go after her. She'd have to soothe Florina's feathers later.

She looked around the room for Robert Wildcat and Victor Halland. Both Kawayas were back at their table, turned toward each other, engaged in a heated conversation. Molly would love to know what they were saying.

After some hesitation and conversation with Lily, Regina had gone back to her table too, and Steven was with her. Visitors were beginning to follow. But the two boys were nowhere to be seen. And where was Maud Wildcat?

Conrad returned with a small glass jar which Lily Roach had given him. He unscrewed the lid, knelt, maneuvered the dart into the jar without touching it, and put the lid back on. He handed the jar to Molly, who lifted it to eye level.

"Looks like the point is gone."

"Maybe somebody stepped on the dart and broke it," Conrad said. They spent a few minutes looking for the point near where they'd found the dart, but didn't find it.

"It could still be in his neck," Conrad suggested. "If so, they'll find it at the hospital."

"We should have enough here for fingerprinting," Molly said.

Conrad muttered, "Something is very wrong here."

He seemed to be reading Molly's mind. It didn't add up. Molly looked anxiously toward the exhibits. She still didn't see Robert or Victor.

"Just a minute," Molly said to Conrad. She left him and went to the end of the Kawayas' table. Josiah turned to her, his weathered brown face grim.

"It might be a good idea to put the darts away," Molly suggested.

Josiah stared at her churlishly and cracked the knuckles of his right hand. "Wolf already did it," he grunted, gesturing with his thumb at the table and an open box behind him. Then he cracked the knuckles of his left hand. There were no darts on the table now, they'd been transferred to the box.

Evidently Josiah felt that Molly was taking too much on herself by giving him instructions. Or he was insulted that she thought he needed to be told.

"That's good," she said lamely.

Josiah flexed all ten fingers. "We'll whittle some more for the lookers," he said, "but we'll put them in the box when we finish. We've shown our blowguns and darts at least a hundred times, and nothing like this has ever happened before." He turned his back on Molly.

Wolf rose. "I want to talk to you." He took Molly's arm and led her apart from the visitors. "I didn't know what was happening until Daye screamed," he said defensively.

"You didn't see Robert using the blowgun?"

"I saw him pick it up—from the corner of my eye. But I never dreamed he was dumb enough to shoot a dart in here."

Molly studied his face, searching for a telltale sign that he way lying. She wondered if he'd somehow manipulated Robert into shooting the dart. Egged him on with a dare? She didn't bother asking, because Wolf would never admit it, but she didn't trust the man.

"I gave those kids a piece of my mind," Wolf continued. "Told them to get out and not come back."

"Did you and your father make all the darts that were on the table?"

"Sure. I made most of them at the reception."

"What kind of wood do you use?"

"All the ones we have here are bois d'arc wood."

"You're sure about that?"

He was puzzled by the question, seemed to be trying to figure out its significance. Molly wasn't sure herself what she meant. But Conrad was right. The facts, as she knew them, didn't add up to a grown man's collapse.

"Hell, yes, I'm sure," Wolf said. "I gathered the wood myself."

"You don't do anything to the wood?"

He considered this in silence. When he finally spoke, his voice was tight. "Look, I don't know what you're getting at, but we make them the way the old Cherokees did. Gather the wood and whittle the darts. That's all. Did Daye say I'd made up a special dart or something?"

Molly shook her head. It was a thought, though.

"Well, it wouldn't surprise me," he muttered. "She's out of her head, attacking me in front of all those people." Had it escaped his mind that, only last night, he'd verbally attacked Daye in front of a crowd?

"She was upset."

He snorted. "Don't you mean *nuts*?" He gazed around the exhibit area almost furtively. Nobody seemed to be paying them any mind. "Listen," he went on, "maybe I should have been keeping a closer watch on Robert and Victor. I know they're full of vinegar."

"I wish you had," Molly said.

His brow puckered. "Listen," he said again, "it's no secret I don't have any use for Battle, but if I wanted to hurt the man I'd use my fists. I was mad as hell at Robert for shooting the dart, but that wasn't what caused Battle to collapse. Impossible. He must have had a stroke or something."

"Lily Roach told me he was agitated when he arrived this morning. Somebody vandalized his house last night."

"You think it was me?" he demanded.

"I didn't say that."

He smiled maliciously. "It wasn't me, but it didn't break my heart when I heard about it. Battle's made a lot of enemies."

"Among the True Echota Band?"

He laughed contemptuously and looked around to see if his father was listening. Josiah was talking to a visitor, but he had an ear cocked in their direction and he was cracking his knuckles again. A nervous habit, apparently. "TEB members aren't the only ones who think Battle's a traitor to his people. You probably don't understand that, being an employee of the Nation."

"TEB members work for the Nation too."

He shrugged. "That's their choice. There aren't that many jobs to be had in Cherokee County."

Was he as understanding as he appeared? Or did he see band members who worked for the Cherokee Nation as traitors?

Conrad came up to them and put a hand on Molly's shoulder. "I'm going home now."

"Where's Florina?" Molly asked. "She didn't look too well to me. I think all this has shaken her badly."

"She's gone already. She's upset with both of us, mostly with me. She caught me coming out of the house this morning and I told her she couldn't come with me because I had errands to run first."

"Then you came straight here," Molly said, shaking her head.

"It didn't occur to me she'd follow me. It should have, though, knowing Florina."

"Well, she'll get over it—eventually," Molly said. He shook his head doubtfully and left.

Wolf had started back to his table. "Wait a minute," Molly said as she caught up with him. "I'd like to ask you one more question."

He paused, looking at her impatiently.

"Did you see Victor or Robert pick that particular dart from the ones on the table?"

He shook his head. "I wasn't paying that much attention to them until I heard you yell. Then I saw Robert's face and realized what had happened. But you're barking up the wrong tree. The darts are all alike. At the hospital, they'll probably find out Battle had a stroke or a blood clot, something like that."

"Probably," Molly responded. It was the most reasonable explanation. So why didn't she believe it? She went out to the reception desk. Brenda was taking money from a young couple. She closed the cash register and they held their hands out to be stamped, then hurried toward the exhibits.

Brenda looked at Molly and then at the door. "Didn't I tell you Robert Wildcat and Victor Halland were trouble?"

"You did," Molly sighed.

"Maud is so worried about Robert she doesn't know what to do," Brenda said. "When the boys left, she ran out after them."

"Where is she now?"

"I don't know—oh, here she is."

Maud had opened the door just enough to slip inside. Her compact body seemed to have shrunk. She clutched a shawl around her shoulders, one hand gripping it together beneath her chin. Her brown complexion had taken on a gray tinge. She looked on the verge of collapse herself.

Molly ran to her side. "Are you all right, Maud?"

Brenda came over too, and took Maud's arm. "Couldn't you find them?"

Maud's eyes shifted nervously from Molly to Brenda. "What?" She sounded like somebody coming out of a trance.

Brenda exchanged a questioning glance with Molly. "Robert and Victor."

Maud's hand, the one that wasn't clutching her shawl, gripped Molly's arm tightly. "I'd better sit down."

They led her behind the desk and settled her in Brenda's chair. Brenda got a Styrofoam cup and filled it at the drinking fountain. She placed the cup in Maud's hand. "Did Robert go home?" she asked.

Maud lifted the cup and took a long swallow of water. Her hand was shaking. "The boys—" she said vaguely, as though she were having trouble focusing on what she was saying. "They left in Victor's car." She released the shawl to grasp the cup in both hands.

Molly patted Maud's shoulder. "Robert will be all right, Maud. I saw what happened. I don't think he meant to hit anyone."

Maud bowed her head. "No, he didn't mean to," she murmured. "He was taken over."

"What—?" Brenda began. Molly cut her off with a quick shake of her head. Maud was beginning to scare Molly. She still sounded vague and unfocused. Molly's concern increased when Maud looked up at her with terror-stricken eyes. Molly pulled a chair over and sat down beside Maud. She took the cup and handed it to Brenda, then she took both of Maud's hands in hers. They felt cold.

"Would you like me to call your doctor?" Molly asked.

Maud's silver-streaked head swung in negation. "I don't need a doctor. I need to get away from this place." She grasped Molly's hand agitatedly. "We all do."

"Why?" Molly asked gently.

"It's the wampums," Maud said. She spoke softly but with absolute certainty. "They should never have been brought here. Now the power has been released. It killed Tom."

Brenda looked at Molly over Maud's head and rolled her eyes. "Tom will be all right," Brenda said. "We have to hang on to that thought."

Maud glanced up at her pityingly.

"We can't give up hope until we know," Brenda insisted.

Maud shook her head. "There's no hope. He's dead, and one of us could be next." She squeezed Molly's hand desperately. Molly winced, but Maud didn't notice. "If they'd take the wampum belts away, maybe nobody else would have to die. Can you make them do it, Molly?"

"I—I don't know. I'll talk to Lily."

Maud took a deep breath and released Molly's hand. "I won't go back in there with the wampums."

She sounded adamant, and Molly suspected it would be a waste of breath to try to talk her into it. "Would you feel better if we moved your exhibit out here?" Maud wouldn't be able to demonstrate the use of her loom, but she could continue the finger-weaving demonstrations in the lobby.

Maud thought about it for a moment and reluctantly nodded. "Near the door," she said. "I don't want to be able to see them from where I'm sitting. But if anything else happens . . ."

"I'm sure it won't," Molly said. "You stay here with Brenda and I'll find Lily."

"Wait. I want you to take Robert's case."

"Oh, Maud, you're overreacting. I doubt there will be a case. And, anyway, I'm no lawyer."

"I know that, but Tom's dead." She was convinced the situation was hopeless, no matter what anyone said.

"Brenda's right. We can't give up hope," Molly said, even though she agreed with Maud that there was little hope. Tom had been so still when they carried him out on the litter.

Maud went on as if she hadn't heard. "Tom's death will be investigated by outsiders. They won't understand about the wampums. Robert won't have a chance with white men. You said Robert didn't mean to hit anyone. You can talk to people, get evidence to back that up. Prove what really happened."

Did Maud expect her to come up with evidence to convince a judge or jury that Robert had been possessed by the power of the wampums? Oh, sure, and while she was at it she'd walk on water. "I'll see what I can find out, Maud."

Maud seemed satisfied with Molly's reply. "I want to go to the rest room," she said and rose shakily to her feet. The rest rooms were at the rear of the museum, behind the exhibit area.

"I'll go with you," Brenda offered.

"Not through there," Maud said, pointing toward the door leading to the exhibits.

"We'll go outside and come in the backdoor," Brenda said. "Molly, would you cover the desk for me until we get back?"

Molly agreed and watched them leave, Brenda with a protective arm around Maud's shoulders. Left alone in the reception room, Molly went to the doorway separating the lobby from the exhibits to look for Lily. Finally, Lily saw her and came over.

Molly explained Maud's state of mind. Lily listened intently, her forehead furrowed. "This exhibition is falling apart," she lamented. "Tom and Daye are gone and who knows—" She paused, then decided to finish what she'd started. "Who knows if either one of them will be back. We can't lose Maud too. I'll find a couple of men to move her table out here."

"Good. I think that will make her feel better. For now, anyway."

"For now?"

"Well, she's terrified. I'm not sure she's going to stay in the museum for a week."

Lily dragged a hand through the wide silver streak running down the middle of her otherwise black hair. "Maybe I should ask the Nighthawks to remove the wampums," she said fretfully. "What do you think, Molly?"

Did Lily also believe the wampums were dangerous? "We've advertised that they'll be on display during the exhibit," Molly said. "A lot of people will come just to see them."

"That's true, and if they're not here, I'll catch all the flak," Lily murmured.

"They're behind glass," Molly said. "Nobody can touch them."

Lily chewed her bottom lip for a moment. "All right. We'll leave them for now." She walked over to the telephone. "Before we move Maud's exhibit, I'll call the hospital and see if I can find out anything about Tom."

She dialed as Molly waited on four visitors who'd just entered the museum. Molly could hear Lily, whose back was turned, speaking softly in the background, but she couldn't make out the words.

After dealing with the visitors, Molly glanced over her shoulder to see Lily drop the receiver in the cradle. For a moment, Lily stood with her hand on the receiver and her back still to Molly. Then she took a deep breath and pinched the bridge of her nose between thumb and index finger. A full minute passed.

Molly couldn't stand the suspense any longer. "Lily—"

Lily turned around. "That was the emergency-room doctor." Her voice was heavy.

More silence. Several moments passed, until Molly asked, "What did he say? Did they bring Tom around?"

Lily shook her head and, overcome, she covered her face with her hands. But when she looked up her eyes were dry.

Molly went to her. "Sit down, Lily."

Again, Lily shook her head. "They couldn't save Tom," she said. "He's dead. Maud knew it all the time."

# 11

"We'd better let Chief Mankiller know," Lily said after she had composed herself. She looked uneasily at the phone. As director of the museum, she probably feared that she would be held responsible for what had happened.

"She's out of town," Molly told her. "Won't be back till the end of next week."

"Oh, darn. I'd forgotten." She tapped her foot nervously. "We still have to tell somebody in authority right away," Lily insisted. Clearly, she wanted to shift the responsibility for deciding what to do with the news to somebody else. Molly liked that idea too.

Lily's tapping foot stilled. "I'll try to get hold of the deputy chief." She looked up the number and caught the deputy chief at home. After a brief conversation, she hung up and said, "He'll talk to the hospital people. If they haven't notified Tom's dad, he'll do it. I think Mr. Battle lives in Wagoner. Tom's mother passed away a few years ago."

"Did the doctor say anything about the cause of death?" Molly asked.

"He said it hadn't been determined. There'll be an autopsy. The deputy chief said something about calling the sheriff's department and the tribal police, asking them to do a preliminary investigation while there are still so many witnesses here." She tidied a few loose pieces of paper on the reception desk, a nervous reaction. "Oh, dear—" She cleared her throat and looked up. "I know it sounds terrible even to be thinking about it, but I'll have to find another storyteller."

"Yes," Molly agreed, even though it did sound crass. "We'll have a lot of disappointed people otherwise."

Lily frowned. "Maybe Regina or the Kawayas can suggest someone. If you'll keep an eye on things out here, Molly, I'll be in the exhibit area."

When Brenda and Maud returned, Maud moved a chair near the door. Her skin was no longer gray, but she seemed acutely alert and poised for flight. It was plain she wasn't going to set foot in the exhibit area as long as the wampums were there. Maud perched on the edge of her chair, tensely waiting for her exhibit to join her. Molly smiled reassuringly, but Maud didn't return the smile.

"Lily called the hospital," Molly whispered to Brenda. "Tom's dead."

Brenda's hand flew to her mouth. Had she really convinced herself that Tom would be all right? "Don't tell Maud till you have to," she whispered.

Molly didn't think the news would have much effect on Maud, who had already accepted Tom's death. Brenda's attention was diverted by the arrival of three new visitors. While Brenda took care of them, Molly found a box of color postcards and replenished the circular rack near the desk.

If it turned out that Tom had had a heart attack, she mused, or some other fatal physical ailment, then the dart might not have contributed to his death. Maybe she was refusing to accept the obvious, but Tom hadn't seemed himself before the dart was blown. Recalling how he'd kept perspiring and wiping his face, Molly realized that he might have been feeling ill, rather than agitated over the break-in at his house. She wished now that she'd asked him what was wrong.

If Tom had died of natural causes, there probably wouldn't even be a manslaughter charge. There'd be no way of proving the dart hastened his death.

But if they found something unexpected. Such as, the dart hadn't been made of bois d'arc wood, as Wolf Kawaya claimed, but some toxic wood—there must be such a tree or shrub. Molly shuddered. She didn't even want to think about murder. A capital crime on Indian land meant the federal government would get involved. Unless the tribal police and sheriff's department had a suspect and the evidence ready to hand over to the agents when they arrived. Not likely. Nobody wanted the feds running around, asking questions, but there wouldn't be much in the way of conclusive evidence until they had the results of the autopsy. Perhaps not even then.

No matter what the autopsy showed, Molly still didn't think there would be enough evidence to indict Robert. She couldn't believe he had meant to hurt Tom. He hadn't even taken time to aim the blowgun before he blew. So if that dart was lethal, she didn't think Robert Wildcat had known it. Which left Wolf and Josiah.

Or Victor Halland, who had handed the dart to Robert. Victor? That opened up another line of thought. Suppose the dart hadn't been made by Wolf Kawaya. Suppose Victor had brought it with him.

But why?

She tried to stop her imagination from running wild. All this speculation might be a lot of wasted energy.

Lily was still in the exhibit area, and Brenda was talking to a visitor. Molly went around behind the desk and moved the telephone as far away from Brenda and Maud as the cord would stretch. She dialed the county morgue and asked for Dr. Pohl, the medical examiner.

She'd witnessed an autopsy performed by Pohl on an elderly Cherokee man the previous summer, and Pohl remembered her well. She'd almost fainted and had to leave the room.

"I'm doing the Battle autopsy this afternoon," he told her. "You want to watch this one?" After the other autopsy, he'd invited her to come back anytime, assuring her that viewing autopsies was like riding a horse. When you got thrown, you had to get right back on. All she had to do was watch a few more autopsies and she'd get over her queasiness.

Then, as now, Molly declined the offer. "No, thanks, doctor. I need to know what you find, though. Could you call me?"

"Sure, but I'd like to talk to his next of kin first."

"That'll be his father. He lives in Wagoner, so he may be in touch with you today. Tell him I asked about your findings. Tell him I'm looking into Tom's death and will want to talk to him later."

"Will do," Pohl said.

Molly replaced the phone, noting that Brenda was watching her curiously. Brenda's question was forestalled by the appearance of two men carrying Maud's exhibit table. Molly left Brenda to deal with them and returned to the exhibit area.

A half hour later, Sheriff Claude Hobart and D.J. arrived at the museum, followed closely by Sam Davey, a tribal policeman. D.J. barely had a chance to say hello to Molly before he and Claude rounded up the visitors who had witnessed Tom's collapse and questioned them. Sam interviewed the exhibitors, as well as Lily, Brenda, and Molly.

From what Molly could gather, nobody had seen anything more than she had. Most of the witnesses had seen less. They hadn't noticed Robert with the blowgun until Molly's shout alerted them.

Several dozen pairs of feet had trampled the area where Tom had fallen, after he'd been transferred to the ambulance. Claude and D.J. took a close look at it, anyway, but Molly doubted if they'd find anything. She and Conrad had already been over it and found nothing but the dart, which she turned over to the sheriff, who would take it to the OSBI satellite lab in Tahlequah when he returned to town.

The sheriff wanted to know where she'd found the dart.

She showed him. "Somebody kicked it over here after it hit Tom," she said.

"Did you happen to see who?" Hobart asked, his tone less than congenial. He was a hefty, sixtyish man, looking forward to retirement in a couple of years. In the meantime, he'd just as soon the Cherokees took care of their own investigations and left him to see to the county's. But as somebody whose job depended on his standing with the voters, he was sensitive to criticism and, therefore, cooperated with the tribe when asked. That didn't mean he had to like it.

"No," Molly replied. "I'm assuming it was kicked because of where we found it."

Finally, all the witnesses had been questioned and the three lawmen left. By the time Molly's stint at the museum was over at one, Lily had located an elderly Cherokee storyteller who had agreed to take over for Tom Battle, starting the next day.

Life, for everybody but Tom Battle, went on.

"The M.E. found no heart damage, no evidence of stroke or a blood clot," Molly said to D.J. that evening. "As of now, the finding is death by respiratory failure." She had heard from Dr. Pohl shortly before D.J. arrived at the apartment.

As soon as she got home that afternoon, she'd called D.J. at work. He confirmed her impression that none of the witnesses gave them much to go on. Sam Davey had told him that Wolf and Josiah Kawaya adamantly denied having anything to do with Robert's shooting the dart. Exactly what Molly had expected. D.J. had taken the opportunity to question Wolf as to his whereabouts Friday night when Tom Battle's house was vandalized. Wolf had gone straight home after the reception, he'd said, where he'd stayed until Saturday morning. Since he lived alone, there was no one to back up his alibi. Or to contradict it.

After leaving the museum, D.J. had tried unsuccessfully to track down Robert and Victor.

At the moment, D.J. was laying out the ingredients for tacos on her kitchen counter. "But what caused the respiratory failure?" he pondered aloud.

"Exactly. Pohl released the body but he's running more tests on the samples he took," Molly said as she poured a cup of English-caramel coffee for D.J. to drink while he made the tacos. "He may know more within the next day or two. In the meantime, maybe the dart will tell us something."

"I talked to Daye Hummingbird at her house this afternoon—or tried to," D.J. said. "Battle's death has devastated her. She's a lovely woman, but she looked terminally ill when I saw her today."

"She was in love with Tom," Molly murmured.

"I know, and I hated having to ask her about her attacking Wolf Kawaya at the museum and accusing him of shooting that dart at Tom. I only got a few sentences out of her before it became obvious that she couldn't go on. She claimed she hadn't meant that Wolf had shot the dart, but that he'd orchestrated it somehow." Since the same idea had occurred to Molly, she wasn't surprised that Daye had thought of it too. "She has no evidence that he did, though," D.J. continued. "She was just lashing out."

Molly's heart ached for Daye. "Wolf's still highly suspect in my book," she said. "But we have to know the real cause of death before we'll even know where to start investigating."

"What do you mean 'we,' *kemo sabe?*" D.J. inquired dryly. "It'll be turned over to the feds, and the sheriff's department will be out of the loop. That should please Claude."

"But my investigation will go on until Robert Wildcat is either cleared or charged. And unofficially I could still use your help."

D.J. shook his head. "Seems to me I've heard that one before. Claude rimmed my butt for letting you get involved in the investigation of those nursing-home murders last summer."

As it turned out, Molly had caught the killer in the act of trying to murder a third victim and saved a life. D.J. had been out of town, but she didn't think this was the best time to remind him of that little detail. "This is different. I'm already involved. And you'll still be investigating the vandalism of Tom Battle's house, won't you?"

"I've got a few more people to talk to on that, but so far I've turned up nothing. Nobody saw or heard anything. Battle doesn't have any close neighbors. Now that he's dead, the vandalism isn't going to be a top priority with the department." D.J. unwrapped a package of ground beef. "What gets me about this whole thing is that dart. It didn't look very lethal, did it?"

"The dart may have had nothing to do with Tom's death."

"Hell of a coincidence, then."

"True."

"It looked to me like the point had been broken off. We looked for it, but didn't find it."

"Conrad and I had already searched for it," Molly said. "Dr. Pohl didn't find it in the body, either. There couldn't be more than half an inch missing, so if there are identifiable fingerprints or anything else, the lab should find them on what they have."

D.J. got a fork from a cabinet drawer.

"The last few days have been strange," Molly went on. "Even my grandmother isn't herself. She's been having bad dreams and waking up at night, thinking about a man she saw drop dead at a stomp dance when she was a child."

"Has she been sick?"

"No, but she's pretty depressed. It's almost as though she sensed trouble coming. She even gave me a charm for protection."

"Insomnia isn't uncommon in elderly people, Molly. It's old age, that's all. And you know how you always think of the worst that's happened, or could happen, when you're lying awake in the middle of the night."

"It's not only Grandmother. Maud Wildcat's convinced the wampum belts made Robert shoot that dart at Tom."

D.J. gave her a perplexed look. "How did they do that?" D.J. was a quarter Cherokee, but his Indian relatives weren't traditional. He hadn't grown up hearing the old stories, as Molly had.

She shrugged. "I've heard tales about the wampums all my life. Some of the old people say it's dangerous to touch them, that an evil force can be released if you do."

"Did Tom Battle or Robert Wildcat touch them?"

"No, but somebody had to, to bring them to the museum and put them in an exhibit case. Several people probably."

"Let me get this straight. Maud Wildcat thinks these people who touched the wampums revived some evil force that has been lying dormant all these years?"

"I know how it sounds," Molly admitted. "But before this, probably nobody's touched them for years except the leader of the Nighthawk Keetoowahs. The old people would say the wampums recognize his touch, I guess." D.J.'s smile was wry but attempting to be tolerant. "Anyway," Molly continued, "we managed to get Maud to stay at the museum by moving her exhibit table into the lobby where she can't see the wampums. If anything else happens, though, she's out of there. Meanwhile, Lily Roach is going nuts, trying to hold the exhibition together. Maud's also worried that the FBI will get involved in the investigation."

"With inconclusive autopsy findings, it's possible. More likely it'll be the BIA criminal investigator from Muskogee, Tony Warwick."

Molly knew Tony and liked him well enough. If she had to deal with a federal agent, Tony would be her first choice. And she didn't think he'd have any trouble accepting whatever help the sheriff would allow D.J. to provide.

"Maud asked me to get evidence to help clear Robert. She doesn't believe he can get a fair shake from the government." Understandably, many Cherokees were suspicious of anything the federal government had a hand in. In their long association with the government, they had usually come out holding the short end of the stick.

"Lots of luck," D.J. said, opening cabinet doors. "You saw the kid shoot the dart with your own eyes."

"But he didn't seem to be aiming at Tom."

"Tell that to the feds." D.J. opened another door and scanned shelves. "I give up. Where's your skillet?"

Molly found her infrequently used frying pan and set it on a burner of the apartment-sized range. D.J. took a bowl from the cabinet, dropped the meat in it, and broke up the ball of ground beef with the fork. He reached for a jar of taco sauce. "How about shredding some lettuce and dicing tomatoes," he said.

She found a small cutting board at the back of the cabinet and set to work. "Another weird thing. Tom had just finished telling the origin-of-death myth when he collapsed."

D.J. lifted a brow. "Come on, Molly. You just said touching the wampums is what set them off."

"I said that's what Maud believes."

He grinned. "Sorry, but now you're telling me they got ticked off by Tom's story. They can hear?"

Molly managed a smile. "Not funny, D.J."

"Hey, you want funny? Did you hear about the planeload of American lawyers that were captured by a band of terrorists?"

"Nope."

"The terrorists sent word to the president that if he doesn't meet their demands, they'll begin releasing the captives, one by one."

Molly laughed and actually felt a little cheerier, until she remembered that Tom Battle had been a lawyer. She was sure D.J. hadn't made a conscious connection between that fact and the joke, but it didn't seem right to be laughing at lawyer jokes right now.

Before D.J. could tell another one, she said, "We're having carrot cake for dessert." She had picked it up at a local bakery that afternoon.

The corners of his mouth twitched. "You bought it."

"Why should I go to the trouble of baking a cake when I can't improve upon the bakery's?"

"You've got no nesting instinct, woman."

"What's baking a cake have to do with nesting?" Her knife tap-tap-tapped against the cutting board as she diced a tomato. "Would you really like me better if I baked cakes?"

He grinned and bent over to kiss her cheek. "I couldn't like you any better, sugar. Don't you know that by now?"

Molly knew it. He'd told her in as many ways as possible without actually using the word *love*. That's what he really meant, though. Luckily, she wasn't in love with D.J. She told herself that all the time, but it was getting harder to believe it.

The trouble was that there had been too many people in her past who'd said they loved her and then had betrayed her. Her father. Her mother. A man named Kurt Williams who, in the eighteen months they were together, neglected to mention that he had a wife and two kids. She was gun-shy. She couldn't let her defenses down far enough for the possibility of love to enter her mind, and she didn't want D.J. to talk about it.

Sensing his eyes on her, she felt her face flush and she frowned and concentrated on the tomatoes. D.J. stirred the meat mixture in the skillet. She knew he wanted to say more but was restraining himself.

"Did you have a busy day?" she asked in a small voice.

"Okay, I'll let you change the subject. But I know what you're doing." She didn't respond, and he went on. "Well, let's see. Did I have a busy day? Sure. Saturdays are always busy. Two cars were stolen last night. We found one abandoned on the highway to Tulsa this morning. The gas tank was empty. I figure it was kids joyriding. No trace of the other car, though. And there was another break-in overnight too. Out at the nursery."

"Green Gardens Nursery?"

He nodded. "An employee found the backdoor standing open when he got to work at nine. A window had been broken. He called and waited for me to get there before going inside."

"What kind of thieves steal plants?"

"Good question. I can't believe there's much of a black market in trees and shrubs. Anyway, it didn't look like the plants were disturbed. I stayed while the employee looked around, but he didn't notice anything missing."

"Like at Tom's house," Molly murmured.

"Only the nursery wasn't vandalized. The burglar probably wanted the money from the cash register, but they don't keep any there overnight. I dusted the register for prints, but the clear ones turned out to belong to employees."

Four crimes, at least, had been committed in the darkness while Molly slept. "When I was a kid," Molly said sadly, "I don't remember hearing about many crimes around here, except maybe somebody breaking the speed limit or a DUI. Now we have stolen cars and burglaries. And murder."

"It happened then too. Adults protect kids from things like that, and kids are too self-centered to wonder about what's going on if it doesn't affect them. Hey, I deal with crime all day. Let's change the subject again."

"Let's. When have you heard from Courtney?" D.J.'s ten-year-old daughter lived with his ex-wife in Colorado.

"Talked to her last night. We're making plans for our ski trip in December." Gloria, D.J.'s ex-wife, was getting married in December and D.J. got to have Courtney for ten days while Gloria was on her honeymoon. "I mentioned that you might come along."

Molly stiffened. "You shouldn't have done that," she said, piqued. "I haven't decided yet. I only said I'd think about it."

"You've had plenty of time to think about it." D.J. sounded a little piqued himself. "It's not a complicated decision. What's it going to be, Molly?"

She resented his pressing her, while realizing that she shouldn't. She *had* had plenty of time to think it over, and D.J. needed an answer. "Courtney would probably rather have you all to herself," she equivocated.

D.J. stirred the meat mixture in the skillet. "I want her to get to know you."

She let that pass without comment. "I'll give you an answer soon, okay?" She already knew what her answer would be, and he probably did too. If she went on vacation with D.J. and his daughter, she felt she would be making a statement. Molly wasn't ready to make that kind of statement, didn't know if she'd ever be. And she'd be damned if she'd be pressured into it.

They talked of other things as they ate dinner.

If D.J. was put out with her, he got over it quickly. When they finished dessert, he said, "Leave the dishes."

She was glad to agree. She could clean up later.

D.J. grinned devilishly and pulled her to her feet and wound his arms around her waist. "Let's neck."

He kissed her and she leaned against him, enjoying the taste of his mouth and his warm body wrapped around her. She wasn't in love with him, though.

Yeah, sure.

What did she call this excitement she felt when he kissed her? The little lift of her heart whenever he came on the scene?

The sudden clump of tears in her throat surprised her. "D.J." She planted both palms on his chest and shoved him down on the sofa, but he held on to her as he fell and they tumbled together on the cushions.

# 12

The medical examiner reached Molly in her office Monday afternoon. "Ken Pohl here," he barked when Molly answered the telephone. "Got the results of my antigen tests." She may have heard the term *antigen tests* before, but the context eluded her. "I have to tell you, Molly, I see a pattern developing here."

She had been about to leave when the phone rang. Now she dropped her purse and leaned back against the desk. "What kind of pattern?"

"This is the second autopsy I've done in which you had a special interest, and there are definite commonalities." Pohl got a kick out of stringing her along. It could be maddening.

"Yes?"

"It's downright spooky."

She hitched one hip up on the desk. "Could you cut to the chase?"

Pohl expelled a sigh. "A bit of morgue humor, Molly. If we're going to go on working together, you must learn to appreciate my little attempts at levity. I'm hinting that you may be putting some kind of Indian hex on these people. It's a joke."

This was a sick man. "*What* commonalities?"

"No time for small talk, eh, Molly? Always so serious. You must learn to lighten up." Molly remained silent. "Well, shoot." She heard the sound of papers rattling. "Both victims were poisoned," Pohl said. Now she knew where she'd heard of antigen tests before.

As Pohl's words sank in, so did she—into the chair behind her desk. She gazed at the scarred desk top and saw Tom Battle's face, bathed in perspiration as it had been Saturday morning at the museum before his collapse. He *was* sick before the dart was blown.

"A poisonous alkaloid," Pohl said. "Commonly known as nicotine."

The word seemed to have no rational connection to death. "Nicotine," Molly repeated uncomprehendingly. "But Tom didn't even smoke."

"The poison was much too concentrated to have come from smoking. But this is one case where the victim might have been better off if he had been a smoker. He'd have had a higher tolerance."

"Where did it come from, if not tobacco?"

"I said it didn't come from smoking. A lethal dose could probably be distilled from the tobacco in several cigarettes. But it's available as an insecticide too, in highly concentrated liquid form."

"Then it was in something he ate or drank?"

"No. I didn't find it in the stomach contents. And there was no excess concentration in the nostrils, either, so it wasn't inhaled. I found it in several upper-body tissue samples. Absorbed through the skin."

This got crazier all the time. Molly pressed her lips together and told herself that if he kept talking, he would begin to make sense eventually.

"Do you still have the dart that hit him?" Pohl asked.

Now she saw what he was getting at and hoped, for Maud's sake, that he was wrong. "It's at the OSBI lab."

"Tell them to check it for nicotine."

Molly felt suddenly queasy. If Conrad hadn't stopped her, she might have picked up that dart! Wait a minute. Both Robert Wildcat and Victor Halland had touched it.

It couldn't be the dart, and she still had the feeling that some important link was missing. "Tom collapsed instantly when the dart hit him," she said.

"Instantly? You mean like within a few minutes?"

"I mean instantly. Is the stuff that lethal?"

"It's lethal, if enough of the poison is present, but it rarely kills instantly. It can take up to three or four hours, even if no counteractive measures are administered. But there is a case or two on record where the victim died within a few minutes. Nicotine causes cardiac irregularity, slows the respiration, and finally paralyzes the muscles, including the respiratory system. Not a pleasant way to die."

In Tom's case, at least, it happened very quickly. Small comfort for Daye Hummingbird and Tom's father.

"Instantaneous death is still a problem, though," Pohl continued. "There shouldn't have been time for so much to be absorbed by body tissue. Of course, everybody's different." He paused. "But instantly? Are you sure he wasn't hit earlier?"

"Absolutely. I saw it happen."

"What I mean is, could he have been hit by another dart, sometime before the one you saw?"

"No—well, not unless it happened before I arrived at the museum." Someone would have mentioned it, wouldn't they? "I'll check into it."

"Do that. Let me know what you find out."

"I will. Thanks, Dr. Pohl."

Molly disconnected and immediately dialed the sheriff's department and gave D.J. the autopsy findings. He said he'd ask the OSBI lab to check the dart specifically for nicotine. Then she went home to put on a dress. She had less than an hour to get to the Baptist church for Tom Battle's funeral.

The church was packed. Molly saw Maud Wildcat, Josiah Kawaya, and Regina and Steven Shell sitting near the front. Lily Roach and her husband sat together at the back. Brenda, the museum receptionist, was there too. They must have closed the museum for the funeral. Molly didn't see Robert Wildcat or Victor Halland. Wolf Kawaya had also had the good sense to stay away.

Daye Hummingbird sat with Tom's father on the front pew. She wept quietly throughout the short service. Afterward, Molly pulled the Civic into the line of cars going to the cemetery.

At the grave site, the pastor read scriptures and prayed with the small group assembled there. ·

> In my father's house are many mansions . . .
> I go to prepare a place for you.

Molly thought about the heaven described by her Sunday-school teacher at the little Baptist church that she'd attended with Eva, growing up. Streets of gold and gates of pearl and everybody laughing and singing. It was nice to imagine Tom there. Then she thought about the ancient Cherokee belief that spirits of murdered people wander restlessly in a Ghost Land until their murders are avenged. Only then can they travel to the Night Land and be at rest. Not so nice to imagine Tom's restless spirit, seeking revenge.

Perhaps Daye was thinking the same thing. She did not seem in the least comforted by the minister's words. She stared at the ground throughout the minisermon, never moving except to wipe her eyes.

Molly joined Regina and Steven as the group dispersed.

Regina seemed preoccupied, but the faraway look in her eyes cleared as she focused on Molly. "I still can't believe Tom's dead," she said. "We were with him two days ago, and now . . ."

"Unexpected death is tough to accept," Molly agreed. "There's no time to get ready for it."

"Poor, poor Daye," Regina murmured. "She's taking it so hard."

Steven's eyes still had that disconcertingly vacant look. He kept blinking in the hazy sunlight, like a cave creature who'd crawled out of the dark. Molly was glad Regina couldn't read her mind, but there was something animallike about Steven under the influence of his medication, his humanity muted by it. His face was stony, expressionless, and he shifted from one foot to the other, taking no interest in the conversation. He hadn't looked directly at Molly, even when she spoke to him.

"Can I have the car keys?" he asked.

Regina dug them out of her purse and handed them to him. "I'll be there in a minute." Molly watched him walk away, disturbed by the image that had sprung to mind. Steven, standing behind Robert and Victor at the museum. She had forgotten that Steven was there too, when Robert shot the dart at Tom Battle. He had shown no interest in any of the other exhibits, yet twice he'd walked over and stood near the blowguns and darts for several minutes. What had attracted him to the Kawayas' table?

"He's not getting any better," Regina said, staring anxiously after her brother. "I'm going to check into some private hospitals. They don't give him any serious counseling at

Eastern State. There aren't enough psychiatrists and social workers to go around. If a good psychiatrist worked with him, he might at least learn to interact with people, hold a job. Maybe even get by with little or no medication."

And live on his own, Molly thought, wishing that it could happen. Regina seemed to want Molly's agreement, so she said, "It's worth a try," but she thought Regina was indulging in wishful thinking. From what she had read, schizophrenia was caused by a chemical imbalance in the brain. Drug therapy was the major method of treatment.

"I can't live with myself until I've tried every way I know to help him," Regina said, still looking toward her parked car. "I better go. He's liable to get tired of waiting and wander off. Or drive off, and his driver's license expired years ago."

Molly hugged her and said good-bye, and Regina hurried away. The funeral-home limousine was leaving with Tom's relatives. Almost everyone had gone now, eager to leave the oppressive atmosphere of the cemetery behind. Molly looked around for Daye Hummingbird, who had driven there in her own car. She saw Daye's Toyota still parked where she'd left it and caught up with the artist as she walked down a grassy, grave-lined path.

"How are you doing, Daye?" Molly asked. Daye's beautiful face was haggard. Purple splotches, like bruises, sat beneath eyes swollen from crying. She wore a high-necked black dress that made her look half dead. Black wasn't Daye's color.

Daye squinted sideways at Molly, as though, like Steven, the sunlight hurt her eyes. "The man I love is dead. How do you think I'm doing?"

Molly didn't take offense. Daye wasn't usually sarcastic, but at the moment she was in so much pain she wasn't responsible for anything she said. "I'm sorry. It's hard to know what to say."

Daye dabbed at fresh tears with a tissue. They had reached her car, and she opened the door and sat sideways in the driver's seat, her black pumps resting on the ground. "I didn't mean to be hateful. I know it's awkward. I never know what to say to other people at funerals, either." She wiped her eyes again. "God, where does all this water come from? I've been crying for two days now. I have to get a grip on myself. I should go back to the museum tomorrow."

"It's a good idea to keep busy," Molly said gently.

"I know, and I need to sell some paintings. I just don't know if I can handle it, with Wolf there."

Molly wanted to question her, but she wondered now if this was the time. Would a day or two matter to Daye's state of mind? She couldn't wait long.

Daye helped her make up her mind by asking, "Have you heard that the medical examiner found poison in Tom's body?"

"Yes. I talked to Dr. Pohl and he raised some questions I couldn't answer. Maybe you can." Daye looked up at her, her swollen lids narrowed against the western sun. "Tom didn't seem himself Saturday morning," Molly went on. "I noticed it when I first arrived at the museum. That was more than half an hour before he started his story."

Tears welled up in Daye's eyes. She blotted them with the now-wet tissue. "He had a headache," she said when she could speak. "A really severe one. The pain was so bad it made him dizzy and nauseated."

"Did he suffer from migraines?"

She shredded the wet tissue in her lap. "No. He thought it was a sinus infection. He started feeling sick about the time he got to the museum at eight forty-five. I thought it was probably stress. He was upset over the mess he found at his house earlier that morning."

"I heard that nothing was taken," Molly said.

She shook her head. "It was vindictiveness, pure and simple."

"Wolf, you mean?"

She opened her purse, dropped in the shredded tissue, and took out a fresh one. She blew her nose. "Of course it was Wolf. I know the man. Smashing things is what he does when he's mad."

Molly wondered if Wolf had ever smashed Daye. "Dr. Pohl asked me if Tom was hit by another dart, before the one that struck him when he collapsed. When he first arrived at the museum?"

She looked confused but shook her head. "I was with him every minute. He was hit by one dart, and Wolf made it happen." She glanced up sharply. "What became of that dart? Do you know?"

"It's at the lab. They're running tests."

"They'll find the same poison that was in Tom's body." She clenched a handful of her black dress in her fist. "He killed Tom and he's going to pay for it—one way or another."

"Daye, Robert Wildcat shot the dart. I saw him."

She twisted the black fabric of her dress even tighter. "Wolf made him," she said stubbornly. "I don't know how, but that's what happened. Wolf can always manipulate things around to make them come out the way he wants. Except for me," she added with something like satisfaction. "He can't make me go back to him."

"Wolf says he didn't know Robert was going to do it until it was too late to stop him."

She looked at Molly with tortured eyes. "Of course he says that! Are you defending him?"

"No, but—"

"He told me that if he couldn't have me, nobody could. Wolf doesn't make idle threats. He's responsible for Tom's death."

"Are you so sure you're right?"

"Totally." She released her dress and turned in the car seat to grip the steering wheel. "Will the tribal police investigate?"

"They're doing a preliminary investigation with the sheriff's department. But if there's a trial it will be in a federal court. A federal agent will probably be around asking questions later in the week."

Daye put her head down on the steering wheel, as though it were too heavy to hold up any longer. After several moments during which she seemed to gather strength, she straightened up. "Can you conduct an independent investigation?"

"I already am," Molly told her. "Maud Wildcat asked me to."

"Good." She nodded. "I'm asking too. We can't let Robert take the blame for this. Wolf has to pay."

"If he's guilty," Molly added, knowing that Daye wasn't open to reason at the moment. She needed to blame *somebody*.

Daye didn't bother to respond. She had left the car key in the ignition, and she reached out and turned it, starting the engine. "I'm going home now and try to rest. I'll be at the museum tomorrow. I'll watch Wolf. Maybe he'll make a mistake and say something to implicate himself."

Daye was no match for Wolf Kawaya. Molly wondered if *she* was. "I think you should stay away from him, Daye."

Her dark eyes were hard and defiant between the swollen lids. Without another word, she closed the car door and drove away.

Dusk was creeping over the cemetery, and Molly was the last person to leave. The cemetery had grown chilly as the lowering sun withdrew its heat, and Molly shivered. Squinting at the orange sliver of sun still visible on the horizon, she thought of Tom's story about the Sun, who had brought death into the world.

As she hurried down the path to the Civic, she remembered the time, in high school, when she'd come there at night with three friends, another girl and two boys. The boys had challenged them to a walk among the graves. Everybody did it at least once during their high-school years, or claimed to have done it. It was a local rite of passage.

The boys had escorted them to the center of the cemetery and identified a grave as that of a murder victim whose ghost roamed the graveyard at night. Molly learned later that an old woman had been buried there in 1918. She'd died in her own bed of influenza.

Suddenly one of the boys had grabbed Molly's arm. "There he is now, behind that gravestone!" Molly had seen nothing, but the other girl screamed and Molly had been infected with her panic. Meantime, the boys deserted them and dashed back to the car. Which is what they'd planned all along. Molly had grabbed the other girl's hand and they had started to follow at a speed that Molly had never reached on foot before or since.

But before they reached the car, Molly had had time to think, and she hauled her companion to a halt. "Let's teach them a lesson and leave by another way."

They'd slipped away and gone home. The boys were waiting anxiously for them at school the next day and pelted them with questions. Molly and the other girl had merely smiled mysteriously and said they'd had an amazing experience, but they weren't telling because you had to be there to believe it. Naturally, that drove the boys crazy.

Now, as Molly drove away from the cemetery, she wondered if local teens still followed the custom, but decided they were probably into more daring and dangerous exploits these days. Everything was more dangerous these days. Even arts-and-crafts exhibitions.

\*    \*    \*

That evening, as Robert was getting ready to go out with his friends, Maud went into his bedroom. He glanced at her, then zipped his jeans and pulled a sweatshirt over his head.

Maud stood at the foot of the bed, gripping the iron footboard with both hands. "I have to talk to you, Robert," she said.

"What about?" He turned to the dresser mirror and picked up a comb.

"They did an autopsy on Tom Battle. He was poisoned."

"I heard," he said, carefully parting his black hair. "Maybe the cops won't be on my back now."

Maud moved to the side of the bed and sank down on it. "I wouldn't be too sure."

He looked around at her. "Stop worrying, will ya? The dart didn't kill him. He ate something that was poisoned."

"I don't know what to think. There are so many rumors going around." Maud shook her head helplessly. "A friend told me that she heard the poison was absorbed through Tom's skin."

"How?" He sounded a little less cocky now.

She watched him comb his hair, squinting at his reflection in the mirror. "Robert, are you sure the poison wasn't on the dart?"

"Well, that's just great!" He threw down the comb. "My own grandmother thinks I'm guilty."

"No, no I don't." Maud got up and went to him, embraced his unyielding body. He shrugged her away. "Friday," she said, "before we went out to the museum, you told me that the Kawayas had their reasons for taking part in the exhibition with Tom Battle."

He scowled and went to the closet for his jacket. "I don't remember saying that."

"Well, you did. What did you mean, Robert?"

"Nothin'." He shrugged into the jacket. "I didn't mean nothin'." At the bedroom door, he turned back. "Don't wait up for me, Granny."

"Robert—"

"Gotta go," he called over his shoulder.

"Be back by eleven. It's a school night." She said it automatically, as she did every evening when he left the house. She had stopped hoping it had any effect on him.

"Sure, sure," Robert said. "But don't wait up."

Maud was too worried to sleep even if, for once, Robert came home on time. She followed him through the house. He went out the front door without saying anything else. She picked up a book and sank down on the couch, tried to read. But her mind wandered. Did Robert really know nothing of the Kawayas' reasons for taking part in the exhibition with Tom Battle? She had always been able to tell when her own children were lying, but Robert was an enigma.

They would test the dart, and if they found poison, word would get around. She should wait until then before she worried that Robert could be implicated in Tom Battle's death.

She should, but she couldn't.

# 13

Early Tuesday morning, Molly drove to Maud Wildcat's house, hoping to find Robert there. Maud was getting ready to go to the museum and said that Robert had already left for school. She stepped out on the porch to talk to Molly, her long hair loose and flying. She had been about to braid it when Molly knocked on the door.

"At least that's where he said he was going," Maud added, catching her flying hair in her hand. "I can never be sure."

"I need to talk to him about what happened at the museum," Molly said.

"I told him you'd be around. Have you found out anything that'll help him?"

"Not yet," Molly admitted.

"I heard Tom Battle was poisoned." She studied Molly's face. "I'm not sure I understand how it happened."

Join the club, Molly thought.

"Has Robert been sick since Saturday morning?"

"Sick?" Maud repeated blankly. "No, and he'd have mentioned it if he had so much as a broken toenail. He likes sympathy." She frowned, then something flickered in her eyes as if a troubling idea had popped into her mind. "You'll keep trying to help Robert, won't you?"

"Yes." An old Ford with two flat tires sat on the grass next to a late-model Chevrolet in the driveway. "Is that Robert's Ford?"

Maud nodded. "He keeps saying he's going to get the tires fixed, get it running again. But I think it's past going."

"Does he walk to school?"

"Usually Victor picks him up."

"Did Victor pick him up this morning?"

"Yes."

Molly had meant to go to Victor's house next, but it seemed she'd struck out all around. She thanked Maud and drove to her office in the old Cherokee Capitol Building. She'd try to track down Robert and Victor after school.

Molly spent Tuesday morning in her office, thinning out old case files to make room for more current ones. By eleven o'clock, she had reduced three file-cabinet-drawers' worth of material to two, gaining an empty drawer. But the culled files lay in three stacks on her desk. There was no other place in her tiny office to put them.

The files would just about fit into two of the cardboard file-storage boxes she'd seen at Wal-Mart, and maybe she could store them at the tribal offices south of town.

She was supposed to meet Moira Pack, a friend since college days, at City Park on the bank of Town Branch Creek for lunch. If she left now, she'd have time to stop at Wal-Mart as well as pick up hamburgers and drinks before going to the park.

As she grabbed her purse from the bottom desk drawer, a young Cherokee woman opened the office door. Two children, about three and four, were with her. The younger of the two, a girl, hung on to the woman's hand. The boy twisted in front of his mother and grinned mischievously at Molly. The grin reminded Molly of a turbo-charged troublemaker named Billy who'd been in her elementary-school class.

"I'm looking for the Native American Advocacy League," the woman said. She was short and plump and discouraged-looked.

"You found it. I'm Molly Bearpaw. How can I help you?"

The little boy darted around his mother, into the hall, and ran toward the Cherokee Fine Art Gallery at the back of the building. The gallery had taken the space formerly occupied by the Cherokee Gift Shop when the gift shop was moved to a building in the tribal complex south of town.

"Bryan! Come back here!" The woman looked ready to cry. "I'd better get him before he breaks something." She pushed the girl into Molly's office and disappeared. The child looked at the closed door, and her bottom lip began to wobble.

"She'll be right back," Molly said hastily.

The child stuck a grubby thumb in her mouth and stared at Molly with chocolate eyes. Never having been around small children, Molly didn't know what to do with them. Where the heck was the mother?

The silence was becoming oppressive. "What's your name?" Molly asked lamely.

The child just looked at her and then at the door, which fortunately opened at that moment. The mother came in dragging Bryan, who clearly had places to go and people to see. The little girl grabbed a handful of her mother's dress without giving up the thumb in her mouth.

Unexpectedly, Molly's memory reached back in time to her four-year-old self. When her parents had represented security, before it had all come apart at the seams, and her stomach knotted in sympathetic response to the little girl.

The mother pointed to one of the chairs facing Molly's desk. "Sit right there, young man, and be quiet until I'm through here."

The boy sulked but climbed up in the chair. The mother took the other chair and lifted the girl to her lap.

Having put her purse back in the drawer, Molly shoved the stacked files to one side and sat down behind her desk.

"I'm Sarah Bowling," the woman said. "I called Chief Mankiller's office, and the secretary said I should come here."

Bryan was trying to slide unnoticed from his chair. His mother glared at him until he straightened up. "I'm hungry," he whined.

"We'll eat when we get back to Grandma's," Sarah Bowling said. Bryan began to kick the chair leg with his sneaker. His mother ignored him. The little girl was content to lean against her mother and suck her thumb.

"What can I do for you?" Molly asked.

Sarah Bowling glanced around the small, sparsely furnished office, unimpressed. No official-looking documents on the walls, and the furniture looked like what it was, castoffs.

"I'm not sure exactly what the Native American Advocacy League is."

"We advocate—mediate or speak for—Native American people." *We* meaning Molly, since she worked alone. "This is the northeast Oklahoma office, and I investigate complaints made by enrolled Cherokees."

"You mean, like you try to get wrongs righted?"

"I do my best," Molly said, feeling not exactly like the caped crusader, but close enough. "I'm an investigator. If you're looking for legal advice, I can't help you. I can refer you to an attorney, though."

"I've already talked to a lawyer. The district attorney too. For all the good it did me. They say I have to tell them where my husband—ex-husband—is before they can do much to help me. Wilson was in Oklahoma City the last time we heard from him, but his phone's been disconnected. And the letter I sent came back. He moved and left no forwarding address. His mother—Edith Thompson—lives here, but she's not about to tell me where he is."

Molly was beginning to get the picture. She'd seen other women like Sarah Bowling in this office. At the end of their ropes. Even though their problem wasn't really a civil-rights issue, Molly never turned them down. They'd usually been everywhere else they could think of before they came to her.

She asked, "Why do you want to find him?"

"To make him pay the child support he owes us. It's over four thousand dollars now. The kids and I had to move in with my folks because I couldn't pay the rent." It was an all-too-familiar story to Molly. She nodded understandingly. "They don't really have room for us," Sarah Bowling was saying, unable to ignore Bryan's kicking foot any longer. Her hand lashed out and swatted his knee. "Stop that!" She tried to smile at Molly, an apology of sorts. "The kids get on Daddy's nerves."

Molly nodded again, in total sympathy with Daddy.

"He never had much patience," Sarah Bowling went on, "and he's gotten worse as he's gotten older."

"Do you know where your ex-husband works?"

Bryan blew a spit bubble and Sarah shook her head at him distractedly. She turned back to Molly. "I called there. He left his job two months ago. If they know where he's working now, they wouldn't tell me."

Molly got a pen and note pad. "Give me the last address you have for him, his former employer's name and address, and his Social Security number." She took down the information as Sarah Bowling told her. If Wilson Bowling was out of state, it would be next to impossible to get local authorities to cooperate. Deadbeat dads were way down on their priority list. Most law-enforcement agencies were shorthanded; they couldn't even do justice to the murders and rapes.

If Bowling was in Oklahoma and she got lucky and found him, it still wouldn't be easy to get the police to pick him up. Their attitude was understandable because, even if a warrant was issued and they arrested Bowling, he'd be back on the street in twenty-four hours, after promising the judge he'd be a good daddy and mail the checks from now on. After all, he couldn't earn money for child support if they put him in jail.

There was no money in Molly's budget to hire a private investigator. She had to do it all herself. If she found Wilson Bowling and he was employed, Sarah could file a request for garnishment of his wages. But Molly had her own priority list and, at the moment, Tom Battle's death was on top.

"I had a job at the Sizzlin' Sirloin," Sarah said, "but I had to quit. I can't pay for day care without the monthly child-support checks. And I can't leave the kids with my folks. Mom's out at the museum most of the time, anyway."

The museum? "What's your maiden name?" Molly asked.

"Roach."

"You're Lily's daughter?"

Sarah nodded. "I didn't mean to sound like I was blaming her for not wanting to baby-sit the kids. After my brother was killed in that car wreck, she almost grieved herself to death. Working at the museum saved her sanity."

Molly couldn't remember that Lily had ever had a son. "How long ago was your brother killed?"

"It's been thirteen or fourteen years now," Sarah said. "Doug—that's my brother—was a student at O.U. at the time."

Molly pulled her mind back to the problem at hand. "I'll need to see your blue card," she said.

Sarah pulled a beat-up billfold from a battered, plastic purse and withdrew several cards. Every enrolled Cherokee was issued a Certificate of Degree of Indian Blood, often referred to as the white card. Three of the four cards on the desk were white.

"The kids' cards are there too," Sarah said.

Molly picked up the white cards. Sarah Bowling was three-quarters Cherokee, her children three-eighths. Wilson Bowling was a non-Indian, then. Caucasian, from the looks of his children. Molly handed back the white cards and picked up Sarah's tribal-membership card, the blue card. She made note of the registry number in the left-top corner of the card. "Is this the address where you're living now?" Molly asked.

"No," Sarah replied and gave Molly her parents' address and phone number.

"I'll need Mr. Bowling's date of birth." Sarah gave the information and Molly added, "Do you know where your ex-husband banks?"

Sarah looked puzzled. "It's been so long since I got a support check. Let me think. . . The last check he sent was on an Oklahoma City bank. United something—United Federal, maybe."

"Do you know any of his credit-card numbers?"

She shook her head. "He canceled them when we split. I guess he got new ones, but I don't know for sure."

"I'll start on this as soon as I can," Molly promised. "It may be a few days before I can get to it, but I'll be in touch with you."

Sarah Bowling's face relaxed from within. She had transferred her problem to Molly and naively expected miracles. "Thank you." It sounded like a sigh.

Molly watched Sarah leave, carrying her daughter and dragging Bryan, who had decided he wanted to stay after all. Sarah Bowling would give out, or give up, long before Bryan did. Unless Sarah was very lucky, the boy would be out of control before he was a teenager.

Every time a woman came into this office, wanting help finding her children's father, Molly felt as though the scabs had been torn off old wounds. She thought of her father, who had disappeared when she was four, and of Kurt Williams, who'd deserted a wife and two kids in California and moved to Tulsa, where Molly had met him. Fallen for him. Believed his lies. She and Kurt were together for eighteen months before his wife tracked him down. God, she hoped Mrs. Williams had taken him to the cleaners.

Leaving a bad marriage was one thing, but what kind of man walked away from his children? What did they say when they left?

Did they lie? *Going out for a pack of cigarettes. Need me to pick up anything?*

Did they make a joke out of it so the wife wouldn't suspect they were serious? *This family bit has been fun, but I'm out of here.*

Or did they, like Molly's father, just not come home one day?

Molly would do her damnedest to find Wilson Bowling and do whatever she could to force him to support his children. Problem was, her damnedest probably wouldn't be good enough.

She labeled a new file folder, dropped in her notes, and stuck it in the file cabinet with two other like cases that she hadn't yet given up on.

She got her purse and locked the office. She barely had time to swing by a fast-food drive-by window and get to the park in time to meet Moira at twelve.

Maybe she could make it to Wal-Mart after lunch.

# 14

The park was on the bank of Town Branch Creek, an arm of the Illinois River that meandered through Tahlequah. It was filled with people bent on enjoying the mild October weather while it lasted. The long-range weather forecast predicted a cold front was on the way, so there might not be many more of these Indian-summer days.

There were young mothers with toddlers in tow, retirees with time on their hands, and businesspeople and students taking lunch breaks from stores, offices, and the local high school.

When Molly arrived, Moira was waiting at one of the concrete picnic tables. Molly spotted Moira's blond head quickly and negotiated a path around four retirement-aged men engaged in a hot game of horseshoes and three young children playing tag.

Moira greeted Molly with a wave and a grin. " 'Bout time you got here. I was ready to send out a search party."

"How did you manage to get a table in this mob?" Molly asked.

Moira threw her hands out, palms up. "No problem. I only had to tackle a couple of old ladies."

Molly chuckled. "Sorry I'm late," she apologized, setting the sack containing lunch on the table. "I got held up at the office, and then there was a line at the restaurant's drive-by window."

"You brought food. You're forgiven." Moira reached into the sack eagerly and pulled out paper-wrapped hamburgers, french fries, and Cokes in paper cups. "Felix is in court all day, so I don't have to rush back." Molly's boss, Felix Benson, was an attorney with an office on Muskogee Avenue. "He took Marquita with him."

"How's she working out?" A few weeks ago, Felix had hired a female associate fresh out of law school.

Moira wrinkled her nose. "She's terribly eager, but she'll mellow with time. Meanwhile, it's tiring as all hell." She unwrapped a burger. "I'm starving." She took a bite, then groaned ecstatically. "Oh, this is scrumptious." She popped a french fry into her mouth and chewed happily, tossing her stylish cap of blond hair out of her eyes.

Molly sat down across from her, tore open a packet of ketchup, and sprinkled it over her french fries in their paper envelope.

"First decent meal I've had in two weeks," Moira said, taking another bite of her burger.

"How come?" Molly asked, picking up a ketchup-drizzled fry.

"Dieting."

Molly ate the fry and unwrapped her burger. "Whatever for?" She scrutinized what she could see of Moira's slender figure in a jade shirtwaist dress. Moira didn't appear to have gained a pound since Molly last saw her.

"Have to," Moira said, "if I want to get in my wedding dress."

Molly's burger-filled hand halted on the way to her mouth. "You already bought a dress?" Moira had told her three weeks ago that she was getting married in January. To Chuck something, whom she'd been seeing for several months. Molly could never remember his last name, which didn't seem important because he probably wouldn't be around long. At thirty, Moira had had so many fiancés that their names ran together in Molly's mind. She had taken the news that Moira was once more altar-bound with a large grain of salt. Every other time, Moira had gotten cold feet and backed out before the wedding.

"Yep," Moira told her. "I wanted to convince skeptics like you that I'm serious this time."

Molly wondered if Moira's convincing herself wasn't more to the point. From the corner of her eye she saw two young boys get into a pushing match and deftly snatched her drink out of the way as they bumped against the table. Laughing, they tumbled on the grass nearby, wrestling, until one got up and ran away. The other boy gave chase.

"Oh, to have that much energy," Moira said. She turned back to Molly. "The dress is a size six, so I need to lose ten pounds. It would be a lot easier if I'd start smoking again." She raised a hand as Molly opened her mouth to protest. "But I won't, so save your breath." She twirled a french fry. "I'll do it the hard way, which doesn't mean I can't indulge in a good old greasy burger and fries now and then."

Molly tore the paper off a straw and stuck it through the plastic lid on her Coke. "You don't need to lose any weight, Moira."

"You can never be too thin."

"Has it occurred to you," Molly asked, "that maybe there's another reason you bought a wedding dress that's too small for you?"

Moira's plucked brows shot up wonderingly. "Such as?"

"Not being able to get into the dress could be an excuse to call off the wedding. In case you need one."

Moira looked wounded, though it might be an act. "That dress cost the earth, Molly. Besides, do you really think I'd deliberately sabotage my own wedding?"

"Not deliberately. Unconsciously, maybe."

Moira sniffed and took a bite of burger. Mustard dripped down her chin. She grabbed a paper napkin and wiped it off. "That's the kind of twisted logic I'd expect from a psych major," she said, but there was a hint of amusement in her eyes. Molly grinned good-naturedly.

"I told you," Moira insisted, "I'm going to lose ten pounds. The dress will fit perfectly on my wedding day."

Molly shrugged. "Not if you keep eating greasy burgers and fries, it won't."

"Don't be so cynical. I can get away with eating a meal like this every couple of weeks," Moira insisted. "It's like a reward for staying on my diet for fourteen days."

Molly nodded. "I see." She watched her friend finish off her burger with relish. "So," she said, "you're actually going to do it this time."

"Ah-ha. You're starting to believe me."

"Well, I figure you'll take the plunge eventually. This may be the time."

"My sister's going to be my matron of honor. I want you to be my bridesmaid."

Molly pressed a hand against her breast. "I'm flattered, but you don't mind if I wait awhile before buying my dress, do you?"

Moira made a face. "Go ahead, scoff. You're entitled, I guess. But I'm getting married. Get used to it."

"I can if you can," Molly retorted.

Moira wadded up the burger wrapping and stuffed it in the sack. She ate the last of her fries and eyed Molly's. "Are you going to eat all those?"

Molly laughed and pushed the fries across the table. "Help yourself. I have a Snickers bar at the office for dessert."

"Don't gloat, Molly," Moira said, attacking the fries. "It's downright cruel." She plucked another fry from the dwindling pile. "God, what I wouldn't give to have your genes."

Molly had inherited her grandmother's metabolism. At five feet seven inches, she stayed within a couple of pounds of a hundred and fifteen, no matter what she ate. She envied Moira's curves. Apparently it was the way of women to want what nature had denied them.

"I'd make the exchange if I could," Molly assured her.

"Are you still seeing D.J.?"

"On occasion."

Moira eyed her impatiently. "And?"

"And what?"

"How are things progressing?"

"Oh, you know . . ."

"Details, Molly," Moira urged. "I need details."

"We had dinner at my place last night. D.J. cooked." Molly took a sip of Coke and waved at an acquaintance who caught her eye. The woman was seated with a friend at another table.

"I think you're crazy about him."

Molly shrugged. "I like him," she amended. "He wants me to go on vacation with him and his daughter in December."

"Great! Where are you going?"

"I'm not."

Moira eyes widened. "Can't you get off work?"

"It's not that. I think Courtney would resent it. She sees too little of her father as it is. She deserves to have his undivided attention when they're together."

"Bull," Moira said. "You're scared to spend too much time with D.J. You're afraid you'll like it too much. So you're using Courtney as an excuse. You're worse than I am, Molly."

Molly didn't bother denying it. Moira was right. "The older you get, the more relationships you see going bad. Maybe that's both our problems. It makes you think..." Her voice trailed off. Over Moira's shoulder, she saw four teenagers getting out of a car on the street that bordered the park. "I see somebody I need to talk to," she said. "Two somebodies, actually."

Moira turned her head to look. "Who?"

"Robert Wildcat and Victor Halland. They're with those two girls. Looks like they've spotted a table." The four were heading for the other end of the park. Victor was carrying a large paper sack with the name of a local fast-food restaurant on it.

"Robert Wildcat sounds familiar," Moira mused.

"His grandmother, Maud Wildcat, is a well-known weaver."

Moira's brow puckered. "I know, but I think I heard Robert's name recently. Wait. Isn't that the boy who killed Tom Battle?"

"It's not certain he killed Tom, and if he did, it was accidental," Molly said, watching the four settle at a just-vacated table. "At least, I think it was."

"But I heard he shot him with a poisoned dart. I went to The Shack this morning for my coffee break. Everybody in the restaurant was talking about it."

Of course. The story would have spread up and down Muskogee Avenue, juicily embellished by now. "You can't believe everything you hear at The Shack," Molly told her. "We don't know that the dart was poisoned. We're still waiting for the lab report."

"We? You're involved in the investigation?"

"Robert's grandmother asked me to get evidence to exonerate him," Molly said. "Listen." She got up. "I missed him at Maud's house this morning. I'd better talk to him now, while I can."

"I have to get back to the office, anyway," Moira said, gathering up the rest of their litter. "Felix may take a notion to call. Or good old Marquita. Thanks for lunch. Next time's my treat."

Molly was already headed toward the table where the four teenagers sat. "Talk to you later, Moira," she called over her shoulder.

# 15

The teenagers' conversation was animated as Molly approached their table. Victor seemed to be impersonating a particularly disliked teacher, which the other three found hilarious.

"And then old bat-face caught Robert passing a note about how frigging bored he was, only he didn't say frigging. She read it in front of the whole class. Left out the f-word, though."

The girls were doubled over with laughter.

"I tried to slide under the desk," Robert said. "She grabbed my ear and twisted it. You believe it? Hurt like hell." They all hooted.

"She goes, 'Perhaps Mr. Wildcat would like to entertain us,'" Victor mimicked, "'since he's so bored.'"

The girls erupted in more peals of laughter. One of them was a freckled redhead with a turned-up nose, the other a pretty ash-blonde with braces. They looked about fifteen. Nobody noticed Molly until she spoke.

"Hello, Robert. Victor."

The girls looked up at Molly curiously. Victor's expression was blank; perhaps he didn't recognize Molly. But Robert did, and his grin froze, then slid away. He looked a little worried and defensive, and he seemed to be having trouble keeping the adolescent bravado in place.

"I'd like to talk to you," Molly said to Robert.

"Call my secretary," Robert retorted, grinning at the girls, who giggled on cue.

Molly ignored the smart remark. He was showing off for his friends. "I tried to catch you at Maud's house before school, but you'd already gone."

"You ain't the police," Robert mumbled. "I don't have to talk to you."

"No, you don't, but your grandmother asked me to help you."

He snorted. "I'll let you know when I need some."

Molly's patience snapped. "Cut the crap, Robert. You already need help. You could be in very big trouble."

He managed a faint sneer. "What for?"

"Could we talk privately?" Molly asked, glancing at the girls, who were listening with great interest.

Victor scooted off the bench, clearly glad to go. "We'll wait for you over there by that tree," he said, picking up his sandwich and drink. The girls got up too.

"Would you stay here too, Victor?" Molly said and looked at the girls. "It won't take long."

The girls exchanged a puzzled glance and retreated to the tree about a hundred yards away, where they whispered to each other behind their hands. Victor sat back down reluctantly.

"I'm employed by the tribe as an investigator," Molly told them. "Robert, your grandmother asked me to look into what happened at the museum Saturday morning. She seems to think I can get evidence to clear you of any wrongdoing."

"I didn't do nothin' wrong," Robert flared, but he didn't look at Molly. The macho posturing was nothing but a token gesture for the benefit of his friends. The kid was scared.

"You blew the dart that hit Tom Battle. Did you know the autopsy showed Tom died of nicotine poisoning?"

He nodded and met her eyes briefly. "That oughta prove I'm innocent. I never even knew nicotine could kill you, except maybe lung cancer. But that takes years and years. And, anyway, I didn't have no tobacco on me at the museum. I ain't saying I don't smoke sometimes, chew a little too. But not that morning."

Molly explained what the medical examiner had told her, that the poison had been absorbed through the skin, not inhaled or swallowed.

"I already knew that," Robert muttered. "Granny told me."

"I don't get it," Victor put in. "How can you rub tobacco into somebody?"

"The poison was probably in liquid form," Molly said. "You can buy nicotine, highly concentrated, as an insecticide. Or it could have been distilled from cigarettes." She looked at Robert. "Or chewing tobacco."

"I never even heard of that before," Robert said, trying to sound confident. "Nobody I know ever heard of it." He unwrapped his sandwich and began eating, as if that settled the matter.

"I sure didn't," Victor added for good measure.

Molly didn't know whether to believe anything they said. She suspected both boys were good liars. They'd probably had plenty of practice, getting themselves out of scrapes. But her memory of the incident at the museum still led her to believe that Robert hadn't meant to hit anyone with the dart.

"Look, I'm not the police, as you pointed out, Robert. I can't arrest anybody, even if I have evidence that they've committed a crime. But I can't help you, either, unless you're straight with me." She looked from Robert to Victor. They looked back at her warily. "Why did you shoot that dart, Robert?" she went on. "You must have realized you could hit somebody, with so many people around."

He shrugged and swallowed a bite before answering. "I don't know why I did it." He glanced sideways at Victor. "I was just messin' around."

Victor looked glumly at his hands which rested on the table, clutching his still-wrapped sandwich. The girls, who were sitting cross-legged on the grass, were eating and watching the three at the table. One of them giggled and drew a glance and a half smile from Victor. Then he cleared his throat. "I dared him," he said softly. "I never really thought he'd do it."

For the first time, Molly felt she was getting the truth—rather, a little piece of it. She sat down on the end of the bench opposite the two boys, turning to face them, leaning forward, her elbows on the table. "Okay. That makes sense. You handed him the dart, Victor. I saw you."

Victor frowned. He unwrapped his sandwich and carefully removed the pickles, dropping them, one by one, on the paper wrapper. "Yeah, I guess that's what happened. I don't really remember."

"We both picked up darts to look at them," Robert said, coming to Victor's defense. "It wasn't all Victor's fault. I knew it was dumb to shoot the damn thing, but I did it anyway. I do dumb things sometimes without really thinking about it. Ask my granny, if you don't believe me."

"Do you remember where you got the dart, Victor?"

Victor seemed to think this was a pretty stupid question. "There was a whole stack of 'em on the table."

"Are you sure the dart you handed Robert came from the stack on the table?"

He nodded. "Where else would I have got it?"

"You're sure nobody handed it to you?" Molly asked.

"Like who?"

"I'm just wondering if Wolf or Josiah Kawaya gave it to you."

Both boys were silent, frowning, while they worked this out. Robert looked at Victor and lifted his shoulders. Victor shook his head. "No, it was on the table."

Molly wasn't ready to give up on that line of speculation yet. It was the only one that made any sense. "Did either of you see anyone fooling with the darts while you were at the Kawayas' table?"

"No..." said Victor, and after a hesitation Robert shook his head again.

"Somebody might have added a dart to the stack without your being aware of it. While they pretended to examine them or something."

"Nobody did anything like that, that I saw," Victor said.

Again, Robert hesitated before he said slowly, "Wolf was whittling a dart when we came up. He could've put it with the others when he was finished."

"Yeah, now that you mention it," Victor chimed in, "I think he did."

"Is that the dart you picked up, Victor?" Molly asked.

"I don't remember."

"Robert, did you notice if Victor picked up the dart Wolf had just put down?"

"Hell, I don't know," Robert said, black brows drawn together. "They all looked alike to me. Wait a minute . . . Are you saying Wolf put a poisoned dart on the stack?"

"I'm only trying to figure out exactly what happened," Molly said. "It's no secret that Wolf and Tom didn't get along."

Robert glanced worriedly at Victor, who looked quickly away. "Lots of people didn't like Tom Battle."

"Including you?" Molly asked.

Robert stared at his half-eaten sandwich. "I didn't have nothing against him personally. And Wolf didn't put no poisoned dart on the table, he wouldn't do that." But he didn't sound completely sure.

There was nowhere else to go with Wolf at the moment. "Do either of you know Steven Shell?"

Victor rubbed his chin while he tried to remember. "I seen him around," Robert said. "He's squirrel bait. Wacko." He looked at the girls and grinned. They giggled; they had their role down pat.

"He has schizophrenia," Molly said, irritated with the flip way Robert had labeled Steven, written him off. It was the sort of ignorant attitude Regina must deal with all the time. "It's a disease that can be controlled with medication."

"Then how come he's in the nuthouse half the time?" Robert scoffed.

"He goes there so the doctors can adjust his medication," Molly said, oversimplifying the complicated truth.

Victor shrugged carelessly. "Why'd you want to know if we knew him?"

"He was at the museum Saturday morning. He was standing behind you and Victor when you shot the dart."

"I didn't see him," Robert said.

"I did," Victor put in. "Yeah, now I know who you mean. He came up behind us and never said nothin'. Just stood there, gawking around and smiling every once in a while. He acted kind of weird."

"Did he come close enough to the table to touch anything?"

"Hey, I see where you're going now," Robert said, more animated than at any other time during the conversation. "Steven Shell could've put a poisoned dart on the table. Is that what you're saying?" Clearly, he liked the notion, which got him and Victor off the hook. As well as Wolf. Apparently Wolf was a friend, maybe a hero, to Robert.

"No, I'm trying to get you two to remember every detail of what happened while you were at the Kawayas' table. I saw Steven standing behind you, but he never moved closer than five or six feet from the table while I was watching."

"If he came closer, I never noticed," Victor said.

"We could've been lookin' the other way," Robert suggested hopefully. "Or he could've thrown a dart on the table from where he was standing, easy."

"Naw." Victor rejected the idea out of hand. "We would've noticed if a dart had come flying through the air."

"I agree with Victor," Molly said. She had run out of questions. "I won't keep you from your lunch any longer. Thanks for talking to me."

"One thing I don't get," Robert said. "If the poison was on the dart and it can get through your skin, like you said, how come me and Victor didn't get poisoned too? We both touched it."

"I haven't figured that out yet," Molly admitted. She wasn't going to tell them she didn't even know for sure that the dart was poisoned. If the boys were telling the truth, it seemed unlikely. If the lab found no poison on it, she'd inform Robert and Victor, but there was no point in getting their hopes up until she knew.

After leaving the park, she went by Wal-Mart, bought two storage boxes, and lugged them across half a block of lawn, through the dappled shade of sugar-maple trees, to the office.

D.J. had left a message on the answering machine. "Call me as soon as you can," his recorded voice said. "If I'm not at the station, they'll know how to reach me."

She dialed the station and was put on hold while D.J. finished with another call. She unwrapped a Snickers bar and ate half of it while gazing out the window as she waited. An

English bulldog, with a squashed face, ran by, chasing a squirrel. The squirrel dashed up a tree, turned around at the top, and barked at the dog. The bulldog stood at the base and barked back. A middle-aged woman came along and called to the dog, who ignored her. She walked over, snapped a leash on the dog's collar, and dragged him away.

After several minutes, D.J. came on the line.

"Deputy Kennedy speaking."

"It's me," Molly said. "What's up?"

"We got the lab results on the dart. It had nicotine on it, all right. 'Drenched in the stuff,' the lab tech said. All but about an inch and a half at the top. Somebody must've gripped it at that end and dipped the pointed end in the poison."

Molly expelled a long breath. "I really expected it to be clean," she admitted.

"How did you figure that?"

"I talked to Robert Wildcat and Victor Halland a little while ago," Molly explained. "Victor swears he picked up a dart at random from the stack on the Kawayas' exhibit table and handed it to Robert. And Robert agrees that's what happened."

"You believe them?"

She nibbled on the Snickers, then laid it on the desk. She thought back over her conversation with Robert and Victor at the park. "I do, for some strange reason," she said finally. "I know they're smart-mouthed rabble-rousers, but I felt they were telling me the truth today. They're kids, D.J."

He put his hand over the receiver and spoke to someone, then came back on. "Sorry. I had to give Claude a message. Now, where were we? Oh, yes, Victor and Robert."

"I'm inclined to think they just happened to be at the wrong place at the wrong time."

"Kids have been known to murder before, Molly."

She twisted the phone cord around her finger. "I don't believe those two did." Was she resisting the obvious answer because she didn't want Maud to be hurt?

"Then somebody else—" She heard the rattle of papers at the other end of the line. "—somebody else put the dart where they'd pick it up."

She reached for the Snickers. Only one good bite left. She dropped the wrapper in the wastebasket and held the bite between thumb and forefinger. "They did say that Wolf was whittling a dart when they got to his table and that he might have added it to the stack. If that's the dart Robert shot, Wolf had to dip it in the nicotine first." She popped the candy into her mouth and licked her fingers.

"If he had a bottle of stuff handy, he could have done it without being seen," D.J. said.

"How?"

"He could've had his hands under the table."

She finished eating the candy before she asked, "How could he be sure they'd choose *that* dart?"

D.J. made an exasperated noise. After a moment, he said, "By putting it right in front of them. Maybe he moved the other darts off to the side. The boys probably weren't paying close attention."

It could have happened that way, Molly supposed, but there was something wrong with the whole picture. She couldn't quite work out what it was.

"Or maybe," D.J. continued hesitantly, as if he uttered the words as they occurred to him, "maybe more than one dart was poisoned. So the boys could have picked up one of several lying there."

Molly found that even harder to believe. "Only Wolf or his father could have done it, then."

"So we're back to Wolf. He had motive and opportunity. And he's probably the one who vandalized Battle's house the night before."

Molly leaned back in her chair and stared out the window. The bulldog having left, two squirrels cavorted on the grass a few feet beyond the pane of glass. Nothing to worry about but storing enough food for the winter, she thought enviously. "It's a giant step from vandalism to murder," she mused. "And if Wolf poisoned several darts—or even one—he was running a big risk of poisoning whoever picked it up. Maybe it wouldn't have been enough to kill them, but Victor and Robert both touched the one Robert shot. Dr. Pohl said nicotine is highly toxic. They should at least have had some symptoms of poisoning. How do you explain that?"

"Maybe they were both lucky enough to grab the end that wasn't poisoned," he theorized.

"To borrow your phrase," Molly said, watching one squirrel chase the other up a tree, "it's a hell of a coincidence. The poisoner sure couldn't have counted on it."

"What other explanation is there?"

"I don't know," she admitted, turning away from the window. Picking up a pen, she drew a rough sketch of a squirrel on a memo pad. Very rough.

D.J. expelled a heavy breath. "Well, it may be out of our hands, anyway. Has the council contacted the feds yet?"

"I don't think so. They will, though, as soon as I report what you just told me. Which I'll have to do today." She gave the squirrel round eyes and increased the size of his tail.

"If they call in Tony Warwick," D.J. said, "he'll probably be here tomorrow or the next day."

Molly drew a big X through the squirrel and dropped the pen. "Maybe I should ask the tribal police to confiscate that boxful of darts that were on the table when Victor picked up the poisoned one. Although I don't see how any of them could be poisoned—Wolf or Josiah picked them up to put them in the box—unless they transferred them to the box without touching them."

"If any of them were poisoned," D.J. muttered, "you can bet they've already gotten rid of them."

Molly sighed. "You're right. I'm grasping at straws."

They made a date to watch a movie that evening at D.J.'s house. Molly would pick up a video at Computamax when she left the office. D.J. wanted to see *Sea of Love* again, but she was more in the mood for *Who Killed Roger Rabbit?* or one of the old Pink Panther movies. Maybe she'd just settle for a classic.

She'd barely removed her hand from the phone when it rang again.

"Molly."

"Grandmother? What a nice surprise. You hardly ever call me at the office. Is something wrong?"

"No—I don't think so. Is there?"

They seemed to be going in circles. There was something in Eva's voice, a worried note. "Not with me."

"Good, well . . . I won't keep you."

"Don't hang up!" What was going on with Eva? "Why did you really call, Grandmother?"

Eva sighed. "I wanted to make sure you're all right."

"Why now, all of a sudden? Wait—you had another dream, didn't you?"

"Yes," Eva admitted.

"About me again?"

"You were in it," Eva said. "I couldn't remember much about the first one, but it left a bad feeling behind. This time some of the dream stayed with me. You were in trouble. I saw your face, and you were scared, and you were surrounded by—by red. Like a red sea."

"Grandmother, I wish you wouldn't worry about me. I'm okay. Honestly." Except for worrying about Eva. Maybe these troubled nights *were* a symptom of aging. "When was the last time your doctor gave you a thorough physical?"

"A few months ago," Eva said, her tone a little lighter this time. "You think I'm going off my rocker or something?"

"No, but you're not yourself lately."

Eva let that pass. "Have you still got that Venus's-flytrap root I gave you?"

"Of course."

"With you?"

Molly had put it in the Honda's glove compartment. "Not right now."

"That's what I thought," Eva said. "I know I'm an old lady and not very educated, but I want you to get it and keep it with you. Hear?"

"I'll carry it in my purse, if it means so much to you."

"It does. Now, I'm going to go and let you get back to work."

Molly hung up, wondering if she should have a word with Eva's doctor. She'd give it a few days.

The notes she'd taken during her conversation with Sarah Bowling still lay on top of the desk. She read what she'd written, then picked up the phone, dialed information for the Oklahoma City area, and asked for United Federal Bank.

"There's no listing under that name in Oklahoma City," said the operator.

"I must have it down wrong," Molly said. "It's United something."

"I have a United American Bank and a United Savings and Loan."

Molly took down both numbers, deciding to use a ruse that had worked for her once before. The person she talked to at United Federal Bank could find no record of an account in the name of Wilson Bowling. She dialed the other number and asked for the bookkeeping department.

"Hi," Molly said, "this is Laura Devoy over at the United Federal Bank. We're having some problems involving a Wilson Bowling. We checked our credit-bureau sources and the only thing that came back was your savings and loan. Could you check your records and see what address you have for him?"

"Sure, hold on a minute."

Molly drummed her fingers on the desk and waited. She didn't expect much, but she might get lucky.

Finally the woman came back on the line. "Wilson Bowling closed out his account with us three months ago. His address at that time was 6013 Northwest Fifteenth Street."

That was the address where Sarah Bowling had sent her last letter, which had been returned. "That's the address I have, too, but he's no longer there."

"Wish I could be of more help."

"So do I. Thanks for trying, anyway."

Well, she hadn't expected it to be that easy. What next? Check public records.

She should have time later today to write the state department of public safety for an abstract of his driving record, which was public information. If Bowling had renewed his license or been stopped for a traffic violation in the last couple of months, the abstract should contain his current address.

When Molly got home later that afternoon, she stopped at Conrad's house to give him the news about the dart. They sat at Conrad's kitchen table, drinking strong coffee and eating the last of a cinnamon coffee cake one of the neighborhood widows had brought over, their conversation following much the same route as the one she'd had with D.J. earlier.

Then Conrad got a book on poisons from his extensive library and read the entry for *nicotine.* It was described as a yellowish-brown liquid with a slightly fishy odor. A few drops could be lethal, whether inhaled, introduced into the eye, ingested, or absorbed through the skin. Death, according to the entry, usually resulted from respiratory failure due to paralysis of the muscles, and occurred within five minutes to four hours.

"Basically, that's what the medical examiner told me," Molly said. "He found the poison in tissue samples taken from the upper body, so it was absorbed through the skin."

"That fits," Conrad said. "The dart punctured Battle's skin."

"The only problem Dr. Pohl had with what happened as I described it to him," Molly said, "was that Tom collapsed instantly and stopped breathing within a minute or two. Given the amount of poison found in the samples, he was surprised at the brief time-lapse between when the dart hit Tom and his death. He wanted to know if Tom had been hit by another dart earlier."

Conrad looked at her sharply, setting down his cup. "Are you sure he wasn't?"

Molly picked up coffee-cake crumbs and a couple of raisins with her fork, pressing them between the tines. "I talked to Daye Hummingbird," she said. "Daye was with Tom from the time he arrived at the museum around eight-forty-five until he collapsed about an hour later. She's sure there was no other dart. She was keeping a close eye on Tom because he wasn't feeling well. Had a severe headache. His house was vandalized the night before, and she assumed that worrying about the break-in had given him a tension headache. They both thought it was Wolf Kawaya who broke into Tom's house, but Wolf denies it."

A little frown appeared between his bushy eyebrows. "Which is what you'd expect, if he did it." Molly nodded. Conrad picked up the poison book again. "Headache is one of the symptoms of nicotine poisoning listed here. Also nausea and confusion."

"Tom did seem slightly confused once or twice," Molly mused.

Conrad looked up. "He could have already been suffering from nicotine poisoning. There might well have been two sources, as Dr. Pohl suggested. The dart the lab tested and an earlier source."

"After I talked to Pohl and remembered how Tom was acting before the dart hit him, I gave that a lot of thought," Molly said. They were talking in circles and getting nowhere. "But there was only one dart. Daye's sure of it, and she should know."

"It couldn't have been introduced by a handshake or anything like that," Conrad offered thoughtfully, raking a hand through his unruly silver hair. "The poisoner would have poisoned himself in the process. Unless he wore gloves."

"*Everybody* would have noticed somebody wearing gloves," Molly said wearily.

"Probably. Well, it could have been on something else. A glass, a chair . . . You need to go back and ask Daye Hummingbird some more questions."

Molly thought about Tom's behavior both before he started the story and during the telling. He hadn't felt well, but was that the result of poisoning? Pohl *had* said that everybody's different. Tom may have had the sort of physical makeup that absorbed the poison very quickly.

She tapped her fork on the table thoughtfully, seeing Tom in her mind's eye, anxious, sweating . . .

Suddenly she sat bolt upright in her chair. "The handkerchief! Tom was perspiring heavily and he kept wiping his face with his handkerchief. Oh, good Lord, that could be it!"

Conrad's eyes met hers. "Do you know where the handkerchief is now?"

Molly dropped her fork and jumped up. "No, but I'd better find out before somebody else handles it."

# 16

With Homer at her heels, Molly bounded up the stairs and let herself into her apartment. She dropped her purse on the table, went straight to the phone, and called the county morgue. Pohl was in.

The words spilled out of Molly. "What happened to the clothes Tom Battle was wearing when they brought his body to the morgue?" she asked in a rush.

"Molly, is that you?" Pohl drawled.

He knew very well who it was. "Yes."

"What, you don't even have time to say hi now before you get down to business?"

Molly clamped down on her impatience and backpedaled. He would dawdle even more if she didn't. "Good afternoon, Dr. Pohl," she said and took a deep breath.

"Ah, that's better. Practically civil."

"I'm pleased you think so," Molly responded, her impatience making the words curt.

"Just trying to get a little sunshine in your life," Pohl said. "Speaking of which—aren't we having great weather?"

"Lovely," Molly snapped.

He clicked his tongue. "You must bone up on the art of social conversation. Take a course," Pohl said, sounding a little hurt.

Molly relented. "I can chitchat as well as the next person," she said. "How are you, Dr. Pohl?" she added to prove the point.

He chuckled. "I'm doing about as well as any fifty-three-year-old man who lives a sedentary life-style could expect. And you?"

"Great. Super," she replied, then plowed on, unable to dally any longer. "I learned today that the dart that hit Tom had nicotine on it, and—"

"Can't say I'm surprised," Pohl interjected, giving up on chitchat.

"Remember, you said the body tissue had absorbed too much poison for it to have been on the dart?"

"Don't put words in my mouth, Molly. I seem to remember that I was puzzled by what sounded like instant death."

"I stand corrected," Molly said. "You suggested there might have been two darts."

"Yes, I remember."

"From everything I can find out, there was only one dart. But Tom had a handkerchief in his hand that morning. He was perspiring and he kept wiping his face with it."

"I *see.*" Pohl sounded faintly excited now. A rare occurrence. "The handkerchief might have been poisoned. Intriguing."

"It must have been in his pocket when he was brought to the morgue. I don't suppose you examined it, did you?" Molly asked.

"There was no handkerchief," Pohl said flatly.

"But there had to be!"

"*Au contraire.* My assistant undressed the body, put everything in a bag, and labeled it. The bag went to the funeral home with the body so the family could pick it up there."

"And you're sure there was no handkerchief?"

"I have an excellent memory, my dear," he said with exaggerated patience. "But I'll check the record to satisfy you. My assistant lists every item of clothing, jewelry, and anything found in pockets. One moment." He put down the phone and she heard him whistling to himself. He was back in a few seconds. "Here it is. Contents of pockets: one wallet containing thirty-eight dollars in bills, driver's license, tribal-membership card, two credit cards, two snapshots, pocket knife, a dollar sixty-two cents in coins. No handkerchief, Molly."

Deflated, Molly propped her chin in her hand. "What happened to it?" she wondered aloud.

"I wish I had the answer for you." He paused. "I keep remembering how much poison was in that body tissue. My advice is find out what happened to the handkerchief posthaste."

"I'm going to make some more calls right now," Molly said. "Good-bye, Dr. Pohl, and thanks."

She hung up and called the hospital emergency room. After being handed off to a second and then a third person, she finally got a nurse who was on duty the day Tom Battle was brought in.

The nurse didn't recall seeing any handkerchief, but things had been hectic. Anyway, if it was in Tom's pocket, it should have ended up at the morgue. The nurse agreed to ask around and see if anyone else had seen a handkerchief. If anybody had, she'd get back to Molly.

Molly thanked her gloomily and dropped the receiver in the cradle. She had been so sure she was on to something. Now that she'd had time to think about it, though, somebody else must have handled the handkerchief. But she hadn't heard of another poisoning. Still, it was odd that it seemed to have disappeared. She wasn't willing to forget it just yet.

She looked up Daye Hummingbird's number and got no answer. Perhaps Daye had gone to the museum today, as she'd said she might. Molly dialed the museum and got a busy signal. A few minutes later the line was still busy.

Pressed by an urgency to do something, Molly grabbed her purse, called Homer, and ran out to her car. He looked at her pleadingly from behind the fence. She melted like a heated marshmallow, went back, and opened the gate. "I'm a sucker for a sad face," she told him. "Come on."

Homer leaped in the car, settled on the passenger seat next to Molly, and sniffed her arm.

Molly backed out of Conrad's driveway. "What happened to that handkerchief, Homer?" she asked as she shifted gears.

Homer tilted his head, ears cocked inquisitively, his tongue hanging out one side of his mouth.

Molly rubbed his head absently, absorbed in thought as she drove toward Park Hill. She couldn't remember seeing the handkerchief after Tom had collapsed. She hadn't even thought of it. Too much had been going on and it hadn't been important until now.

"You think the murderer took it?" she mused. Homer wagged his tail.

"That's what I would have done," Molly told him. He dipped his head and slobbered on her jeans. "If I'd put poison on Tom's handkerchief," she went on, "I'd have got rid of it in all the commotion after Tom collapsed."

Homer barked and gave her a friendly lick on the cheek. She waved him away. Not the least offended, he pressed his nose against the glass to watch the scenery.

Lily Roach was at the reception desk when Molly entered the museum, but she didn't look up. Maud Wildcat sat at her table near the door. "I talked to Robert and Victor at noon," Molly told Maud. "They were very cooperative."

Maud looked up at her eagerly. "Then you've found evidence that Robert didn't mean to shoot Tom?"

"Not exactly," Molly admitted, and watched Maud's face fall, "but I'll keep working on it."

"Robert is being used," Maud said darkly. "Somebody has to stop this—if it can still be stopped."

Stop what? Molly wondered. And how? She wanted to ask Maud but Maud's head was bent now over her finger-weaving. She seemed lost in her own thoughts, as if she'd given up on Molly's being able to help Robert and was working on a plan of her own. A worrisome thought.

Molly went to the desk. "How's business?" she asked Lily.

Lily jumped as though she'd been struck and jammed one hand into the deep pocket of her skirt. "Good grief," she gasped, pulling her hand out again and fanning her face with it. "I didn't see you."

How could she have missed seeing her, Molly wondered. Everybody seemed to have wandering minds today.

"Is everything all right?"

Lily blinked. "Of course. Busy, though. We've had a steady stream of visitors all afternoon, but they're thinning out now." She seemed frazzled and she looked tired. She must have been there all day. But it was after four and the exhibition would close at five-thirty.

"Are you taking on painting projects too?" Molly asked, indicating the black-capped aerosol can of spray paint which sat on the desk.

"What? Oh, that," Lily said vaguely. She grabbed the can and bent to set it beneath the counter.

Did she imagine it, Molly wondered, or was Lily being furtive? Perhaps, having shared the reception area with Maud all day, she'd been infected with Maud's fear. Lily seemed to be struggling to gain her composure. Then she straightened up and smiled too brightly at Molly.

Something about the can Lily had been so anxious to get out of sight nibbled at the back of Molly's mind. A half thought which she couldn't grab hold of. Maybe it would come to her later.

"How's the new storyteller working out?" Molly asked.

Lily seemed to relax a little, as though she welcomed the change of subject. "He's not Tom," Lily said gloomily, "but he's okay. It's not easy to step in with little prior notice."

"You sitting in for Brenda?"

Lily nodded. "All afternoon. She had to leave early today. Her baby-sitter got sick."

Molly glanced toward the exhibit area, seeing several visitors through the open doorway as well as Regina Shell, who was seated at her table, working on a basket. Absorbed in her work, Regina didn't look up.

Molly walked into the next room, exchanged a few words with Regina, and looked around for Daye. The storyteller, Ed Corn, an elderly Cherokee, had just launched into a story.

My great-uncle told me this story. A long time ago, when the animals were made, they were allowed to choose something for their food. The Rabbit chose the sycamore because it bore so many seeds. He thought he would always have food to eat. All the other animals took everything else.

The Rabbit kept waiting for the sycamore seeds to fall, but instead they were blown away by the wind. He didn't have anything to eat. So he went to the other animals and asked for food, but they all turned him down. Last of all, he went to the Bear and asked for something to eat. The Bear said, "If you'll bring me something I like, I'll give you some food."

The Rabbit went out to hunt something, but whatever he brought, the Bear didn't like. He couldn't find anything the Bear liked. So the Rabbit said, "I'll just have to go eat up old women's gardens. I'll eat up their cabbage and steal everything. They'll have their dogs chase me, but I can run fast and get away."

That's how it happened that the Rabbit chose garden vegetables for his food. That's why he is a garden thief.

The storyteller finished, and Molly, not having caught sight of Daye, returned to the reception room. "Daye said she would be here today," she said to Lily.

"She was," Lily said and sighed. "She came in less than an hour ago, left again not long after. I think she was crying. She looks wretched."

"But I thought I saw her car outside. Isn't it that blue Toyota?"

"Yes. Didn't you see Daye?"

"No."

"That's odd. Well, maybe she went for a walk," Lily suggested, frowning. "I should have gone after her, I guess, but I thought she'd rather be alone."

"I'll find her," Molly said, "and make sure she's all right."

Daye had stumbled through the wooded grounds, not knowing where she was going, not caring so long as it was away from the museum. Trees and the fading daylight wavered, seen hazily through the shimmer of tears.

She had found herself, at last, facing a weathered placard raised on wood posts and a narrow path leading to a tiny, circular stone chapel. Blinking to clear her vision, she had read the words on the placard:

Ho-Chee-Nee "Trail of Tears Memorial Chapel."
Dedicated to the memory of all those Cherokees who

failed to complete their journey over the "Trail Where They Cried," 1838–39. This chapel is a memorial bequest by Jimalee "Ho Chee Nee" Burton, 1913–77, erected in 1978.

She had forgotten about the chapel, removed some distance from the other heritage-center buildings, dignified somehow in its isolation. Rarely if ever used for religious services, it was too small for a gathering of any size. Occasionally, someone wandering over the grounds found it and went in to sit for a few moments in the quiet.

The heavy wood doors, beneath a stained-glass depiction of weary Cherokees on the Trail of Tears, were rarely locked.

Inside, two sections, three rows each, of curved, red-upholstered benches—each a step below the one behind it—looked down on a wood pulpit which rested on the lowest level.

In the dimness, Daye sat on the middle bench next to the center aisle, listening to the silence. The tears had stopped, leaving her cheeks and throat feeling raw.

She had known that being in the museum again would be difficult, and she had thought herself prepared, had planned to spend only an hour or two today and return for the full day tomorrow.

She had talked briefly to Lily and Maud in the reception area. She had walked past Wolf and Josiah, back straight and eyes ahead, feeling Wolf's eyes on her but never acknowledging him.

She had spoken to Regina and Edgar Corn, the old storyteller Lily had found to take Tom's place. She had stood by her easel and talked to visitors, feeling fragile and brittle and removed from it all, as though a glass dome had dropped over her, but standing and talking nonetheless.

And then Edgar Corn had begun a lighthearted folktale about why the possum's tail is bare.

The content of the story was irrelevant. After the first few sentences, Daye couldn't hear the words for the roaring in her ears.

Instead of the old man, she saw Tom standing there in the jeans and ribbon shirt he'd died in. Across his forehead the beaded headband. Red and yellow. She had shut her eyes, blotting out the image and all the images and memories that overwhelmed her in the wake of the vision of Tom falling, dying. Dead.

She had known that the glass dome was about to shatter, and when it did there would be no distance, no protection from the black pit of grief all around her. She would start screaming. She might never stop.

She had stood perfectly still to keep the glass from breaking, but it had begun to crack, anyway. A tiny hairline crack, and then another, the blackness seeping in.

She had bolted from the museum, ignoring sympathetic voices, well meant but futile. Outside, the roaring in her ears had diminished until all she could hear were her own tortured sobs.

Now there was only silence, vast and impenetrable in a world without Tom.

# 17

Lily Roach gripped the edge of the desk to stop the trembling in her hands. Dear God, what had she done?

And what was she going to do now?

Nobody but Molly would have noticed the can of paint. Molly had also made sure that Lily knew she'd noticed, after she'd slipped up on Lily like a cat.

Well, maybe that was a bit strong. She had to get a grip on this thing.

To be fair, she'd been lost in her own thoughts, unaware of Molly until she spoke. Lily wasn't really sure Molly had meant to sneak up on her. Either way, she had made the situation worse by reacting like an idiot. If Molly hadn't been suspicious before, Lily's reaction took care of that.

Molly had looked at her with that speculative expression she got sometimes, her head cocked to one side, as though her brain were scrolling through propositions and deductions like a computer. What *had* Molly been thinking? Was Molly really onto her or was it Lily's guilty conscience that made her sure she would be exposed any minute?

Lily forced her fingers to release their grip on the edge of the reception desk and very deliberately walked to the window. Resting her forehead against the glass, she squeezed her eyes shut. She had never been any good at subterfuge. She should have said something. If only she'd had time to think it through and decide what to do before Molly appeared as if from nowhere.

She watched a car pull into the parking lot. Two women got out, looked around, and then walked toward the museum.

I have to tell someone, Lily thought as she thrust her hand guiltily into the pocket of her dress. Perhaps the pocket was empty. Perhaps she'd imagined the whole thing.

Perhaps she'd imagined this whole terrible week.

Her fingers touched a hard, smooth object. Of course she hadn't imagined it—or anything else.

I have to tell someone, she thought again. But who? She should have told Molly, but she wasn't sure she could trust Molly to keep an open mind. Especially when Molly learned what had happened all those years ago. Anyway, she hadn't told her and now it would be harder to do. And the longer she waited, the guiltier she would look.

All at once she realized that Maud was watching her. Lily had grown so used to Maud's sitting in the reception area, speaking quietly to visitors as her nimble fingers manipulated her yarn, that she often forgot Maud was there. How long had the woman been studying her in that curious way? Lily forced a smile as the two women she'd seen get out of their car entered the museum. She took their admission money, then walked to the closed office door. "I'll be in the office if anyone comes in," she said to Maud.

Inside, she twisted the button on the doorknob to lock position. For a few minutes, she stood there, undecided. She glanced at the phone, but she could think of no one she could confide in.

Sighing, she opened the bottom desk drawer, took the object from her pocket, and wiped it carefully with a tissue from the box on the desk. She wrapped the object in the tissue and wedged it at the back of the drawer behind a stack of ledgers.

Maybe she wouldn't mention it to anyone. She'd pretend it hadn't happened, banish it from her mind. The object might stay at the back of the drawer for months before it was discovered. There would be no way of determining who had put it there.

Molly hesitated at the back of the chapel. Daye hadn't heard her come in, at least she hadn't looked around. She sat bent over with her face in her hands, a portrait of desolation. Molly's strongest impulse was to slip away and leave the woman to her misery, her own private trail of tears. But on the heels of that thought came another. Finding the handkerchief might save a life.

"Daye," Molly said.

She turned then to look at Molly, broken but dry-eyed. Daye didn't seem surprised to see her. She didn't seem anything except drained of emotion.

Molly took two steps down and sat on the end of a bench, the narrow red-carpeted aisle separating her from Daye. "I guess it was harder than you expected, coming back," Molly ventured.

Daye squeezed her eyes shut. Whether in surprise that Molly understood or in resentment at Molly's intrusion on her grief, Molly couldn't have said.

"Yes," Daye murmured. Lily was right; Daye did look wretched, even worse than she had at the funeral. "I was all right until Edgar Corn started a story," Daye went on, and Molly wondered what she considered *all right*. "Then, I suddenly felt claustrophobic."

"Are you getting any sleep?"

"Enough."

Molly doubted it. "When have you eaten?"

Daye seemed to search her mind as though it were an unfamiliar landscape. "I had breakfast . . . sometime this morning."

"It's turning colder out," Molly said, eyeing Daye's thin sweater. "It'll soon be too chilly to stay here."

The ghost of a smile touched Daye's lips, a hopeful sign. "I didn't plan to spend the night."

Good, Molly thought, if she can joke, she's not in shock. She didn't think Daye was suicidal, either. Molly's mother, Josephine, had killed herself when Molly was six, and as far as she could remember there had been no levity, hardly any conversation, in the house in those last weeks.

Her memories of that time with her mother were hazy impressions. Silence—Josephine had lain on the couch, drinking or passed out—silence so thick it had sometimes seemed an effort just to breathe. Dark rooms—Josephine had kept the shades drawn night and day. Mostly the memories were of feelings, a lonely child's sense of abandonment and the resulting fear, though at six she hadn't been able to give the feelings names. She realized now that Josephine had lost all hope for the future. Daye, on the other hand, was devastated, but Molly didn't think she was without hope.

"I have an idea," Molly said, "let's go to The Shack and eat something fried with thousands of calories. Then we'll have pie with ice cream on it."

The smile flickered again. "Comfort food?" Daye seemed to turn it over in her mind. "I could use a little comfort." She ran her hands up and down her sweatered arms. "It *is* getting chilly," she murmured, as though she hadn't noticed before. Then, "All right," she said, surprising Molly, who had expected to have to coax.

"Right now?"

"Yes, I've realized I'm hungry. I'll meet you at the café."

"You may have to wait a few minutes. I need to take my dog home first."

Daye nodded. "I'll be there."

"I'll make it as soon as possible."

"Don't hurry. I'm not eager to get home these days."

They sat in a corner booth. Few of the other booths were occupied. It was only a little after five; they had arrived before most of the dinner customers. Outside, the overcast sky deepened a slate-colored dusk to charcoal, and people walked quickly, having left home in shirt-sleeves or at most a sweater. The temperature must have dropped fifteen degrees since Molly drove out to the museum in search of Daye, hardly more than an hour, and the wind had come up.

Molly and Daye ate chicken-fried steak and mashed potatoes, talking, by unspoken agreement, of inconsequential things. Daye seemed to have put aside her depression for now and finished most of her dinner before she folded her napkin beside her plate.

"I needed that," Daye said. "I'm glad you suggested dinner. I haven't been much interested in food since . . . " Her voice trailed off. She couldn't say the words yet.

"Want dessert?"

"Oh, I couldn't."

"Neither could I," Molly admitted, giving up the idea of warm blackberry cobbler with ice cream. Another time.

They settled for coffee. "Daye," Molly said, "I didn't just happen into the chapel this afternoon."

Daye looked puzzled. "I hadn't thought about it. I've been centered on me, my feelings. Have to get past that." She sighed. "Obviously you were looking for me."

Molly nodded. "I'm trying to track down Tom's handkerchief."

"Which handkerchief?"

"The one he had Saturday at the museum," Molly said, "before they put him in the ambulance. It wasn't left at the museum and they didn't see it at the hospital." She couldn't bring herself to mention the morgue.

"I have it," Daye said, blinking, "but I don't understand why you'd want it."

"Then you've touched it," Molly said, stating the obvious but wanting to nail it down.

Daye made a faintly impatient noise. "*Of course* I've touched it. What is this all about?"

Molly explained about the poisoned dart and the medical examiner's puzzlement over the amount of poison in Tom's body and Molly's now-dead theory that the handkerchief had been poisoned too.

"Oh." Daye shivered. "I've already laundered it, but it couldn't have been poisoned. It fell out of Tom's pocket in the ambulance and I picked it up and kept it in my hand all the time I was at the hospital with Tom. I even took it to bed with me that night. It smelled of him—" Her voice broke.

Feeling helpless, Molly reached across the table and clasped Daye's hand until Daye regained her composure. Outside the restaurant, the wind moaned like a lost child.

At length, Molly said, "Probably Tom was just highly susceptible to the poison, more than the average person, I mean." But she couldn't shake the feeling of having missed something.

Beyond the café's windows, the leaden sky seemed to be closing in around them, squeezing out the fragile remnants of daylight. "That morning," Molly went on slowly, "Saturday morning. Did you see anyone hand something to Tom?"

Daye swallowed hard and, letting go of Molly's hand, leaned forward on her elbows, in control of herself now. "No, I did not. Why are you trying to find some other way for Tom to have gotten the poison? The dart was covered with it. Wolf's dart. You said so yourself." Clearly, she didn't want to be confused by the medical examiner's reservations. "I don't understand why he hasn't been arrested by now."

"You're forgetting," Molly reminded her gently, "Wolf didn't shoot the dart."

She brushed this aside as of no consequence. "I told you," she flared, "he got Robert to do it for him. Robert was merely there. You should be spending your time trying to figure out exactly how Wolf made that boy shoot the dart, instead of chasing after missing handkerchiefs."

Molly looked at her unhappily and gave a little shrug. "I've been working on that. Wolf's still a suspect, but the police can't arrest people without hard evidence."

Daye stared into her coffee cup as though she might find there some evidence against Wolf. "I'm sorry," she muttered after a moment. "I know you're doing your best. I'm not angry with you. If I'm angry at anyone, I guess it's God. Can you understand that?"

"Oh, yes," Molly murmured.

"I'm feeling kind of trapped too. I—I have to do something I dread, and I'm wishing I'd never agreed."

"What is it?"

"I promised Tom's father I'd pack Tom's things and take them to Wagoner. I could tell Mr. Battle wasn't up to it, and there isn't anyone else. Tom was only renting the house. His father will send a van to pick up the furniture, after the insurance adjuster has assessed the damage. But somebody has to deal with his clothes and personal belongings." She stared at the napkin beside her plate, making tiny pleats with her fingers. "When I offered," she went on, "it seemed one last thing I could do for Tom. I had a crazy notion that touching his things might be comforting." She frowned and dropped the napkin. "Now, I'm not sure I can go through with it."

"Would you like some company?"

Hope flickered in her eyes. "I couldn't ask . . . "

"You aren't. I'm volunteering."

"Oh, would you, Molly? It would help so much if I didn't have to be there alone."

"Just say when."

Molly's words eased Daye's apprehension a little. "Would tomorrow afternoon be all right? I'm going back to the museum first. I have to face up to—" She hesitated. "—face up to it, sooner or later."

Molly suspected she'd started to say she had to face up to Wolf. Daye's implacable conviction that Wolf had killed Tom worried Molly. If he had, and Daye kept accusing him, he might try to shut her up.

"I could meet you at Tom's place at four o'clock," Molly said.

The chill wind brought a cold drizzle. If the predicted dip in the overnight temperature materialized, the drizzle could turn to sleet by morning, fulfilling Eva's prophecy of an unusually early freeze. Indian summer had been cut short abruptly and probably would not return in full force, even though there would undoubtedly be more balmy days before winter.

D.J. had bought a bottle of red wine. They drank it while they watched the movie Molly had rented. *Dial M for Murder*, one of Molly's favorites. All that business with the keys was classic Hitchcock.

Outside, the rain continued in sporadic bursts, and thunder rumbled like a restless lion in the distance. Inside, Molly and D.J. were settled comfortably, warm and dry, on the couch, Molly leaning back against his chest, his arms around her.

"Why is it," D.J. asked as the final credits scrolled across the TV screen, "I usually rent sexy movies and you invariably go for mysteries?" He reached over her to retrieve the wine bottle and empty the dregs into their glasses.

Molly smiled and fingered the stem of her glass. "I think," she murmured, "it says something about the way our minds work." She covered a yawn. She felt cozy and contented, but she had forgotten that wine made her sleepy.

"Are you suggesting my mind's in my pants, and the mysteries are your attempt to lift it to a more intellectual plane?"

"Succinctly put," she said and giggled. The wine had gone to her head. She rarely drank, even wine. Josephine had had a drinking problem, and Molly feared the tendency was in her genes. She set her glass on the floor next to the sofa. Settling back, she laid her head on D.J.'s shoulder. She never wanted to move again.

His arms tightened around her. "Your strategy isn't working," he said, his lips touching her hair.

She turned to kiss him. "Good thing the wine's gone," she whispered. "I think I'm a little drunk."

D.J. chuckled.

"Are you planning to take advantage of me?"

"Why do you think I brought the wine?"

It was slow and lazy and, for once, Molly was able to shut off her mind. The wine made everything but the moment's shivery physical pleasure dim and distant.

Time enough later to worry about where the relationship was going and whether she was already in deeper than she had ever meant to be.

"You shouldn't drive," D.J. said as she stood beside the bed in the dark. "Stay the night."

Cold sober now, she felt around for her underclothes and put them on. Her dreamy contentment was gone, replaced by a clarity that left no gently shadowed corners in her mind where she could hide her doubts. She fought her desire to crawl back in bed.

D.J. sat up in bed, and she bent to kiss him lightly on the lips. "I'm all right to drive, and it's stopped raining. Don't get up."

"Why won't you sleep over?"

For the same reason that she had never suggested he stay overnight at her place. Because it felt like giving in. Or giving up too much of herself. At the moment, though, the distinction between staying a few hours and overnight seemed meaningless. "I need fresh clothes and a toothbrush to start the day." She pulled her sweater over her head and reached for her jeans.

"Molly?"

She tugged on the jeans. "Hmmm?"

"We need to get something settled. The ski trip. Are you going with me and Courtney?"

It seemed a separate issue altogether, but it wasn't, and they both knew it. Well, she couldn't put it off any longer. "I can't, D.J."

"This," he said, "whatever *this* is for you, for me it's not just getting laid. It never has been."

"I never thought it was." She touched his face. Then, with a little shake, she sat on the bed to put on her shoes and hoped he wouldn't say any more tonight. She was tired and vulnerable.

"I'm falling in love with you, Molly."

The words hung in the dark silence. Molly's heart thudded and contracted, and down there somewhere were the words *I love you, too,* but something had lodged in her throat and wouldn't let them come up.

"D.J., please—"

"I'm tired of tiptoeing around it," he said.

"Oh, D.J.—I don't know what to say," she whispered. "It's just—your timing couldn't be worse."

"*Timing?*" he said incredulously.

She couldn't begin to describe the jumble of feelings she was experiencing. She didn't even try, but finished dressing as he lay back down.

She didn't want to leave it like that, but if she left at all it would be on an unhappy note now. "Good night, D.J."

# 18

Before going to the office the next morning, Molly stopped to tell Conrad that tracking down Tom's handkerchief had been a wild goose chase. Conrad said she shouldn't give up on the idea of a second poison source just yet. He'd done a little research into nicotine-poisoning deaths and was as uncomfortable as Dr. Pohl with the instant-death scenario.

"There is an explanation, Molly," he said. "It's like a logic problem. The known facts don't fit together because there are too many gaps."

Conrad's most recent passion was logic problems. He bought books full of them, but lately he'd complained that the problems were too easy once you got the hang of how the publishers put them together. He was toying with the idea of compiling a book of his own creations.

"Do you ever run across a logic problem you can't solve?"

"Sometimes you think you can't," he said. "When that happens, you have to make an assumption and follow it to the end. It lets you see the facts you do know in a new light. If things don't fall into place, you go back, throw out that assumption, and make another."

Molly wasn't sure how she could apply that to her investigation of Tom Battle's death. She thought about it on the way to town. The medical examiner was a logic-problem buff too, which reminded Molly that she'd promised to report back to him. She took care of that as soon as she got to the office, but Pohl had nothing new to suggest.

Tony Warwick, the BIA investigator from Muskogee, showed up at eleven o'clock. He was a small man, about five-feet-six and whipcord lean, with a swarthy complexion which he said was a legacy from a Sioux ancestor on his mother's side. Personally, Molly thought he looked more Mediterranean than Native American. She wondered if he'd fabricated the Sioux ancestor to give himself more credibility with the Indians he dealt with.

Tony had several pairs of cowboy boots, which added an inch or two to his height. Today the boots were made of ostrich skin. With them he wore a tan windbreaker over a plaid shirt and brown trousers.

Tony greeted her and flopped into a chair beside Molly's desk. "Been out to the museum. Talked to Lily Roach, the receptionist, and the craftspeople. It was sort of like getting a filibuster out of a bunch of deaf mutes, except for the artist. Pretty woman."

"Daye Hummingbird."

"Yeah, that's her." He scratched his shiny pate in front of a rapidly receding hairline. "Are the rest of 'em covering up for somebody?"

"I don't think so. Except maybe Maud Wildcat." Every time she thought of what Maud had said yesterday at the museum, she felt troubled. *Somebody has to stop this—if it can still be stopped.* Somebody who? Maud? Lily had acted strange too. Maybe the two women had hatched up something between them. Something illegal, or at least questionable. It would explain why both of them were being so secretive.

"She's the weaver, right?" Tony asked.

Molly pulled her mind back to Tony's question. "Yes. Her grandson shot the poisoned dart."

He tented his fingers in front of his face. "I got that much out of Lily Roach. All Maud Wildcat would say was, 'He was a tool.' What'd she mean by that?"

Molly explained Maud's fear of the wampums' power.

He nodded morosely. "I may represent the BIA, but I can't compete with ancient curses. Except for the artist, they aren't talking to me."

Molly shrugged. No point in denying it.

"I understand you've been on this from the beginning," Tony said. "How did you get involved?"

"I was there when it happened, and Maud Wildcat asked me to investigate. Maud's worried Robert won't get a fair shake from you big-city types who work for the government."

Tony grinned. "Don't think I've ever heard Muskogee called a big city before. But I'm used to being seen as an out-sider." He fingered the edge of a file folder on Molly's desk. A shadow touched his face. "What do you think? Is the kid a murderer?" Tony rarely mentioned his family, but Molly knew he had a son about the age of Robert Wildcat.

"Technically. I saw him shoot the poisoned dart. But I don't think he knew it was poisoned or that he meant to hit anyone. I've talked to him and the boy who was with him when it happened."

"That would be Victor Halland."

"Right. Victor handed the dart to Robert, but they were just horsing around."

He smoothed a thick, black brow with his thumb. "Prob-ably scared them worse than anyone when the dart hit Tom Battle." He leaned back in his chair. "Are you planning to continue your investigation?"

She nodded. "I'll try not to get in your way."

"Actually, I was going to suggest that we join forces. Those people will talk to you. You're one of them."

Molly relaxed and beamed at him. "I was hoping you'd feel that way." She filled him in on what she'd learned and mentioned the vandalism of Tom Battle's house the night before he died.

"I heard about that. You think whoever vandalized his house killed him?" Tony asked.

"Don't know. The sheriff's department doesn't have a hot suspect for the vandalism, as far as I know. But Tom Battle was well liked. It's hard to imagine there were two people who had it in for him. Much more likely the same person committed both crimes."

"I agree. Daye Hummingbird came right out and said she thinks the same person did both jobs. The guy who made the dart and blowgun, Wolf Kawaya. I asked her how come it couldn't have been the old man, Josiah Kawaya. She said because Josiah doesn't have a motive. Said she divorced Wolf and he can't get over it."

Molly told him what she knew of the strained relationship between Daye and Wolf, about Daye's romantic involvement with Tom Battle, about the scene between Wolf and Tom the evening before Tom's death, and the fact that Tom and Wolf were on opposite sides of the TEB–Cherokee Nation conflict. Which reminded her of the sign painted on the tribal office building the night before the pre-opening reception at the museum, and she told him about that too.

"Great," Tony muttered, "I hate getting in the middle of tribal politics. No matter what you do, you're wrong."

"Just keep in mind," Molly added, determined to be fair, "that Daye's not exactly an impartial witness in all this."

Tony mulled over her words. "Did Sheriff Hobart handle the investigation of the vandalism of Battle's house?"

Molly shook her head. "D.J. Kennedy took the call."

His boney face relaxed. "Good. I know D.J. We can work with him. I'll clear it with Hobart."

"Claude won't be happy to have you taking up D.J.'s time," Molly warned.

"I know Claude's territorial," Tony said, "but he's also a politician. I'll send a letter to Washington saying how cooperative Claude is being. He'll like that."

"You're not bad in the politics department yourself," Molly said, wondering how D.J. would feel about working with her after last night. "What's next?"

"I'll try to talk to Robert Wildcat and Victor Halland today. They probably won't tell me anything they haven't already told you. Hell, they'll probably tell me to shove it, but I want to get a firsthand impression. And I'd like to set up a meeting—you, me, and Kennedy. Make sure we're all singing out of the same book."

"I won't be free until about six today," Molly said.

"Let's make it a dinner meeting then, if Kennedy can do it. Where can you get a decent meal around here?"

"Oak Hill will give us more privacy than anywhere else. It's south of town, on Highway 62."

"Seven o'clock?" Tony asked and Molly agreed. "I'll check with Kennedy and get back to you," he added.

"If I'm not here, leave a message on my machine," Molly told him.

Molly arrived at Tom Battle's house Wednesday afternoon, a few minutes after four. No sign of Daye. Molly suspected Daye was intentionally late, giving Molly time to arrive first. Several large cardboard boxes were stacked on the porch. Daye or Tom's father must have dropped them off earlier.

It was a dull, gray day. At the moment, a fine mist was falling, but the temperature hadn't hit freezing during the night, so the shedding of bright fall foliage hadn't been hurried along just yet. And no freeze was predicted for the next twenty-four hours. Still, it was definitely jacket weather.

Molly got out of her car and ran to the front door, shaking drops of water from her hair. The top half of the door was divided into nine small panes of glass. A door that practically invited a break-in. The pane closest to the knob was broken, evidently by Friday night's vandal. The hole was big enough for a man's hand to pass through.

Before sticking her hand in, Molly tested the knob. The door wasn't locked. What was the point? She went in.

A rectangular piece of plywood lay on the floor just inside the door. Somebody had used it to cover the broken pane, but they hadn't done a very good job of it and it had fallen out. Molly picked it up, noting four small nail holes in the corners. Two of the nails were still in the wood. She picked up the other two nails from the carpet and walked through the house.

It contained five rooms: living, dining, kitchen, two bedrooms, and a single bath. All the damage had been done in the living room and kitchen. Sofa and chair cushions had been slashed, and bits of the foam padding had spilled out. The curtains had been ripped off their rods and lay in heaps where they'd landed. The contents of several manila folders had been shredded and thrown on the carpet.

The kitchen floor was littered with broken dishes and glassware. From the faint dents in the wall opposite the cabinets, Molly concluded the dishes had been dashed against the wall. The upper cabinet doors stood open, revealing mostly bare shelves.

Oddly, the dining room separating living room and kitchen appeared untouched. As though the vandal had done his work in haste, first the living room, then on to the kitchen where he could do more damage than in the dining room. The nearest house was a half mile away, so it was unlikely anyone would have seen or heard anything. But maybe the vandal had expected Tom to return home at any time.

Molly picked a careful path across the kitchen to the broom closet, crunching glass and pieces of pottery beneath her Nikes.

She swept up the pieces and deposited them in a tall can beneath the sink, then went out to the porch to bring in the boxes as Daye's Toyota turned in the driveway.

Daye was wearing a tan raincoat over red sweats, her black hair caught up in a French braid that hung down her back, and she looked considerably more rested than she had the day before. She splashed through a puddle next to the driveway and came up the walk.

"Hi, Molly. Thank you for coming. Oh, good, Mr. Battle left the boxes. I hope we have enough."

"I was about to take them in."

Daye picked up a box in each hand. Then she hesitated at the door, as though to brace herself. "Let's get this over with quickly, okay?" Molly followed her inside with the other boxes.

Daye, who hadn't been there since Tom's death, stopped in the living room. "My God, what a mess."

"It's not as bad as it looks," Molly told her. "The vandal only got to the living room and kitchen."

"That must have been enough to vent his spleen," Daye muttered darkly.

"Mmmm," Molly said. Daye would not be moved from her conviction that Wolf had done it, and maybe he had, but Molly was trying to keep an open mind. Admittedly, it was getting harder to do. "I've already swept up the glass in the kitchen," Molly went on. "Should I have done that before the adjuster saw it?"

"He came by this morning." Daye touched the brass stand of a floor lamp and shivered. Being in Tom's house was difficult for her, and Molly wished she'd offered to do the whole job herself. But Daye had said it was one last thing she could do for Tom. Even though it wasn't easy, perhaps she needed to be there to finally say good-bye to him.

"It's cold in here," Daye said, "and I think they've already turned off the gas."

"Once we get moving, we won't notice. Do you want me to pack what's left of the dishes and the other kitchen stuff?"

Daye looked around gloomily, seeming at a loss. Then she appeared to shake off whatever memories the house had called up and said briskly, "Yes, and I'll take the bedrooms. Throw away any food in the cabinets that's been opened. We'll save the refrigerator for last and clean it out together."

Molly found a trash bag for the open food containers. The rest she packed. A stack of old newspapers on the small, screened back porch provided plenty of padding for the dishes that escaped the vandal's tirade.

Twenty minutes later she had finished the kitchen and went in search of Daye, who was in the back bedroom, the one, Molly had determined earlier, that Tom had used. An eight-by-ten photograph of Daye in a wood frame sat on the dresser. Molly's glance stopped on the photograph. Odd that Wolf didn't smash it or take it with him. Then she realized that she was falling in with Daye's conviction that Wolf was the vandal, and she told herself again to keep an open mind.

Daye had packed the clothes from the closet and had started on the dresser. The top drawer was open. She sat on the bed, already stripped of its bedclothes, poring over a handful of snapshots. Molly thought she'd been crying.

Daye glanced up at Molly standing in the doorway, then back at one of the snapshots. "I found these in the dresser drawer," Daye said. "They were taken on a picnic Tom and I and a couple of friends had last summer at Fort Gibson Lake."

Molly sat down beside her on the bed and Daye handed her the snapshots, which showed Tom and Daye in shorts, wind-blown, smiling, happy. "That day, he asked me to marry him for the first time," Daye said desolately.

"I didn't know you and Tom were engaged."

"We weren't. I turned him down." She wiped her eyes with the ribbing at the waist of her sweatshirt. "And I kept turning him down. I liked things the way they were." She sighed. "I was afraid marriage would spoil it. My marriage to Wolf turned out so badly. He thought he owned me. Sometimes I think he still does. After the divorce, I swore I'd never marry again."

"That's understandable."

"It seems ridiculous now," she said. "I thought Tom and I had all the time in the world. I loved him, Molly. He was nothing like Wolf. I—I only wish I'd agreed to marry him before. . ." She still couldn't say it. She took a deep breath and, accepting the snapshots from Molly, put them on the dresser. "I'll take these home with me." She lingered over the snapshot on top of the stack for a moment. "I don't know why he put up with me and my hang-ups. I'd marry him now in an instant. Do you think people always look back, when it's too late, and wish things had been different?"

"Probably," Molly murmured, thinking of D.J. Thinking that people did eventually reach a point where they couldn't tolerate a particular situation any longer. "I'll get the towels and whatever else is in the bathroom."

"Okay," Daye said, lifting underwear from the drawer.

In the bathroom, Molly started with the medicine cabinet. Comb, brush, shampoo, an aerosol can of shaving cream, a bottle of cologne which had never been opened, deodorant, toothpaste, toothbrush, twin-bladed razor and extra blades, dental floss, two bars of soap still in wrappers. Exactly what you'd expect to find in a man's medicine cabinet.

She hesitated, looking down at the contents of Tom's medicine cabinet piled in a small cardboard box. Odd. There was no after-shave lotion. Didn't all men use after-shave?

She shrugged. Maybe Tom had kept it in the bedroom. Or maybe he'd run out and hadn't bought a new bottle yet.

She closed the medicine-cabinet door and looked around, remembering that Tom had showered in that room and stood before the mirror to shave the morning of his death. He would have called the sheriff's department first and waited for D.J., then covered the broken pane. The shower and shave were probably the last thing he did before dressing and driving to the museum. His mind would have been on the break-in and on Wolf Kawaya. What else had he thought about in his last hour or two on the earth? Was there a premonition of his death?

Molly wanted to get out of the bathroom suddenly, but she still had the linen closet to empty. Hurriedly, she packed towels, washcloths, and bed linens, finishing as Daye came out of Tom's bedroom. They went together into the second bedroom. Not much to pack there. The bedspread which covered a bare mattress and a few jackets and sweaters in the closet.

They tackled the refrigerator last. Fortunately the electricity was still on, so they didn't have to deal with spoiled food, but they threw out everything anyway. Daye unplugged the refrigerator, leaving the door open, and Molly carried the trash to the cans out back.

"That's it, I think," Daye said when Molly came back. She sounded about equal parts relieved and reluctant to go, now that the work was finished. Probably, for Daye, a little of Tom lingered in these rooms. But once his furniture was gone, it would be just an empty house.

They began carrying the boxes out to Daye's car, filling the trunk and backseat. Molly found the piece of plywood which she'd dropped in a chair earlier. "I'll put this back in place before we go," she said.

"The insurance adjuster was supposed to leave the door unlocked," Daye told her. "I guess he forgot."

Molly realized that Daye assumed she'd removed the panel to reach in and unlock the door. "It *was* unlocked." She set the panel in place and began fitting the nails back in their holes. "The panel was out when I got here—I found it on the carpet."

"That's strange," Daye said. "Tom nailed it over the broken pane Saturday morning, before he came to the museum. It couldn't fall out on its own with four nails holding it."

"Maybe the insurance adjuster removed it to get in."

"No," Daye said, "I gave him my key."

"Well—" Molly shrugged. "It's back in place, but it won't deter anyone who really wants in."

"There's nothing here to take now," Daye said, "except the furniture, and it will be gone tomorrow." She frowned as she set the lock and closed the door behind them. "I don't know if Mr. Battle has a key," she mused. "Maybe he removed the panel." She shook her head. "Well, I don't guess it matters, since nothing seems to be missing."

"I helped Daye pack Tom's things this afternoon," Molly told Tony and D.J. that evening. "She didn't want to go into the house alone."

The three of them had met at the Oak Hill Restaurant, as planned. The atmosphere between D.J. and Molly was restrained, and Molly was exquisitely aware of his every glance. Tony evidently did not know that they'd been seeing each other, and he didn't appear to notice the tension.

Tony said, "I gather she and Tom Battle were pretty thick."

"They were very much in love," Molly said, carefully avoiding D.J.'s eyes.

"Tom spent Friday night with Daye," D.J. put in, giving Molly a flickering glance. "He found the mess when he went home Saturday morning to shower and change clothes before going to the museum. So we can't even get close to the time the vandalism took place."

"Somebody knew he wouldn't be at home that night," Tony suggested.

"Not necessarily," Molly said. "Only two rooms were touched, as though the vandal were in a hurry. Which he would have been if he thought Tom might come home any minute."

"You say nothing was taken?" Tony asked D.J.

"Tom Battle went through the house and didn't notice anything missing," D.J. said.

"So, it was kids raising hell or somebody wanting to shake up Battle," Tony theorized. "I'm beginning to understand why Daye Hummingbird thinks Wolf Kawaya did it. She told me he sometimes parks outside her house and sits there for an hour at a time. She's afraid of him."

Molly hadn't known Wolf was stalking Daye. No wonder she was frightened. "Wolf says he went straight home Friday night but he might have gone by Daye's house first," Molly said. "He could have seen Daye and Tom going in."

"Or Tom's car parked outside," D.J. said.

And the house dark, Molly thought suddenly. "Wolf does have an explosive temper."

"I'll check with Daye Hummingbird's neighbors," D.J. said. "Somebody might have noticed a car parked on the street outside her house Friday night."

"Daye Hummingbird may not be an impartial witness," Tony observed, "but it sure seems like Wolf Kawaya is the prime suspect in both the break-in and the murder."

"The problem is that poisoned dart," Molly said. "If Wolf is responsible for it, he had to get it into Robert's hand someway. But Robert and Victor swear they picked up a dart at random."

Tony nodded. "Yeah. I talked to both of them at Maud Wildcat's house after school today." He smiled humorlessly. "Scared the crap out of them, a federal investigator showing up at the door. They could be lying about the dart, I guess."

Molly remembered then to tell them about Steven Shell's being near the Kawayas' table for several minutes before the dart was blown. She gave Tony a brief sketch of Steven's history.

"We'd better talk to him," Tony said.

"If Regina will let us," Molly said. "He's living with her and she's very protective."

"He wasn't at the museum with her today," Tony said.

"If he stays away tomorrow," Molly said, "we can probably find him at Regina's place."

Tony volunteered to visit the museum the next morning and give Molly a call if Steven wasn't there. "Since he knows you, he'll be more likely to talk if you question him." They left Oak Hill an hour later, having pooled their information, which didn't result in their being struck by any dramatic new insights.

Tony's car was parked nearest the restaurant. He said good night and got in, leaving Molly and D.J. to walk on together. Cold wind whipped Molly's jacket open and she pulled it closed, shivering.

"About last night," D.J. said quietly, and Molly took a deep breath. All right, so they were going to have to talk about it. "I'm sorry I snapped at you," he continued.

The tight feeling in her chest eased. It wasn't what she'd expected to hear. She looked down. "You didn't snap, and my reaction wasn't exactly subtle. You took me by surprise."

"Really?" He smiled faintly. "Don't tell me you didn't already know how I feel."

Molly hesitated, tempted to feign ignorance, until she realized D.J. would see right through her. She gave a long sigh. "I guess I realized," she admitted, "in a way." She wasn't making a lot of sense, she thought, and struggled for the words to explain how she had felt when he dropped his announcement on her without any warning. It was no easier than it had been last night. "Your saying the words made me feel—well, responsible."

"Responsible?"

"As though something was expected of me in return." She knew at once that she was only making things worse. She hadn't said it right. She shouldn't have tried.

There was a pause. They had reached her car and he looked down at her, his eyes lost in the shadow of his brow.

She pulled her jacket more tightly around her. "I'm trying to tell you what I felt," she said defensively, "not accusing or assigning motives to you. I realize I'm not doing a very good job of it."

"You're doing fine. I get the picture. But I never intended to make you feel—obligated." He hesitated as though tasting the word. "Obligated. Good God."

She had hurt him, when that was the farthest thing from her mind. Why did relationships have to progress or end? Why couldn't they remain in an easy, uncommitted limbo indefinitely?

"You don't feel the same about me, is that it?"

"I'm not sure how I feel, D.J."

He looked at her suspiciously. "Okay, but do me a favor."

"What?"

"When you figure out how you feel, give me a clue."

She lifted her eyes. "Deal."

He waited for her to say more. When she didn't, he kissed her hair and walked away.

# 19

Molly was awakened during the night by lightning striking something nearby. The crackling was so loud that it must have awakened everybody within a mile's radius. Molly sat bolt upright in bed, disoriented for a few moments, before she realized what she'd heard. Just then the sky opened up and let loose a downpour.

Homer barked shrilly and scratched at the door. He was terrified of thunderstorms. Molly let him in and he promptly showered her with raindrops by shaking himself.

"Thanks a lot," she muttered and trudged to the bathroom for a towel. When she came out, Homer had crawled under her bed, as far away from the storm as he could get.

As she climbed back into bed, she checked the luminous dial of the bedside clock. It read 1:22. She drifted back to sleep to the steady beat of rain on the roof.

The next morning, Molly was already outside on the landing on the way to work, having locked the door and dropped the key in her purse, when she heard the telephone ring. She had to dump half the purse's contents out on the landing to find the key again. Finally she got the door open, ran for the phone, and grabbed it off the hook, expecting to hear the dial tone.

"Hello," she panted.

Instead of the dial tone, Tony Warwick said, "Glad I caught you."

"You couldn't have cut it any closer. I was practically in the car. Where are you calling from?" Tony went back home to Muskogee each evening.

"The museum."

Molly looked at her watch. It was only eight-ten. "It doesn't open till nine."

"They made an exception, just for me," Tony said dryly.

"So you phoned to brag? Gee, I'm impressed. Now, what's the real reason for this call?"

"We got a small problem here. The security guard discovered it when he made his rounds at seven. He called Lily Roach and Lily called the tribal police, who called me, since it was probably going to end up on my plate, anyway."

"It? What?"

"Somebody broke in last night and stole one of the exhibits."

"When?"

"Using my great powers of deduction, I'd say sometime between dark and dawn."

Another comedian, Molly thought, cut from the same cloth as Ken Pohl, the medical examiner. "But the guard should have heard the alarm." The guard lived in a small house on the grounds.

"It didn't go off," Tony told her. "The burglar worked around it."

"How?"

"Easily. Come on out and I'll show you."

"I'll be right there." He'd hung up before she had a chance to ask him which exhibit had been stolen. Occasionally the museum staff discovered books or prints missing from the displays in the reception area, but they'd never lost an exhibit before.

For some reason, she thought of Daye Hummingbird's paintings. Daye was becoming pretty well known, her paintings beginning to be in demand. Maybe it was an art theft. A Daye Hummingbird painting would be worth two or three thousand now, and it would undoubtedly increase in value with time. Also, there was Wolf Kawaya, who would surely like to have one of Daye's paintings—as a memento, rather than an investment.

The theft of a painting might be one thing more than Daye could cope with right now. Molly had gotten the impression that Daye was strapped for cash and needed to sell as many of her works as possible during the exhibition.

As Molly drove to Park Hill Thursday morning, the sun shone brightly in a pristine blue sky, the trees alongside the road dripping the last of the previous night's rain.

When she got out of her car at the museum, a cardinal landed on wet leaves nearby and cocked his head at her, and she thought of the origin-of-death myth that Tom Battle told, the last thing he did before he died.

The Sun's daughter—who happened in this instance to be male—flew away, and Molly wondered if every redbird she saw for the rest of her life would remind her of Tom.

Walking toward the museum, she could see the building's solid wood door. It had a gaping hole in it. A square about eighteen inches on a side had been sawed out of the bottom half. The piece of wood thus removed was propped against the wall of the building.

Tony Warwick and a beefy security guard with a square face and no discernible neck were bent over, examining the hole, as

Molly joined them. It was eight-forty, twenty minutes before the museum would be open to visitors.

"Hell of a way to start the day, eh, Molly?" Tony greeted her.

The guard, whom Molly knew only as Tip, shook his head unhappily and touched a finger to the bill of his green John Deere cap. "Mornin', Miss Bearpaw."

"The alarm system encircles the door's perimeter," Tony said to Molly. "It goes off if the lock or hinges are tampered with. So the burglar sawed a hole in the middle, avoiding the alarm system altogether."

"That's incredible," Molly said, stooping to look through the hole into the museum.

"No, it's just so simple that it didn't occur to the people who installed the alarm system," Tony told her. "They tend to think in more complicated terms."

In that case, Molly thought, the museum should get a new security company.

"All the burglar needed was a brace and bit," Tony said, "for boring four holes at the corners of the square, and a key-hole saw." At Molly bewildered expression, he added, "That's a saw with a skinny blade. The tip was inserted in the holes made with the brace and bit, then it was a simple matter of sawing from one hole to the next. Anybody could do it. Probably didn't take more than five minutes."

"Crawled in on his belly like a snake," Tip muttered.

"He had to know how the alarm system worked," Molly said, "if he came prepared with the right tools. Did you find fresh footprints, Tony?" she asked, thinking of last night's rain.

"On this gravel?" Tony indicated the area in front of the museum and shook his head. "No such luck. All the good luck was on the side of the thief. Sawed his hole and, once he was inside, he had the run of the museum. There are no alarms on the individual exhibit cases. He simply broke the glass and took what he wanted."

"Good grief," Molly said, examining the hole more closely, "he could have cleaned out the place."

"Reckon he only wanted one thing," Tip said.

"What was that?"

Tip hung his head. "The wampums. He didn't bother nothing else."

Molly straightened up. "Oh, no . . . " She hadn't even thought of the wampums. On the drive to Park Hill, she'd imagined everything else being stolen, assuming the wampums' value was more sentimental than monetary.

She walked into the museum, outraged at a burglar who would steal the tribe's most ancient and cherished relics. Tony and Tip, who had already turned on all the lights in the reception room and the exhibit area, followed her inside.

The glass exhibit case on the back wall of the exhibit area had been shattered. Only a few pieces of glass remained around the edge of the frame, and there was a blank wall where the wampums had been.

"I picked up the glass," Tony said, "and put it in a box. I'll get the lab to dust it for fingerprints. Of course, we have to have a suspect to match them with before they'll do us any good. He probably wore gloves, anyway." He glanced at Tip, who stood with his hands in his overall pockets, rocking back and forth on the balls of his feet. "You must be a real sound sleeper, Tip."

Tip stopped rocking. "Not hardly," he said. "I got the arthritis. If I lay the same way long, I get to aching and it wakes me up. Sometimes I have to take four aspirin and walk around awhile to get it to quit hurting enough so I can go back to sleep."

Molly pictured the security guard's small house. The only road to the museum passed a few feet from it.

"Runs in my family, the arthritis does," Tip was saying, getting into his narrative. "My mama suffered with it for years before she died. Walked all bent over, Mama did." He seemed launched on a tale of family illness that could go on indefinitely. "My older sister, now—"

"How did you sleep last night?" Molly interrupted, before he could give them a rundown on the other members of his family and their various afflictions.

Tip blinked at her, as though startled by the interruption. "Last night was pretty bad," he said mournfully. "My right hip's the worst. Felt like I was getting stabbed with a knife. Went to bed about eleven. I got up three different times to limber up my hip. Don't think I closed my eyes for more'n fifteen minutes at a stretch all night long. The doctor says—"

"So you probably would have heard a car going by," Molly cut in.

Tip nodded emphatically. "No doubt about it. Last night especially. I was as wide-eyed as a tree full of young owls, with the pain and all. Downright excruciating. Heard every little sound, but I never heard no car."

"He must have walked in," Tony said.

Which meant he knew a car was too risky, since it would have to pass close to the guard's house. Which meant the burglar was familiar with the layout of the heritage center. But then lots of people were.

Someone ran into the museum, high heels clicking. Tony, Tip, and Molly turned simultaneously to see Lily Roach in a denim skirt and a knitted white tunic hurrying toward them. Her usually carefully coiffed hair looked a bit ragged, as though she'd run a comb through it on her way out the door. "I got here as fast as I could," she said breathlessly and came to a dead halt as her gaze took in the empty exhibit case. Her face sagged. "It's true then." She glanced at Tony. "I was hoping you were mistaken, Mr. Warwick. I wasn't sure you knew what was in that case."

"Tip told me," Tony said.

"Oh dear, oh dear," Lily moaned. "What am I going to tell the Nighthawk Keetoowahs?"

"Obviously, you'll have to tell them what happened," Molly said. "And you should probably do it right away, Lily, before word gets out."

"Oh dear," Lily said again and caught her bottom lip between her teeth. After a thoughtful pause, she added, "I'll call the deputy chief first. Maybe he will get word to the Nighthawks. After all, he's in charge when Chief Mankiller's gone." She brightened a little. "I'm sure he'll want to do it. Don't you think so?"

Molly had no idea how the deputy chief would want to handle it, but since Lily seemed to need reassurance, she said, "Probably."

"Then," Lily went on, "I'll have to find somebody to put in a new door today." She consulted her wristwatch. "It's five of nine. Brenda should be here any minute. Oh, wait—I just remembered. She said she'd be a little late this morning. She's having trouble with baby-sitters." She looked pained then, as a new thought struck her. "Some of the visitors are coming especially to see the wampums. What'll we tell them?" She sounded as though she might wring her hands any minute.

"Simply say they're no longer on display," Molly suggested. "You don't have to explain why." Once the story hit the papers, most people would know why, anyway.

Lily scrutinized Molly's face, nodding slowly. "That sounds good. Yes. That's exactly what we'll say. I'll tell Brenda and the others as soon as they get here. Molly, could you stay until Brenda comes? It shouldn't be any longer than half an hour. I need to go in the office and make my phone calls."

The exhibitors began arriving then. Regina and Daye first, followed shortly by the storyteller Edgar Corn, the Kawayas, and Maud Wildcat. One by one, they stopped to wonder over the gaping hole in the door. To a person, they seemed genuinely shocked about the missing wampums. Molly made a point of watching Maud's face as Tony explained what had happened. Of the six, only Maud had been overtly upset about the presence of the wampums. Only Maud had refused to stay in the same room with them.

*Somebody has to stop this*, Maud had said.

Molly was sure Maud wouldn't have taken the wampums herself. She'd have had to touch them, which Maud wouldn't do with a ten-foot pole. That didn't mean she hadn't found somebody else to remove them. Like her grandson. Was that what she meant when she said "this" had to be stopped? But Maud seemed as stunned as everyone else by the news.

"If you don't need me no more, Mr. Warwick," Tip said, "I got work to do."

"Can't think of anything else you can do right now," Tony said. "Thanks for your help." Tip limped off and Tony turned to Molly. "When can you break away here?"

"Half an hour."

"I'd like to meet with Kennedy again." He paused, looking at Molly questioningly. "Unless you have a problem with that."

"Why should I?"

He shrugged. "I got a funny feeling last night. What's going on between you two?"

And she had thought Tony was oblivious. "Working with D.J. is no problem."

He cocked his head. "Which doesn't exactly answer my question."

"Mind your own business, Tony."

He threw up his hands. "Okay, okay. I'll call him. See if he can meet with us today."

Visitors began trickling in by twos and threes, keeping Molly occupied at the reception desk. Tony used the phone behind the desk to set up a meeting with D.J., then clear it with Claude Hobart. Listening to Tony handle the sheriff, Molly decided he'd missed his calling. He should be in the diplomatic corps.

When he hung up, he wandered around, talking to the exhibitors and waiting for Molly to finish.

Lily came out of the office. "One problem's solved. We can get the new door installed today. Now I want to call the security people who put in the alarm system, but I can't remember the name of the company." She began rummaging around beneath the reception desk. "I saw a packet they left with us down here the other day."

Molly bent over to help her and knocked over an aerosol can. She righted it, remembering that this was the can she'd seen Lily put beneath the desk the last time she'd been to the museum Tuesday afternoon, the can Lily had seemed eager to get out of sight. Molly turned the can to read the label—it was black enamel—and suddenly her mind made the connection it had tried to make earlier. The message on the tribal office building had been sprayed on with black paint.

Of itself, it meant nothing. There must be several cans of black enamel within a five-mile radius, except that Lily had acted furtive when Molly had called attention to the can.

Molly set the can on top of the desk as Lily said, "Oh, good, here it is," and straightened up with a manila envelope in her hand.

"Where did this paint come from, Lily?" Molly asked.

Lily glanced at the can, then at Molly before her eyes slid away to focus on the envelope in her hand. "You mean where was it purchased?" she asked vaguely. "I have no idea."

Lily would not meet Molly's eyes. The woman was hiding something. "The last time I was here, Lily," Molly said, "you hid it under the desk."

"Put it back where I found it," Lily corrected.

Molly shook her head. "It wasn't there last Saturday, or I'd have noticed it when I was helping Brenda."

With an effort, Lily lifted her eyes and met Molly's doggedly. "I must have found it somewhere else then. What difference does it make?"

Clearly, it made a great deal of difference to Lily. "Last Friday night," Molly said, "somebody used black spray paint to write a message claiming the tribal office building rightfully belonged to the TEB."

"Well, for heaven sakes," Lily sputtered, "it couldn't have been this paint that was used. That's ridiculous."

"Is it?" Lily didn't respond, so Molly asked, "Does the museum have any use for black enamel?"

Lily shrugged and studied the bare desk top.

"Where did you find it?"

Lily chewed the inside of her cheek and looked toward the door, as though giving serious consideration to flight. Molly waited, and after a moment Lily seemed to make a decision. "I've done a stupid thing," she said. "I'm in big trouble, aren't I?"

"Because you found a can of black spray paint? That's hardly grounds for a criminal indictment."

Lily didn't look reassured.

Molly repeated her question. "Where did you find it, Lily?"

After a hesitation, she blurted out, "In the men's rest room."

"When?"

"Tuesday afternoon."

"What were you doing in the men's rest room?"

"The janitor left a note on the desk Monday night after he'd cleaned, saying there was something wrong with the toilet in the men's rest room. It wasn't flushing right. With everything else I had to do, I put the note aside and forgot about it until Tuesday afternoon."

Molly nodded encouragingly, wishing Lily would get to the point.

Lily took a deep breath. "I flushed the toilet a couple of times and I heard a rattling noise inside the tank. So I took the lid off and there it was."

"The can was inside the tank?"

Lily nodded. "I wouldn't have thought anything of it if it had been sitting there on top of the tank or on the floor. But somebody hid it."

They were interrupted by a visitor wanting to buy a ticket. Molly took care of it while Lily stood there, thinking and turning the manila envelope over in her hands.

As the visitor walked away, Maud came in from the exhibit area and sat down at her table. She looked as though a weight had been lifted from her shoulders. Now that the wampums were gone, they could move her table back in with the others.

Molly glanced at Maud and took Lily's arm, moving toward the windows so that Maud couldn't overhear the conversation. "When you found the can," Molly said, "the first thing you thought of was the sign on the office building, the same as I did. Isn't that true?"

Lily nodded reluctantly. "Only because it was hidden like that. But then I thought it couldn't be the same can, Molly. Why would whoever painted that sign leave it here?"

Molly didn't know the answer. It did seem pretty far-fetched. "Then why did you try to hide it from me?"

She sighed and fingered the flap of the manila envelope. "All right. For one thing, Wolf came out of the men's room shortly before I went in."

"And you thought he'd left it there."

"I didn't see him take it in," she said quickly. "I just didn't want to cause any trouble for him. He's got enough with that dart he made being poisoned. People are saying he gave it to Robert Wildcat to shoot. Not that I believe that for a second."

"Wait a minute," Molly interrupted. "The toilet wasn't flushing right before that. You said the janitor noticed it Monday night."

"It wasn't the paint can that was causing the problem. There was something else wrong with it."

Molly asked, "Do you know if the janitor looked in the tank Monday night?"

"I asked him," Lily admitted, "and he said he did. Nothing was in there that shouldn't be, until after he left Monday night."

"So the can was hidden in the tank sometime Tuesday." But why in the men's rest room? Molly wondered. The sign on the tribal office building was painted last Thursday night. The culprit had had four days to dispose of the can where it would not be found. Why bring it to the museum?

"As for painting the office building," Lily was saying, "that's not a serious crime, Molly. The letters have already been painted over. It's forgotten."

This might be true, but Molly remained troubled. She was missing something here. Tuesday afternoon, before Lily whisked the paint can out of sight, she'd put something in her pocket. "You said 'for one thing.' If there's something else you're not telling me, Lily, now's the time to speak up."

Lily folded her arms and gazed out the window. "Are you going to tell Tony Warwick about the paint can?"

"Yes."

"Even though it has nothing to do with Tom Battle's death?"

"The fact that it was hidden makes it suspicious," Molly said. "Tom represented the Nation against the TEB. If that's the paint used on the office building, then maybe there is some connection to Tom."

Lily glanced over her shoulder at Maud, who was talking to a visitor. "I've done a terrible thing," she blurted. "I'm in big trouble, but I can't keep it to myself any longer. It's eating me up."

"Calm down, Lily. You tried to hide a can of paint. It's no big deal."

"There's more," Lily said. "Come with me."

Mystified, Molly followed Lily to the office. They went in and closed the door. Lily pulled open the bottom desk drawer and reached down behind a stack of ledgers. She brought out something wrapped in tissue and handed it to Molly. "This was in the tank too, with the paint can."

Molly removed the tissue, revealing a small, rectangular glass bottle with a screw cap, about half full of brown liquid. The bottle had been marked with a skull and crossbones and the word *Nicotine*.

"I wiped it off," Lily said. "The paint can too."

"You dried them when you took them out of the tank?"

"That too," Lily said. "And before I put that in the desk drawer, I wiped it all over with a tissue."

Molly stared at her. "Why?"

Agitated, Lily clenched her hands together in front of her chest. "I know I shouldn't have. I tampered with evidence, didn't I? I wasn't thinking, Molly. I was so scared."

Lily may have been scared, but she'd had the presence of mind to remove any fingerprints that might have been on the bottle or paint can. Wiping off fingerprints wasn't ordinarily what a frightened person did. It was what a guilty person did. Or a person who wanted to protect somebody else who was guilty. And Lily had come to Wolf's defense on several occasions.

The Roaches and the Kawayas were all members of the True Echota Band. Lily might be worried that if Wolf were accused of the murder it would reflect badly on the band. But was that enough reason to destroy evidence?

Molly wondered suddenly if she knew Lily Roach as well as she'd thought. "Wait here," she said, "while I find Tony. You need to tell him everything you've told me."

While Tony and Lily were closeted in the office, Molly took care of a sudden flurry of visitors. During the lull that followed, she stood in the doorway leading to the exhibit area as Ed Corn performed.

Long, long ago there lived a Cherokee man whose name was *Tseg'sgin'*. Now, *Tseg'sgin'* was a great trickster. If he wanted anything, he always found a way to get it. This is the story of how *Tseg'sgin'* got a woman.

There was a beautiful woman who lived nearby, but her father wouldn't let *Tseg'sgin'* come calling on her. So *Tseg'sgin'* had to think quite a long time about how he could get that woman. One day, on his way to her house, he saw a cow in a field. So he cut off the cow's tail and took it with him to the woman's house. When he came near her house, just out of sight, he stuck the tail into the ground. Then he cried for help so that the father of the woman would hear him.

Sure enough, the father came out and asked what was wrong. *Tseg'sgin'* said, "My cow went into the ground here. I don't know how I'm going to get her out. If I pull the tail too hard I might pull it off, then the cow would be gone forever. Do you have a shovel so I can dig my cow out?"

"I do," the other man said.

"Here," said *Tseg'sgin'*. "If you'll hold this cow's tail, I'll go get the shovel. Don't pull too hard. If you do, the cow will be gone forever."

So *Tseg'sgin'* went to the woman's house and the woman was there alone. She was young and very beautiful.

"I saw your father over there," said *Tseg'sgin'*, "and he said you could leave with me if you want to."

"I don't believe my father would say that," the woman said. "I'd better shout to him and ask."

"All right," said *Tseg'sgin'*.

So the woman called to her father, "Did you really tell this man to come up here?"

"Yes, that's what I told him," the father said.

So *Tseg'sgin'* took the woman away. And that's how *Tseg'sgin'* got a beautiful woman.

Only as Ed finished the story did Molly become aware of a vaguely familiar sound to her right, the sound of Josiah Kawaya cracking his knuckles. He glanced away when she turned toward him, but not before she realized he was watching her intently. She had the feeling he'd been doing so for some time.

# 20

Molly, Tony, and D.J. met in Claude Hobart's office at two o'clock. The sheriff wasn't expected back that afternoon, and his office was the only place in the sheriff's building for a private meeting, since the deputies' desks shared a large common room between the office and the dispatcher's cubicle.

D.J. had instructed the dispatcher to hold his calls, barring an emergency. He sat behind the sheriff's desk, his rumpled khaki shirt open at the neck, his forearms resting on the desk. He tapped a ballpoint pen idly against the wood.

Tony had already filled D.J. in on the burglary at the museum and related his conversation with Lily Roach.

Molly and Tony pulled two chairs up to the other side of the desk, facing D.J. The can of black enamel and the nicotine bottle rested on the brown desk between them.

D.J. seemed perfectly relaxed, and Molly was relieved that Wednesday night's tension had evaporated. At least their professional relationship was on an even keel.

"How do we know Lily found the paint and nicotine, like she says?" D.J. asked. "If she's an innocent bystander, why would she wipe them clean?"

"She claims she was too scared to think straight," Molly said.

"That's her story and she's sticking to it," Tony agreed. "But, hell, what's she scared of?"

He looked at Molly, who suggested, "Maybe that whoever hid those things in the men's room would find out she'd removed them. She thinks it was Wolf Kawaya, by the way, though she would deny that if asked. She's trying to protect him for some reason. She told me that Wolf came out of the men's room shortly before she went in and found these things."

"Doesn't sound like she's trying to protect him to me," Tony observed.

That brought Molly up short. "You've got a point," she said slowly. As Conrad had said, it helped sometimes to look at facts from a different angle. "If she really wanted to protect him, why would she tell me she saw him coming out of the men's room?" She shook her head, frowning. "But when anybody suggests that Wolf vandalized Tom Battle's house or knew the dart that killed him was poisoned, Lily comes to his defense."

"What if she only wants to seem to be protecting him," D.J. said. "It keeps us from viewing *her* with suspicion. If she's involved somehow in Battle's murder, you'd expect her to encourage our suspicions of someone else. If she can do it by seeming to defend that person, so much the better."

"I guess it makes a convoluted sort of sense," Tony said. "But if she's involved, what's her motive?"

"The Roaches are TEB members," Molly told him, "but I can't believe Lily would murder Tom because he was a lawyer for the Nation. If she's got a motive, it's something else. Something more personal."

"Unless she's crazy," Tony said half seriously.

"No way," Molly said. But wait. Hadn't Lily's daughter said that working at the museum had saved Lily's sanity? Had she had psychological problems in the past? She repeated what Sarah Bowling had told her.

"Maybe I'd better check into her background a little more," D.J. said, and Molly suggested he find out if she'd had psychiatric care after the death of her son.

D.J. dropped the pencil he'd been tapping on the desk and picked up the nicotine bottle. "I've got an interesting bit of news for you two. Molly, remember me telling you somebody broke into Green Gardens Nursery?"

Molly nodded. "The same night Tom Battle's house was vandalized, wasn't it?"

"Yes," D.J. replied. "The nursery manager out there called me a little while ago. He'd heard by the grapevine that Battle died of nicotine poisoning. That reminded him that the nursery had a full bottle of nicotine, which they use as an insecticide. They hadn't used it recently, and he had no reason to think of it until he heard about Battle. So he looked where the bottle of nicotine was supposed to be, and guess what."

"It's missing," Molly supplied.

"Yep." D.J. set the bottle down. "He described this to a *T*. I'll take it out there and get him to identify it, but this is it. No question."

All three of them gazed at the small bottle. "*This* is what the burglar was after at the nursery," Molly said, "not money. So it was someone who knew the nursery had the nicotine poison on the premises."

"I quizzed the nursery manager about that," D.J. said as he reached for the pencil again. Tap, tap, tap.

"His employees knew it, of course. And before you ask, I already checked their names against the list of people who were at the museum the morning Battle was killed. No matches. The manager said they carry a large stock of roses, and anybody who knows something about roses might guess they'd have nicotine on hand. Evidently it's the most effective method of killing rose aphids."

"Works pretty damned well with people too," Tony muttered, sitting back in his chair, hands linked behind his head and one booted foot propped on the other knee. Lizard skin today. He jiggled his foot restlessly. "What have we got here? Nicotine poison swiped from a nursery, a murder by nicotine poisoning, vandalism of the murder victim's house, a pro–TEB message painted on the tribal office building, the theft of the tribe's ancient wampums from the scene of the murder. Hell's bells, we've got us a regular crime spree on our hands. The question is, were all these crimes perpetrated by the same person or persons?"

D.J. mused, "Seems fairly obvious that the nursery break-in, the vandalism of Battle's house, and the murder are all connected."

"That can of paint being hidden with the poison points to a connection between the defacing of the office building and the murder," Molly added. "*If* that's the same paint can that was used on the offices. But if it's not, why hide it?"

"If we buy that," D.J. said, "then have we tied in the TEB to the other crimes?"

Molly shook her head. "No. In fact, just the opposite. It must be somebody who's in sympathy with the TEB cause, but he doesn't have to be a member of the band. I know most of their members. They're upright, law-abiding citizens. Besides, the TEB council has made it clear the sign painter wasn't acting with their approval, or even with their knowledge."

"Molly's right," Tony agreed. "You take your Middle East terrorist organizations. When they kidnap or kill somebody, they call up the newspapers and brag about it. Makes no sense for somebody to commit a crime to make a political point and then deny it."

"So," Molly added, remembering Herb Cochran's suggestion, "it's a loose cannon."

"Maybe a nut case, like I said before," Tony supplied.

"Do we have any evidence that the theft of the wampums is connected to any of the other crimes?" D.J. asked.

"None," Tony admitted, scratching his head, "except the wampums disappeared from the place where Battle was killed."

Molly shifted restlessly in her chair. "I'm convinced there's no real TEB connection. But there may be one in the mind of the perpetrator. Possessing the wampums might, in his mind, give some validity to the handful of radicals' claim that the band's leaders are the rightful leaders of the entire tribe."

Tony looked puzzled. "How come?"

"It's too long a story to go into in detail now," Molly said, "but the principal chief had possession of the wampums until early in the twentieth century. It was like a badge of office."

"I've been wondering why anyone would steal the wampums," D.J. put in. "That may be the answer."

"If so, it's somebody who mistakenly thinks the TEB leaders will welcome the wampums," Molly said. "But the band's leaders are committed to lawful settlement of their claims, so if the thief turns the wampums over to them, they'll give them back to the Nighthawks."

"You mentioned TEB radicals, Molly," Tony said. "You happen to have any names on the tip of your tongue?"

"A couple," Molly admitted. "Wolf and Josiah Kawaya."

Tony's foot began to wobble again. "Every road comes back to those two. To Wolf Kawaya, anyway."

"Wait a minute," D.J. interjected. "Could there be a financial motive for stealing the wampums? Are they valuable?"

"They would be to a museum," Molly said, "but no reputable museum would buy them without a thorough background check. They'd find out right away that the wampums were stolen."

"Yeah, you're right," D.J. said. "The thief probably wouldn't dare offer them to a museum."

"There are folks who might not ask so many questions," Tony mused.

"Private collectors? But they'd have to suspect the wampums were stolen," Molly protested. "They couldn't risk showing them."

"People are weird," Tony said. "Some of them get their jollies out of owning rare stuff. They're like a miser who hides his money in a mattress and gets it out every now and then to count it. *They* know it's there. That's what matters."

"You'd have to have connections to sell stolen relics," Molly said.

"Yeah," D.J. added, "it's much more likely to be a local thing. A lone ranger who thinks he's making a political point."

Tony thought a moment. "If only we knew what time the wampums were taken."

"The janitor cleans at night," Molly said. "I think he finishes and leaves the museum around midnight. I'll confirm that with the security guard."

"Okay, so the burglary occurred between midnight and dawn," Tony said. "Likely between midnight and three or four in the morning. The thief could count on the security guard sleeping during those hours."

"Except he didn't," Molly put in and told D.J. about Tip's restless night. "But Tip didn't hear anything."

"Yeah, but the thief believed he'd be sleeping," Tony went on.

"A lot of people knew the wampums were in the museum this week," Molly said.

"Well, let's say for now there's a connection between the theft and the other crimes," Tony said. "That'll limit our list of serious suspects to a few names. We need to know where they were between midnight and dawn."

D.J. grabbed a memo pad and began a list of names: Wolf Kawaya, Josiah Kawaya, Lily Roach, Robert Wildcat, Victor Halland.

"Better add Maud Wildcat," Molly said. "She wanted those wampums out of there. And Steven Shell. I'm planning to talk to him this afternoon."

"Might as well add the others who were there when Battle was killed too," Tony said. "Regina Shell and Daye Hummingbird."

"Daye?" Molly asked. "That's ridiculous."

Tony gave her a crooked smile. "Probably, but let's cover the bases."

"What about the receptionist, Brenda Farley?" D.J. asked.

"Put her down," Tony said with a wolfish grin, "Let's shake 'em all up."

"And hope it's one of them," D.J. added. "If the thief is somebody not connected to the museum, we'll never track him down."

"If we could get a break in one of the crimes, that might be all we need to tie 'em all up," Tony said.

"I'm not getting anywhere on the investigation of the break-in at Battle's place," D.J. said. "I talked to the people who live within a mile of the house—that's only three houses. No one noticed anybody around Battle's house the night of the vandalism. They were all asleep before eleven."

D.J. had yet to check with Daye's neighbors to see if anybody noticed Wolf Kawaya's car parked outside her house Friday night, or to get the nursery manager to ID the bottle of poison, in addition to working on unrelated cases, the cases the sheriff had instructed him not to put on the back burner to help "the damned feds."

Tony said, "I'll try to find Robert Wildcat and Victor Halland this afternoon while you look up Steven Shell, Molly."

"He didn't come to the museum with Regina this morning," Molly said. "So he should be at home."

Tony and Molly agreed to team up on the other people on the list.

"Well, troops," Tony said, standing. "Let's go rattle some cages."

# 21

The Shell home appeared to be the oldest in a block of fifties-vintage frame houses in Tahlequah. Certainly it was the most in need of a paint job. It sat at the back of the lot surrounded by shrubbery beds that had been neglected about as long as the house.

Molly was shocked by the change in the place since she'd last been there, when Regina and Steven's mother was alive. It appeared that little in the way of upkeep to the yard or the outside of the house had been done since Mrs. Shell's death.

Steven might be less bored, Molly thought unkindly, if he'd lift his hand to do some work around there. Keeping occupied would probably help his mental state as well. Regina didn't have time to do it herself and couldn't afford to hire it done, or the place wouldn't be in its present decrepit condition.

All the shades at the front of the house were drawn. Molly pressed the rusty doorbell button, then knocked in case the bell was out of order like everything else.

She heard movement in the house, but two full minutes passed before the door was opened. Steven, puffy-eyed from sleep, squinted out at her from the dim interior, like a bug exposed to a rare shaft of sunlight.

"Hi, Steven," Molly said with forced cheeriness.

"Hi," he mumbled, scratching his chest through his dirty knit shirt. His gaze seemed to be fixed on her right shoulder, perhaps on her car parked at the curb. He said nothing more.

Was it possible he didn't recognize her? "It's Molly Bearpaw," she said. His eyes flicked to hers and then back to the spot over her right shoulder. "May I come in and talk to you for a few minutes?"

He mumbled something indecipherable and walked away from the door, back into the dimness. Molly took this as assent and stepped inside. He had flopped in a chair, his long arms dangling between his legs. He yawned, looking up at her without curiosity, waiting for her to explain what she was doing there. Or not. Molly had the feeling it mattered little to Steven.

In contrast to the exterior, the interior of the house was neat and clean. Whatever money and time Regina could spare from her basket making had been expended here. Several of Regina's baskets were set about, ivy and ferns spilling over the edges. Another basket next to the couch held magazines. Through the open doorway to the kitchen, Molly could see gleaming white floor tile and part of a drying rack on which a blanket was spread. The vague lemony scent of furniture polish hung in the air. The only discordant note was the rank smell of body odor coming from Steven.

No chair being offered, Molly helped herself to the end of the couch nearer the door. "I'm sorry if I woke you," she said.

"It's all right. Sometimes I sleep 'cause there's nothing else to do."

Nothing to do? Hadn't he noticed the yard? Don't be so critical, Molly, she told herself. Steven's medication sapped energy and dulled the mind. At least he wasn't tearing around at the behest of delusional voices. Furthermore, Steven might actually be making an effort to interact. His response had been a long one for him. Two whole sentences.

"Doesn't sleeping in the daytime keep you up at night?" Molly asked, edging toward her reason for being there. She wanted to get away from that house as quickly as possible. It wasn't that she was afraid of Steven, exactly, but he made her uncomfortable. His shirt had food stains on it, and his mouth hung half open, as though closing it were too much trouble.

"Not really."

He wasn't going to volunteer much, that was for sure. Conversation with Steven was at best a one-sided affair, but Molly plowed ahead. "What about last night?"

"Huh?"

"Did you sleep well last night?"

He rubbed his chin bristles. "Sure."

Molly couldn't stand the murkiness any longer. She turned on the lamp that sat on the table beside the couch. Light fell on a pamphlet that lay beside the lamp, an informational brochure on Serenity Psychiatric Facility in Dallas, Texas. "What time did you go to bed?"

He frowned. "'Bout ten, I think."

"And you slept right through the night?"

He nodded.

Idly, Molly opened the brochure and scanned it. There were several color pictures of the hospital's accommodations—a large dining room, another big room with a fireplace and a piano, and an attractive bedroom. A far cry from Eastern Oklahoma State Hospital in Vinita. But still a hospital. Did Steven know that Regina was thinking of sending him away again?

"What time did Regina go to bed last night?" Molly asked, refolding the brochure and placing it on the table.

"She always goes to bed after the news."

"Ten-thirty?"

"Uh-huh."

"So you were both in bed from ten-thirty last night until sometime this morning."

He shrugged carelessly. "Like always. Regina never goes anywhere, especially not at night. In the daytime, she only goes to the store and places where she sells her baskets." When Steven wasn't around, Regina did have the semblance of a social life, but apparently he didn't realize he was the reason it disappeared when he was home. Or didn't care.

"Do you usually go with her?"

"She tries to get me to, like I'm gonna run off if she lets me out of her sight. Where'd I go?" He sounded resentful of his sister's protectiveness. The fact that he had disappeared on numerous occasions—sometimes for weeks at a time, when he stopped taking his medication—didn't seem to occur to him. But it was the first hint of any emotion in his voice.

"The ancient wampum belts were stolen from the museum last night."

He looked blank for an instant and then something shifted in his eyes as his sluggish mind made a connection. "Is that why you want to know what time I went to bed and all that?" Steven wasn't as out of it as she'd imagined.

"Only because you spent some time at the museum this week, so you knew the wampums were there," Molly said. "We're asking a lot of people the same questions."

"I don't know anything about the wampums," he said, scowling darkly. "Stealing them would be dangerous."

Molly wasn't sure if he was referring to the wampums' evil power or the fact that theft could lead to jail time. "You were with Regina at the museum," she said carefully, "the morning Tom Battle died."

His scowl deepened. "It was boring," he said defensively, "so she said I didn't have to go back there anymore."

Boring to watch a man die before your eyes? Surely not as boring as staying shut up in this house, alone, doing nothing. "You seemed interested in the blowguns and darts."

He pressed a palm against his forehead as though trying to remember. When he dropped his hand, the scowl had disappeared and he looked at her with an expression of bland candor. Or perhaps it was vacuousness. Except for that brief moment earlier, Steven did give the impression that no one was at home behind those dark eyes.

"You were standing behind Robert Wildcat and Victor Halland when Robert shot a dart and hit Tom."

"I guess," he said, disinterested now, and yawned broadly, as though he found Molly quite as boring as his day at the museum. A greasy lock of black hair flopped over his forehead.

"You do know that Tom is dead, don't you?"

"Sure. Regina told me." There was no empathy in his flat tone. Perhaps he was incapable of it.

"Did you see anybody put a dart on the table where Robert and Victor were standing?"

His brows drew together again, but if he was concentrating, it was a surface activity. There were no depths to Steven on his medication, and maybe that was the point. Steven's depths must be very frightening.

"There were lots of darts on the table. Wolf Kawaya was making them."

So he knew who Wolf was, but seemed not to have a clue about what Molly was driving at. "Have you ever made blowgun darts?"

He shook his head and, again, he seemed not to understand why she asked. "My medicine makes my hands tremble sometimes. I could cut myself if I tried to whittle."

"Did you know Tom Battle?"

"Not really." He scratched his chest. "I knew his name, is all."

Molly didn't think he knew anything about any of the crimes. Steven was lost in his own foggy world.

"Regina was real sad when Tom Battle died." He yawned.

"We all were." Molly sighed, admitting defeat. "I have to go now. Nice talking to you, Steven."

He didn't stir as she let herself out.

Driving to the museum from her interview with Steven, Molly thought sympathetically of Regina and her sad, narrow existence. It centered on two things, the baskets that provided her livelihood and the brother who was never going to be well.

Tony and Molly arrived at the museum within five minutes of each other. They went into the museum office and Molly reported on her interview with Steven Shell.

"Sacked out all night, huh? You think he was telling the truth?" Tony asked.

"I have no idea," Molly admitted, "but I can't believe he stole the wampums. He sleeps most of the time. He doesn't bathe or wash his hair often enough. He's so medicated it's a major expenditure of energy to walk across the house. Stealing the wampums required energy and nerve—and planning. Steven doesn't seem able to plan anything. He just drifts along in his medicated fog."

"But he's a nut case," Tony said. "You can't predict what one of those people will do."

"Steven's fairly coherent when he's on his medication, and he has no motive for stealing the wampums," Molly insisted, "and certainly no connection for disposing of them. And if the thief is the same person who killed Tom, Steven has no motive for murder, either. He didn't even know Tom."

"But he's one of the few who had opportunity. He was close to the Kawayas' table when that kid hit Battle with the poisoned dart."

"I'm sure he was only wandering around," Molly said. "Think about it, Tony. Poisoning the dart and getting it in Robert Wildcat's hand took planning and timing. Steven isn't capable of masterminding something like that."

"Okay, we'll put Steven Shell on the shelf for now," Tony said with some reluctance. "I waited outside the high school until school let out. Caught Wildcat and Halland and had a talk with them in Halland's car."

He shrugged off his corduroy jacket and tossed it on a bookcase, then leaned back in his chair in his favorite pose, hands linked behind head, one booted foot resting on the other knee. "Their story is that they were together from eight o'clock until about one last night. 'Just messing around.' When I pinned them down, they finally said they drove to Tulsa, took in a movie, picked up a six pack, and drove back to Tahlequah. At one or thereabouts, Halland dropped Wildcat off at his grandmother's house and went straight home. In other words, they're each other's alibi, for whatever that's worth. I'll check with Victor's parents, see if they know what time he got in, but I'll bet they confirm his story."

"We can ask Maud what time Robert came home," Molly said. "Do you want to talk to her first?"

"Might as well."

The next hour and a half was spent interviewing the exhibitors and museum employees. Maud backed up Robert's story. She'd gone to bed about ten but had slept fitfully until she heard Robert come in. Her bedside clock had read twelve-fifty-five. She'd gone back to sleep soon after the rain started and didn't awake again until almost eight that morning. Robert had overslept too, and wasn't ready for school when

Victor came by for him. Maud had dropped him off on her way to the museum.

Between the hours of midnight and dawn, Brenda Farley, the receptionist, had been in bed with her husband. Ditto for Lily Roach. Josiah Kawaya and his wife had attended a stomp dance at Vian the previous evening, returning home at eleven-thirty, when they had retired for the night. Wolf Kawaya had been at home alone all night, as had Daye Hummingbird.

These were the stories they gave Molly and Tony, at any rate. Any of them who slept alone could easily have gone out after midnight and returned before dawn with no one the wiser.

By the time Tony and Molly got to Regina Shell, it was close to four-thirty and Regina was eager to leave for the day and get home to Steven.

"This won't take long," Tony assured her. "We'd like to know where you were last night after midnight."

Regina wasn't surprised by the question, having talked to the other exhibitors after they were interviewed. "Where I am every night," she said. "At home in bed." She made a wry face. "I'm not exactly a social butterfly. And I sure didn't come out here and steal the wampums."

"Steven says he was home in bed too," Molly said. "Can you confirm that?"

Her expression shifted from impatient tolerance to surprise. "*Steven* says." Regina sat forward in her chair. "When did you talk to Steven?"

"I went by the house earlier this afternoon," Molly told her, squirming in her chair. She felt a twinge of conscience because she'd deliberately picked a time to talk to Steven when he was alone, knowing that Regina wouldn't like it.

But Regina's reaction was even stronger than Molly had expected. Anger turned her eyes to black pebbles. "You got him alone and questioned him?"

"He happened to be alone, yes."

"You knew damned well he'd be alone!" Regina rose slowly to her feet, turned away from the desk where Tony was sitting to face Molly. Her eyes flared with rage; she was so angry all at once that she seemed barely able to contain herself. "How dare you!" With one hand, she reached out and grabbed the back of the chair she'd been sitting in, her knuckles white.

Instinctively, Molly drew back in her chair. "Steven knows me, Regina. He didn't seem to mind talking to me."

"Mind?" Regina's voice rose in a shrill crescendo. "Steven would let in Jack the Ripper! He's not responsible. You know that, Molly. You knew he'd be alone and you took advantage of the situation to interrogate him."

"It wasn't an interrogation," Molly protested. "Regina, you're upset over nothing."

Regina let go of the chair and snatched her purse from the floor. "Don't you understand that Steven will agree to almost anything anyone suggests? You could tell him he was a serial killer and he wouldn't disagree for long. Disagreeing takes too much thought and energy." She stomped to the door. "If you ever try anything like that again, Molly," she said, "I'll get a lawyer and sue you for everything you've got or ever will have. Then we'll see if it was nothing." She jerked open the door and stormed out.

In the silence that followed Regina's departure, Tony and Molly looked at each other in bewilderment.

Finally, Molly said, "I knew she was protective of Steven, but wasn't that a bit out of proportion?"

Tony scratched his head. "She's something else. Maybe scared of what Steven might tell us if she's not there to stop him."

"But he didn't say anything incriminating."

"It's what she's scared he might say."

"What do you mean?"

Tony leaned over and rested his elbows on the desk. "Try this on for size. Steven left the house last night. Maybe she woke up and found him gone, and she doesn't know where he went or how long he was out. She's sure scared to death we'll try to pin something on him because he's an easy mark. You heard her."

"Tony, it's—well, highly unlikely that Steven was on the loose last night. For all the reasons I've already mentioned. Besides which, I'll bet Regina sleeps with one eye open when he's living with her."

Tony raised a hand. "Let's say for a minute that he got out of the house without waking her. The woman is stressed out. Once she falls asleep, she's gonna be dead to the world."

"Maybe . . . " It *would* explain why Regina had been so angry.

"If she did wake up and Steven wasn't in the house," Tony continued, "and this morning she learned the wampums were stolen during the night, wouldn't she the think the worst? Wouldn't she react exactly like she just did when she found out somebody had questioned Steven?"

"I still say Steven didn't steal the wampums. Why would he? He's schizophrenic, but as long as he's taking his medicine, he's not insane. If he did leave the house at night, he'd probably wander around aimlessly for a while and go back home." A memory from the day of Tom Battle's funeral flitted across Molly's mind. At the cemetery, Regina had been worried that Steven, who had no driver's license, would drive off in her car while she was talking to Molly. If she woke up last night and found both Steven and the car gone . . .

Tony interrupted the thought. "It's not what Steven did," he told her, "but what Regina thinks he did."

"I don't know," Molly said. "But now that I think about it, I shouldn't have been surprised by her reaction. She would fly into a rage over anything that she sees as threatening or taking advantage of Steven. She would die protecting him. It's such a strong instinct it borders on pathological. They've always been unusually close, even for twins. When Steven got sick, Regina lost a part of herself. She's been fighting to get it back ever since."

Tony straightened up, planting his hands on his knees, arms akimbo. "Well, we've gone through the list, and I'll lay you odds one of 'em's lying."

"Which one?"

"Yeah." He reached for his jacket, stood and put it on. "Who's your money on?"

Molly shook her head, not wanting to commit herself. "I can't say."

He grinned. "But you're thinking, and the one you're thinking of is Wolf Kawaya."

"His name does keep coming up, doesn't it? Maybe Wolf's a bit too obvious, though—too convenient." For an instant her memory went back to yesterday when she'd caught Josiah Kawaya watching her and nervously cracking his knuckles. What had that been about?

"Don't try to make it complicated. Murders usually aren't." Tony buttoned his jacket. "I'm going home and shoot some baskets with my boy." He looked troubled for an instant. Perhaps thinking about Robert Wildcat, whose grandmother seemed to be the only adult in his life who had any time for him.

Molly followed him out of the office. "Let's meet here tomorrow morning at nine," Tony suggested, adding with a salute as he went out the door, "Call me if you solve the case before tomorrow. Save me a trip."

# 22

It was four-thirty, half an hour before museum closing time. After Tony left, Molly scanned the reception room. Lily Roach was using a lamb's-wool duster to clean the display shelves. Brenda Farley was absorbed in a paperback book.

"Isn't that the janitor's job, Lily?" Molly asked.

Lily flicked the duster across a row of books as she glanced over her shoulder. "Men don't notice little things like dust." She walked around the reception desk next to Brenda and stored the duster beneath. "I'm going in the office, Brenda, and catch up on some book work."

Brenda nodded without looking up from her book, a romance novel, Molly saw now. The cover depicted a busty blonde, boobs halfway out of her dress, shrinking away from the swashbuckling, black-haired pirate who loomed over her.

"I'm sorry we had to take over your office for our interviews," Molly said to Lily. The last few days she'd realized that Lily was truly indispensable to the museum. She doubted that many people knew how hard the woman worked, doing whatever needed to be done, from organizing exhibitions to cleaning up after the janitor. "You're very patient with us, Lily. I hope we'll be out of your hair soon."

"Don't worry about inconveniencing me," Lily said unhappily. "The Nighthawks are absolutely devastated by their loss. If they ever get hold of the wampums, they'll never agree to exhibit them again. The important thing is for you to get the wampums back." She glanced at Molly as if to judge whether information as to the progress of the investigation might be forthcoming. Then she cleared her throat and added, "And catch Tom's murderer, of course."

Molly wasn't too surprised that the murder seemed to be an afterthought. A lawyer could be replaced; the wampums couldn't.

Lily ran her fingers through her hair. "The sooner I get on that book work, the sooner I can go home," she said in a tired voice.

Molly went back to the exhibit area to find Regina and assure her again that she'd meant no harm to Steven, but Regina had already left. Edgar Corn was about to begin another tale, the last of the day, and Molly decided to stay for the story.

Corn, in his seventies, resembled the wise old Indian of Hollywood legend. His long gray hair was braided in two plaits with bright green yarn, his face carved by age and weather, his nose prominent and hooked, his dark eyes gentle and resigned. He even wore deerskin moccasins.

All the seats were taken, so Molly sat on the floor near the first row of folding chairs. Corn spoke in a deep, raspy voice.

This is a story my grandfather told me when I was a boy. In the old Cherokee country back East, a terrible monster roamed the earth, catching men and eating them. The Cherokees called him the *Uk'ten'*. He had horns and a body like a giant lizard, with seven big spots on it. He could kill a man just by breathing on him.

One day, the people decided they had to kill the *Uk'ten'*. They were tired of hiding in caves in the dark. They wanted to come out and live in the sunlight. So they sent their best archer to shoot an arrow and hit the monster on the seventh spot.

When the archer found the *Uk'ten'*, the monster was having a fight with Thunder. They were fighting to see who could live on the earth. The archer drew his bow. But he missed because the monster and Thunder were rolling around on the ground, and tremendous thunder and lightning shook the sky.

The archer drew his bow a second and a third time, and missed. Finally, on the fourth try, he hit the *Uk'ten'* in the seventh spot. The monster fell and floundered about and made hot fire rain from the sky. The fire rained until he was dead. After that, the people came out of their hiding places, and ever since then, Thunder has been a friend to the Cherokees.

Molly didn't move as the other listeners applauded and began to disperse. Corn's story reminded her of her college anthropology professor who had pointed out the similarities between the Cherokee *Uk'ten'* and the mythical European dragon. Was the Cherokee legend derivative—or did it come from ancient racial memory common to all cultures? And why, she wondered, had so many ancient cultures considered *seven* a particularly powerful number? The number appeared in many Cherokee myths and folktales, and in ancient times there had been seven Cherokee clans.

The mythological *Uk'ten'* had represented all that was evil in the world. His death had allowed the people to walk in the sunlight and live like men, but the monster had left some of his evil behind in the hearts of human beings. Evil that sometimes caused men to murder their brothers.

As closing time neared and the visitors began to leave, several of them glanced curiously at Molly, who still hadn't moved from her spot on the floor. She barely noticed them as she continued to sit, staring at a blank wall; thinking about the interviews she and Tony had had.

When absolute quiet descended on the deserted museum, Molly began to make a mental list of the information given by the people they'd questioned.

The only thing she accomplished with this exercise was to fix the details firmly in her mind, which would be useful when she wrote her report. Unless the thief was somebody they hadn't talked to, Tony was right and one of the suspects was lying. But which one?

What was it Conrad had said about logic problems? *You have to make an assumption and follow it to the end. It lets you see the facts in a new light.* Something flitted teasingly through the dark recesses of Molly's consciousness, just beyond grasping. Something she'd seen? Something somebody had said? Or failed to say?

It wouldn't come, so she gave up trying to recall whatever it was and followed Conrad's advice, taking each of the suspects in turn and assuming he or she was both the thief and the murderer.

Lily Roach, Brenda Farley, Josiah Kawaya, Robert Wildcat, Steven and Regina Shell had alibis that could be corroborated by another person. Their spouses, in the first three cases. As for Robert, Victor was with him until one in the morning, and Maud confirmed that he'd come home at that time. The problem was that, if Victor and Robert had worked together to steal the wampums, they could easily have done it between midnight and one. Furthermore, they'd lie for each other. And if Maud thought Robert had done it alone, after Victor left him, she might lie about the time he came home.

Steven and Regina said they were at home all night, and in spite of Tony's suspicions, Molly believed them. Although either of them *could* have gone out after the other was asleep.

Wolf Kawaya's and Daye Hummingbird's alibis for last night couldn't be corroborated at all, nor could Maud's for the time before one in the morning.

When it came to motives for murder, Brenda, Daye, Regina, and Steven had no credible ones that Molly could think of. Robert, Victor, Lily, Maud, and Wolf were TEB members who might, to one degree or another, have disliked Tom because he'd represented the tribe in legal battles against the band. But had any of them felt strongly enough to kill Tom and then steal the wampums so that the band could have possession of them? That made no sense, because killing Tom wouldn't stop the lawsuits. The tribe would simply hire another lawyer. And the wampums could not be turned over to the leaders of the band. Surely the thief realized that would lead to immediate exposure.

From what Molly had seen and heard, only Wolf hated Tom Battle enough to want him dead. And only Maud had been violently opposed to the wampums being exhibited at the museum, enough so that she might have arranged to have them removed. If Molly had to choose between the two, she was forced back to Wolf, who, in addition to wanting Tom out of the way for personal reasons, was a radical in the ranks of TEB members.

Maud had wanted the wampums removed, but Molly had never heard her express an opinion on the Cherokee Nation–TEB conflict and assumed that she would have, if she'd had strong feelings on the subject. Also, Maud had no personal motive for wanting Tom dead, as far as Molly knew.

Indeed, Wolf kept floating to the top of the pool of suspects, but she was no closer to proving that he committed any of the crimes than she had been the day Tom died. Frustrated, she sighed and rubbed her eyes. She wasn't going to get closer to a solution by thinking anymore about the sparse evidence they'd gathered. Like the clues in a particularly tricky logic problem, there were too many gaps.

Time to leave before she found herself locked in for the night.

As she started to get up, her glance caught on the place where the wall met the floor. She'd been staring at it for twenty minutes without really seeing it. Now, she noticed for the first time that there was a narrow crack where the wall and floor didn't quite meet. She moved closer and got down on her hands and knees. Something was wedged into the crack.

She knew immediately what it was and blinked hard to make sure she wasn't imagining it. No, it was still there.

Tom Battle had been standing near the wall at that very spot when he was struck by the poisoned dart. Molly got up and ran into the reception area. Everybody was gone except for Lily, who was working in the office. The office door was open.

"Lily?"

Startled, Lily looked up from the ledger and loose papers spread around her. "Oh, Molly—I didn't know anybody else was still here."

"Didn't mean to frighten you. I'm leaving in a minute. I was wondering if you have some tweezers."

Lily opened the bottom desk drawer and took out her purse. "I always carry a small manicure set. I have a problem with split nails." She drew out the tweezers and handed them to Molly. "What's the problem?"

"Uh—got a splinter in my thumb," Molly lied. "Thanks. I'll bring these back in a sec." She turned away from the open door, hoping Lily wouldn't follow.

Fortunately, Lily stayed where she was and returned her attention to her work. Molly found an envelope at the reception desk and took it into the exhibit area, where she extracted the sliver of wood easily with the tweezers. She dropped it in the envelope, folded it several times, and tucked it in her jeans' pocket. Then she took the tweezers to the ladies' room and washed them thoroughly.

As she left, Molly returned the tweezers to Lily, who was running numbers on a calculator now.

"Make sure the door locks behind you," Lily murmured with barely a pause in her tabulations. "I'm kind of uneasy about being here alone, after last night."

Molly left the museum and ran across the parking lot to her car. If she hurried she might make it to the OSBI lab in Tahlequah before everybody left for the day.

She parked in front of the lab as one of the techs, a middle-aged woman named Sheilah Overman, was locking the door. Molly caught her, explained what she wanted, and handed over the envelope. "If you need authority from the sheriff's department, call D.J. Kennedy."

"That's not necessary," Sheilah said. "I know D.J.'s working with the tribe on an investigation. I'm still holding that poisoned dart for him. How soon do you need this information?"

"Yesterday," Molly said apologetically.

"At least we know what we're looking for this time. It'll still take twenty-four hours to get the results of the antigen test."

"This is a murder investigation," Molly said urgently.

"Yes, I know. I liked Tom Battle. He was a good man."

Molly nodded and the tech studied the folded envelope in her hand. "If this is part of that dart I'm holding, we already know what's on it."

"Unfortunately, when this goes to court, they won't take our word for it. We'll need the lab report."

"Sounds like you guys might be close to making an arrest," Sheilah said with a faint lift of brows.

"Not exactly," Molly admitted, "but I want all the evidence ready to go when we do. If you could start on that right away, I'd be eternally grateful. I wish I could pay your overtime, but I don't have it in my budget. I'll buy you lunch sometime, whenever you say."

Sheilah turned back to the door and unlocked it. "My husband's out of town, anyway. I'm only going home to an empty house. It won't take long to get started on this. I'll call you as soon as I know anything. Give me your phone number."

Molly followed her into the lab and wrote both her home and office numbers on the memo pad Sheilah handed her.

Sheilah unfolded the envelope, spread the opening, and dropped the sliver of wood on a square of glass. Then she went to the shelves against the wall and picked up a small glass jar. "This is the dart with the nicotine on it," she told Molly as she tipped the jar and spilled the dart on the glass with the new specimen. She took two large tweezerlike instruments from a drawer, picked up the dart with one and the sliver with the other, and brought them together, not quite touching.

"Perfect fit," she said.

Molly leaned over her shoulder. Indeed, the points on the jagged end of the sliver matched the notches in the dart like adjoining pieces of a jigsaw puzzle.

Sheilah returned the dart to the jar and replaced it on the shelf.

"Thanks, Sheilah," Molly said.

There was no point in hanging around. Sheilah wouldn't be able to tell her anything until tomorrow or the day after.

# 23

From the lab, Molly drove slowly down Muskogee Avenue, trying to decide if she wanted to stop somewhere for dinner. Actually, she wasn't very hungry and she had leftover meatloaf at home. Since she wasn't ready to go home yet, she turned down the street where the Shells lived. She had to mend her bridges with Regina, and putting it off would make it harder. They'd been friends for too long to let a misunderstanding come between them, and she wouldn't rest easy until she made the effort.

When she rang the bell, Steven moved a front window shade aside a crack and peered out at her.

Molly smiled and waved. "Hi, Steven."

The shade fell back into place and a moment later Steven opened the door. "Hi, Molly."

"Could I talk to Regina?"

"She's gone to the grocery store."

Molly felt let down. She was all primed to apologize, say whatever it took to fix things between her and her old friend. Now she would have to get geared up for it all over again.

"She'll be right back," Steven said. "I guess you could come in and wait for her."

Molly hesitated as Steven held the screen door open. He was wearing a clean shirt and seemed more alert than he had earlier that afternoon. Maybe the effects of his medication wore off as the day went on. "Well, if you're sure she'll be back soon," Molly said, stepping across the threshold.

"I can talk to you," Steven said seriously, "if you won't ask me any questions."

Plainly Regina had had a talk with him when she got home from the museum. Molly sat down on the couch where she'd sat a few hours earlier. "You don't need to stay with me," she said, worrying about how Regina would react if she came home and found Molly and Steven together.

He stood in the middle of the room, undecided whether to go into another part of the house or stay. "Regina said I can't answer any questions," he reiterated, "about anything."

It was a bad idea to wait for Regina, Molly decided. "You know what," she said, standing again. "I think I'll come back later and talk to Regina."

"Okay." Steven seemed relieved that she was going.

Regina drove up as Molly stepped out on the porch. She saw Molly as she got out of the car, but said nothing as she turned back to lift two sacks of groceries from the backseat. Then, dipping her head, she walked across the yard. It was impossible to read her expression.

"I just got here," Molly said quickly. "Steven said I'd missed you, so I was going to come back later."

"You might as well come on in now," Regina said. She didn't seem angry, merely weary.

Molly followed her to the kitchen. Regina set the sacks on the table and began putting away the groceries. Steven had disappeared, and the TV had been turned on in one of the bedrooms.

Regina said, "I'll get you something to drink."

Regina was at least talking to her, but the atmosphere between them didn't feel exactly right. Molly sat at the table, and Regina took a can of cola from the refrigerator and set it in front of her. She really didn't want it but was afraid she'd offend Regina if she turned it down.

Molly sipped the cola and said, "I wanted to apologize to you, Regina. It didn't occur to me that you'd get so upset over my questioning Steven alone. It should have. It was thoughtless of me, and I'm sorry."

Regina stacked cans of soup in the cabinet. She finished and closed the cabinet door, then turned around. "I owe you an apology too." She smiled faintly. "I really went into orbit, didn't I?"

Coming there had been the right thing to do, Molly thought, relaxing a little. "I think I shocked you when I said I'd talked to Steven."

Regina leaned back against the counter, her arms folded. "All those things I said—I didn't mean them, Molly." She sighed. "I don't know what got into me. We've been friends for so long . . . I don't think you'd intentionally hurt Steven."

"I really wouldn't," Molly told her.

"I'm so worn out these days," Regina said. "It's the exhibition, I guess. I don't like having to be there all day while Steven's here. But he doesn't want to go with me, and if I try to force him—" She dropped her arms, came over to the table, and sat down heavily. "—he says I want to keep him chained to me like a prisoner, like they do in the hospital. He accuses me of not trusting him to fix his own lunch and take his medication when he's supposed to."

"I can understand that you'd feel uneasy about leaving him alone," Molly said. "For one thing, Steven has a history of stopping his medication."

Regina gazed at her rough, blunt-nailed hands linked together on the table. "I've found a place in Texas that will work with him," she said quietly.

"I noticed a brochure when I was here earlier today," Molly said. "Is that the place?"

Regina nodded. "He'll get daily individual and group counseling and they want to try him on a new drug. It's produced dramatic results in some schizophrenics." Regina's tone was pathetically eager, her dark eyes suddenly alive. "If it works as well with Steven, he can be independent, Molly. Live a normal life."

"That's wonderful." Provided Regina wasn't making more of what the doctors said than they'd intended. If there was such a miracle drug—and Regina clearly wanted to believe in a miracle—why hadn't it been all over the news?

"I haven't told him yet," Regina said, "but I'm taking him there next week."

Reaching out, Molly laid her hand over Regina's. "Don't feel guilty. It's for his own good."

Regina looked down, blinking hard. "I hope he sees it that way. I'm all he has. If he thinks I only want to be rid of him . . ."

"You'll make him understand. And, Regina—" Molly waited for Regina to lift her eyes. "You have to start making some kind of life for yourself apart from Steven."

Regina nodded, unable to speak.

"But right now," Molly went on, "you need to rest. I'll go so that you can. If there's anything I can do to help—anything at all . . ."

Regina gave her a misty smile and found her voice. "Thanks, Molly. You're a good friend."

When Molly got home, D.J. was sitting on the apartment steps, talking to Homer through the fence. She was ridiculously glad to see him. As she got out of her car, the curtain on Florina's kitchen window fell into place. Florina might be miffed at her, but she was still keeping track of Molly's comings and goings.

"What's happening, deputy?"

"The usual." Homer flopped his plumy tail and barked when she didn't immediately give him her undivided attention. She stuck her fingers through a link in the fence and scratched his ear and promised him a treat later.

D.J. squeezed her shoulder as he followed her up the stairs. Inside, she dropped her purse and went straight to the kitchen to grind beans for coffee.

D.J. sank down onto the sofa, spreading his arms out along the back, and expelled a tired breath. "It's been a long day."

"For me too," Molly agreed. She took a bag of coffee beans from the freezer and poured some in the grinder. When the grounds were as fine as she liked them, she said, "Tony and I interviewed the people at the museum. They all claim to have been in bed long before midnight last night, except for Robert and Victor, who alibied each other."

"I had a little better luck."

"Lord knows we could use some," Molly said, as she finished measuring grounds into the Krups and turned on the machine. "You want a sandwich?"

"That'd be great."

She took the meatloaf from the refrigerator and sliced enough for two sandwiches. D.J., still spread-eagled on the sofa, watched her silently until she paused to look around at him. "Will you talk?" she said impatiently. "The suspense is killing me."

He grinned. "Don't get your hopes too high. First off, Lily Roach went through a very rough time when she lost her son fourteen years ago. I talked to a couple of people who were close to her then. Neither of them would call it a breakdown, but they admitted she saw a psychiatrist on an out-patient basis for several months."

After spreading mayonnaise on four slices of homemade wheat bread, Molly added the meatloaf, lettuce, and tomato and set the sandwiches on the table.

"Tony might think that's a hot flash," she said. "He keeps talking about nut cases. But if she wasn't even hospitalized, she couldn't have been off the deep end, even temporarily. And it was fourteen years ago. Lily's as stable as you or I now."

"Lily might not appreciate the comparison," D.J. told her dryly.

Molly waved him to the table and checked the coffee. Half of it had dripped through the filter. She filled two cups, releasing the tantalizing aroma of Viennese chocolate, and carried them to the table.

"Also," D.J. went on, picking up his sandwich, "the nursery owner ID'ed the bottle of nicotine as the one missing from the nursery."

"No big surprise."

"No, but that brings me to some really interesting information. Last Friday night, long after midnight, a neighbor of Daye Hummingbird saw a car parked on the street outside Daye's house. He couldn't tell if the driver was a man or a woman, but he's sure somebody was in the car, and the description sounds like Wolf Kawaya's Plymouth. It was a dark color—brown or black or blue. The light wasn't good enough for the neighbor to be sure."

"Wolf's Plymouth is dark blue."

"Right on."

"Then Wolf lied to us about going straight home from the reception," Molly said.

"*If* we can prove it was Wolf's car and that he was inside. I wish the neighbor had gotten a better look at the driver." D.J. paused long enough to eat a couple bites of his sandwich.

Still not hungry, Molly took slow sips of her coffee. Of course it had been Wolf in the car. Who else would sit in a parked car at Daye's house in the middle of the night?

D.J. continued, "The witness said the car was there for ten or fifteen minutes before it drove away. It could have been there a lot longer before he noticed it."

"That fits Wolf's pattern," Molly murmured. "Daye says he has parked and watched her house for as long as an hour, several times before."

"He got an eyeful Friday night. Tom Battle's car was parked in Daye's driveway."

Wolf's imagination would have done the rest. Wolf had already had a run-in with Tom at the reception. When he saw Tom's car at Daye's later, jealousy would have painted vivid images of Tom and Daye making love. Pure torture to a man who was obsessed with his ex-wife.

"From what I've seen of Wolf," she said, "that would be enough of a motive for him to break into Tom's house and smash a few things."

D.J. nodded. "But it didn't cool his rage, so he stormed out, decided Battle had to die, broke in Green Gardens Nursery, stole the nicotine, and used it the next morning at the museum."

Absentmindedly, Molly picked up her sandwich and nibbled at the crust. D.J. was probably right. It all fit together so neatly, and Tony had cautioned her not to make it complicated. But she kept remembering what Lily had said: *Wolf's not stupid.* If Wolf was the murderer, he hadn't been very smart about diverting suspicion away from himself. And using one of his own darts to kill Tom *was* stupid. There was no other word for it.

"Why are you looking like that?" D.J. asked.

Molly put her sandwich down. "Like what?"

"Like you don't buy a thing I've said."

"It's not that, but something's missing. I can't think what."
She shook her head. "Maybe it'll come to me eventually. Oh, I
almost forgot. I found the tip of the poisoned dart. It was
wedged into a crack between the wall and floor of the museum. I left it at the OSBI lab this afternoon. Sheilah Overman
started the tests before she went home."

"Good. Maybe our luck is changing," D.J. said. "It had
occurred to me that if we got to court without the tip of the
dart, a clever defense lawyer could make a case for the piece
we found the day of the murder never having touched Battle."

He finished his sandwich while Molly drummed her fingers
on the table and pondered his words. It hadn't occurred to her
before, but a defense attorney *could* have made something of
the fact that the business end of the dart was missing. She
could just hear him:

Where is the rest of it, ladies and gentlemen? Where's
the part that struck Tom Battle's neck? How do we know
it's poisoned if it's never been found? There were dozens
of darts at the museum that day. The prosecution has
admitted that the piece of wood presented in evidence
was found twenty to twenty-five feet from the victim's
body. And it never even touched Tom Battle. As for the
missing tip, the part that did touch the victim, the prosecution doesn't know where it is. May I suggest, ladies
and gentlemen of the jury, that the prosecution has not
proved beyond a reasonable doubt that this broken piece
of dart came from the one that struck Tom Battle.

But she'd found the tip, and the lab tests would leave no
room for such doubts. Piece by piece, they were accumulating
evidence, but they still hadn't tied a particular suspect to the
pieces they had.

"We should confront Wolf Kawaya," she said. "Tell him his car was seen outside Daye's house Friday night."

"A bluff might work," D.J. agreed. "Once he admits he lied about one thing, we're closer to proving he lied about killing Tom Battle."

"I'll suggest it to Tony tomorrow."

They talked about the case for a few more minutes, then D.J. said, "I have to go home. I'm expecting a phone call from Courtney."

At the door, he kissed Molly and drew back to look down at her, his gray eyes crinkling at the corners. "Hey, are we okay?"

"Yeah," she agreed. "We're okay." It felt good to be back on the old footing.

After D.J. left, Molly finished half her sandwich, then let Homer in and gave him the other half.

Homer curled up at her feet as she sat at the computer and typed up her notes. Her file on the Tom Battle case was growing, but its volume added up to a lot of hearsay and a few facts, none of them particularly helpful, except for what D.J. had learned from Daye Hummingbird's neighbor.

She printed out her notes, then took some raisin bread dough from the refrigerator, enough to make a loaf for Conrad and another for Florina as a peace offering. She had already mixed, kneaded, and let the dough rise once before. She turned the dough out on a floured cloth and began kneading again. With her hands thus occupied, her mind was free to drift. Images and ideas floated around in her head like pieces of lint. Of little substance, they wouldn't light anywhere or stick to another piece.

Okay, so she'd think about tomorrow. In the morning, she'd meet Tony at the museum and they'd talk to Wolf Kawaya. And she still had to drive to Wagoner and interview Tom Battle's father. She'd been putting it off, knowing it would be difficult for him to talk about his son's death. Besides, she didn't really expect Mr. Battle to tell her something that would break the case wide open, so there was no big hurry. If she didn't make it tomorrow, she'd do it Saturday.

Before letting the dough rise again, she punched it hard several times, taking out her frustration over the murder investigation, which wasn't exactly progressing at lightning speed. But then most investigations were ninety percent false leads and dead-end trails.

What they had were five crimes, all of which seemed to be interrelated. Like a five-piece jigsaw puzzle. They constituted some kind of whole, but Molly didn't know how to fit them together.

Last Thursday night, a week ago now, the tribal office building was defaced with a message in black paint. The next night, Friday, Tom Battle's home was vandalized, and the same night nicotine poison was stolen from Green Gardens Nursery. Saturday morning, Tom was murdered. And sometime Wednesday night, the wampums were stolen from the museum.

How did the pieces fit together?

A few ideas came to mind, most of which she'd already mulled over with D.J. and Tony. One: A TEB sympathizer orchestrated all the crimes as a political statement. The perpetrator was convinced the TEB council had a historical right to govern the Cherokee tribe, so all tribal land and buildings rightfully belonged to the band. Hence the sign on the office building. Tom Battle was the archvillain because he'd represented the Cherokee Nation in suits against the band, and won. So Tom's house was vandalized. As a warning to Tom that he was treading on dangerous ground? But the nicotine that killed him was stolen the same night. If the murderer intended to kill Tom anyway, what purpose was served by a warning?

Leave that for now.

The theft of the wampums was the final statement on the murderer's political agenda. Carrying this line of reasoning to its ultimate conclusion, the wampums, as the ancient badge of the principal chief's office, belonged with the TEB, not the Nighthawk Keetoowahs. The TEB council had not reported that they'd been offered the wampums yet, so the thief still had them. Perhaps he intended to turn them over to the council later. Or he might keep them indefinitely. Maybe knowing they weren't in the hands of the wrong people was enough for him.

It was possible to loosely connect all the crimes if tribal politics was behind them. But the question remained, why vandalize Tom Battle's house if the plan was to kill him anyway?

Okay, second brainstorm: The wampums were stolen for money. They were destined to be sold to a private collector. The sign on the tribal office building and the mess at Tom Battle's house were meant to throw suspicion on the TEB when the wampums were subsequently stolen. But wasn't that enough to implicate the TEB? Why was Tom murdered?

Both scenarios left one piece of the puzzle that didn't quite fit snugly with the others.

That led to idea number three: The theft of the wampums had nothing to do with the other crimes. The sign on the tribal offices and the vandalism of Tom's house had been arrows pointing to the TEB, meant to throw suspicion on the band when Tom was murdered. A second person, not connected to the other crimes, had stolen the wampums for the money they would bring from a private collector. The timing of the other crimes and the resulting attention on the TEB were merely fortuitous.

All three scenarios required some assumptions in order to make the connections and Molly was inclined to throw out the third one altogether. There was a single perpetrator for all the crimes, she could feel the logic of it.

Or she wanted to believe in a single perpetrator because it made solving the crimes simpler. Catching one criminal was easier than catching two.

Okay, had she learned anything new from all this free association? One thing especially stood out. The hints at TEB involvement were too obvious to miss, which almost certainly meant they were red herrings. There was no TEB involvement. Which brought her back to the loose-cannon theory and, upon reflection, that seemed pretty off the wall.

So the murderer killed Tom Battle for personal reasons, and everything else was meant to falsely implicate the TEB. She had made a full circle back to Wolf Kawaya. The only problem was, she could not believe that Wolf, a devoted TEB member, would implicate the band in a personal vendetta.

While the bread baked, she took a shower and put on an old pair of jeans and gray sweat shirt. When the bread was cooled, she wrapped it in foil and let Homer out of the apartment. Florina's kitchen light was on.

"Time for my act of penance," Molly told Homer as she fastened him in his pen.

Then she walked around to Florina's kitchen door. Florina cracked the door and peered out at Molly.

"I brought you a loaf of fresh bread."

Florina let her in and offered a drink, which Molly declined. Florina was a little stiff at first, but she thanked Molly for the bread, and Molly stayed long enough to drop a few hints about the investigation, vague hints for Florina to interpret as she chose. By the time Molly left, Florina had loosened up.

Conrad had told Molly that Florina still wasn't speaking to him, but that was Conrad's problem.

# 24

Wolf Kawaya stood in the doorway of the museum office with an air of surly combativeness. His big body almost filled the opening. Tony, who stood at the window, seemingly in idle contemplation of the grounds, had asked Lily to fetch him. He thought it was to his and Molly's advantage to put Kawaya in the position of being "sent for," but that remained to be seen.

"You people are starting to make me feel harassed," Wolf snapped at Molly. Tony still had not acknowledged him.

"That's certainly not our intention," Molly responded, indicating a chair. "Would you like to sit down?" She took the chair behind the desk.

"Like?" Wolf echoed. "Hell, no. I don't like one damn thing about this. I'm here to exhibit, not to be at your beck and call." Tony had guessed correctly; Wolf resented being summoned to the office by a third party.

"Sorry to inconvenience you, but we're trying to solve a murder," Molly pointed out mildly.

Wolf stepped in and closed the door. "I didn't kill Tom Battle. How many times do I have to tell you?"

Turning from the window, Tony drawled, "We appreciate your cooperation, Mr. Kawaya."

"Do I have a choice?" Wolf snarled as he lowered his hulking body into a chair.

"There's always a choice," Tony said. "If you don't wish to cooperate . . . " Coming over to perch on the corner of the desk, he left the thought unfinished. From his elevated position on the desk, he looked down at Wolf, which Molly suspected was another deliberate strategy.

"If I don't cooperate, you'll think I've got something to hide," Wolf said. "I'm damned if I do and damned if I don't."

"Since you mention it," Tony said smoothly, "we've come up with some new evidence in the case."

"I didn't mention no new evidence."

"You said you have something to hide."

Wolf bolted to his feet, his chin thrust out and his hands balled. "Don't twist my words, damn you! I said you might *think* I had something to hide."

"Please sit down, Mr. Kawaya," Tony said calmly. Wolf took several moments to make his decision, but finally his hands unclenched and he sat.

Tony glanced at Molly and she said, "We'd like to go over your testimony concerning your whereabouts on the night Tom Battle's house was vandalized." Wolf glared at her as she opened her case file and scanned the top sheet. "If my notes are correct, you said you went straight home from the museum at approximately ten-thirty, following the reception, and did not leave your house again that night." She looked up at him for confirmation.

"That's right."

Molly closed the folder. "Are you sure you don't want to change your statement?"

"Why would I want to do that?"

"Perhaps you have that night mixed up with another one," Molly suggested.

"I ain't the one mixed up here," Wolf puffed. "What—"

"Then why did you lie to us, Mr. Kawaya?" Tony put in.

Wolf's head swiveled toward Tony as he got to his feet again. He was going to wear out that chair with all the sitting down and getting up. For an instant, he seemed to struggle for words. "Listen," he said menacingly to Tony, "you damned little banty rooster, I don't have to take this from you."

Tony's eyes narrowed. "You were seen parked outside Daye Hummingbird's house last Friday night after midnight. We have a witness who will swear to it."

Wolf's eyes took on a trapped look, and he lost some of his bluster. Rubbing his hands over his face, he muttered, "Oh, hell." He dropped his hands. "All right, I woke up and couldn't go back to sleep. So I drove around for a while."

"And parked outside Daye's house," Molly added.

"What if I did? Is that a crime?"

"No," Tony answered him, "but we'd kinda like to know why you lied about it, if you have nothing to hide."

"Because I was frigging embarrassed."

"Or," Molly interjected, "you were afraid of the implications."

"What implications? I want my wife back. Is that what you want me to say? Okay, it's true. I wanted to talk to her, to ask her to come back to me. But I saw Tom Battle's car in her driveway, so I went home."

"That's it?" Tony said with an edge of sarcasm.

"What'd I just say?" Wolf demanded.

"We don't think that's the way it happened, Mr. Kawaya," Tony said flatly. "We think you lost it when you saw Battle's car at your ex-wife's house, and you drove to Battle's house, ripped up a few things, and smashed some dishes. Then you broke into Green Gardens Nursery and stole a bottle of nicotine poison, so you could murder Battle the next morning."

Wolf was shaking his head violently. "I went straight home from Daye's house. You ain't gonna pin this murder on me, Warwick. This meeting is over!" He jerked open the door.

"We'll talk again, Mr. Kawaya," Tony said as the door slammed shut. Tony slid off the desk and grimaced. "I am developing a real dislike for that man."

"It was mean of him to call you a banty rooster," Molly said, barely suppressing a smile.

Tony grinned sheepishly. "It's never easy, is it? I was kind of hoping he'd be so riddled with guilt by now that he'd spill his guts when we said we had a witness."

"Wolf?" Molly scoffed. "You didn't really expect that to happen, did you?"

He shrugged. "No, but it would've been nice. Well, we have to do it the hard way."

"How?"

"Find another witness. Somebody who can place him near Battle's house or Green Gardens Nursery Friday night."

"Preferably both," Molly muttered.

"Yeah."

"D.J. already talked to Tom's closest neighbors. Nobody saw or heard anything that night."

Tony made a sour face. "Looks like I'll be spending the day knocking on doors in the neighborhood of the nursery."

"I wish I could help you," Molly said, "but I have to catch up on some work at the office."

"I can tell you're all torn up over it. I'll come by your office this afternoon."

As they left the museum together, Molly glanced toward the exhibit area where Wolf and Josiah Kawaya were in earnest conversation. Wolf punctuated his words with angry gestures, and Josiah appeared deeply troubled.

*  *  *

The abstract of Wilson Bowling's driving record arrived in the afternoon mail. The only address on the printout was the last one Sarah Bowling had for him. Molly tossed the abstract in the Bowling file and tried to think of another way to trace Wilson Bowling.

She remembered a ruse that D.J. had told her about. It had worked in tracking down a suspect wanted for questioning by the sheriff's department.

It might work if Wilson Bowling was still in the Oklahoma City area. Molly found Wilson's mother listed in the phone book, and a woman answered on the second ring.

"Edith Thompson, please," Molly said.

"Speaking."

"Hi, Mrs. Thompson. This is Cynthia Brown at Advantage Financial Services in Oklahoma City. Wilson Bowling has given your name as a reference on a loan application. Do you have a minute to answer a few questions?"

There was a silence while the wheels turned. Edith Thompson was thinking, These people don't know I'm Wilson's mother, so I'd better be careful what I say.

"Okay."

"How long have you known the applicant?"

"Uh—let's see now. Uh, six years."

"And how long has he lived in Oklahoma?"

"Oh, all his life," Edith Thompson said, and added quickly, "I think."

"Where is he currently employed?" Molly asked.

"He works at the Fitzhannon Metal Works in Oklahoma City."

That's all Molly needed, really, but she might as well see what else she could get from Wilson's mother. "We'd like to check the home address he gave us. What is Mr. Bowling's current address, to the best of your knowledge?"

"He's living in Casablanca Apartments in Bethany."
Bethany was a suburb of Oklahoma City. "I can get the
address if you'll give me a minute to find it."

"That's all right. I have it here. Thank you very much, Mrs.
Thompson."

Molly hung up and slapped her hand on the desk. "All
right!" Then she called Sarah Bowling and told her to contact
her lawyer about garnishment proceedings.

When his mother told him about the call, Wilson would
probably figure out what was going on. He might quit his job
and move again, but not before he had another job lined up.
That would take a little time. Molly hoped it was long
enough for Sarah Bowling to get some of the back child-
support he owed.

Tony arrived at Molly's office at three-thirty. The door-to-
door hadn't turned up a single witness who noticed anybody
hanging around Green Gardens Nursery the previous Friday
night. "I talked to Victor Halland's mother too," Tony said.
"She confirmed that he got home Wednesday night a few
minutes after one. She'd told him to be home by midnight, so
she was waiting up to yell at him."

"Terrific," Molly said glumly. "What next?"

Tony shook his head. "You got any bright ideas?"

"Not a one."

"Okay, let's do some brainstorming."

Molly went through the scenarios she'd conjured up the
evening before, and they did a little fine tuning on them, but
after an hour they were no closer to a solution.

At four-thirty, Tony said, "It's like we're operating in a vac-
uum. We don't have enough data. I might as well go home."

The phone rang and Molly picked it up. It was Sheilah
Overman at the OSBI lab.

"I've some of the results on my tests," Sheilah said.

Molly covered the mouthpiece to say to Tony, "Wait a minute. It's the lab." She removed her hand and said, "Go ahead, Sheilah."

"You're not going to believe this," Sheilah told her. "That tip you found is clean."

"You mean there's no nicotine on it?"

"Not a trace."

Molly stared at Tony, who frowned and leaned toward her. "What's she say?"

Molly held up a hand to silence him. "That's impossible, Sheilah."

"The tests don't lie, Molly."

"Then—" What? There had to be a mistake somewhere. "You couldn't have gotten the tests mixed up or something, could you?"

There was a pause and then Sheilah said stiffly, "I checked my results three times."

"I'm not questioning your methods," Molly assured her. "I'm trying to figure out what could have happened. That piece I found—it must not be the tip of the poisoned dart after all."

"You saw me put the two of them together. It's a perfect fit. No question about it."

"How can it be the same dart?"

"Don't ask me. I run the tests. I don't speculate about the results. I'm going to call D.J. Kennedy now and fill him in."

As Molly hung up, Tony demanded, "What the hell did she say?"

Molly leaned back in her chair, feeling as though she'd been totally stumped by one of Conrad's logic problems, and no matter how many assumptions she made, it didn't help. "The point of the dart wasn't poisoned."

Tony opened his mouth, closed it, scratched his head, and opened his mouth again. "Then it's not the tip of the poisoned dart."

Molly shook her head. "Yes, it is, Tony. They're a match. No two tips could have broken off in exactly the same way. I saw Sheilah fit the pieces together."

"Then, the tests—"

"You heard me ask her about the tests. I think she was insulted, and she told me she'd checked the results three times. There's no mistake."

They could only look at each other as, momentarily, words failed them. Then Molly said, "Let's think this through. I saw Robert Wildcat shoot the dart, and I was watching Tom when it hit—or at least a second or two after it hit—because he grabbed his neck where it struck him. Either way, the tip flew one way and lodged in the crack between the floor and the wall. The rest of the dart may have flown in another direction, or it may have landed near where the tip was."

"You said you found it twenty-five feet from where Battle fell," Tony said.

"Somebody probably kicked it after it landed."

"This is crazy," Tony murmured.

Gazing out the window, Molly chewed her lip and visualized the scene at the museum. Robert Wildcat shooting the dart. Daye screaming. Tom grabbing his neck. Tom collapsing. People crowding around. She turned back to Tony. "The dart was poisoned after the tip was broken off."

"After Battle was hit?"

She frowned. "That's the only explanation."

Tony's brows shot up a good half inch. "You call that an explanation? It makes no sense."

"It has to. We just haven't put it together yet."

Tony stood and buttoned his jacket. "I do my best thinking when I'm driving. Will you be home tonight?"

"Far as I know."

"I'll call you about seven, after we've let this percolate for a couple of hours."

"In the meantime, I'll try to find out what D.J. makes of it," Molly said. Tony left the office, shaking his head and muttering.

As it turned out, D.J. had to agree with Molly. The dart was poisoned after it struck Tom Battle. But why? And how? They speculated, via the telephone, on some possible answers, but they weren't able to make a great deal more sense of the situation.

Two hours later when Tony called the apartment, she'd had more time to think, and the two of them came up with a somewhat workable sequence of events.

The nicotine was already in Tom's body before the dart ever left the blowgun. He'd gotten it earlier, maybe before he arrived at the museum. It could have been put in something at his house, where he'd stopped off to shower and shave and discovered the vandalism.

"Wait a minute," Molly said. "That could have been the purpose of the break-in. To plant the nicotine somehow. The vandalism could have been nothing but misdirection."

"That makes as much sense as anything else about this case," Tony agreed.

It answered the medical examiner's doubts about Tom's seemingly instant death and explained Tom's headache, sweating, and nausea before he was hit. Death was not instantaneous but came about sometime after the nicotine entered Tom's body. This also cleared up another puzzle. It explained why Robert and Victor hadn't been poisoned by handling the dart. At that point, the poison had not yet been applied to the dart.

From there the sequence of events was harder to rationalize. The murderer, who'd put the nicotine in something at Tom's house the previous night, was at the museum when the dart incident occurred. He'd had what remained of the nicotine with him, for whatever reason, and had used it to muddy the waters. Somehow, without being seen, he'd dipped the broken dart into the nicotine bottle and dropped it on the floor, where Molly and Conrad found it. That probably wasn't as risky as it seemed, because everyone's attention was on Tom Battle at that time.

It was hard to escape the conclusion that the murderer had meant to cast suspicion on the two boys or Wolf Kawaya and, by extension, the TEB. The murderer may not even have felt any particular malice for any of the three. He couldn't have foreseen that Robert would shoot the dart but had acted on impulse when the opportunity to divert attention away from himself and direct it at somebody else presented itself.

"He may have outsmarted himself," Tony observed. "The poisoned dart definitely places the murderer at the museum when Battle collapsed."

"Obviously, that's what he intended," Molly said. "The killer couldn't have known we'd figure out the dart was poisoned after the fact—and we wouldn't have if I hadn't found the tip. The killer probably didn't even notice it was missing. Think about it. He must have been nervous, shocked by the dart incident, and thinking fast how he could turn it to his advantage."

Later, the murderer had planted the nicotine with the black spray paint in the men's rest room, knowing it would be discovered eventually. Which meant he wanted to make sure the investigators tied the poisoning together with the sign on the tribal office building, which implicated the TEB.

By the time the wampums were stolen from the museum, suspicion was already focused on the TEB—and Wolf Kawaya, in particular.

Molly's and Tony's speculations answered several of the questions that had been bothering them. It left others unanswered. If things had happened as they theorized, and clues to TEB involvement were planted deliberately, was Tom Battle's murder the ultimate goal? If so, had the murderer then stolen the wampums, thinking to throw more suspicion on the TEB? Talk about overkill, Molly thought. Tony might be right. The murderer may have been too clever for his own good. He hadn't been content to leave well enough alone.

Or were the thief and the murderer two different people?

At the end of the phone conversation with Tony, Molly asked, "Did you ever hear from the lab about the glass from the exhibit case that you left with them?"

"It was wiped clean," Tony muttered.

"Figures."

"They found a few yellow fibers stuck to the glass, which might have come from a sweater or something like that. But there's no way of knowing if the fibers were on the glass or on the floor where the glass fell and were picked up with the pieces."

"They could have been there for weeks—months, even."

"Yeah, and it sure doesn't look like Wolf Kawaya's our man," Tony said reluctantly. "It's one of the others. You want to nominate somebody?"

"Not yet, but I'm going to Wagoner tomorrow and talk to Tom Battle's father. Maybe I'll pick up something there." Now that Wolf was no longer the prime suspect, talking to Mr. Battle was more urgent. He should at least know if Tom had a recent disagreement or confrontation with someone besides Wolf Kawaya.

"We'll get with D.J. Monday," Tony said, "and figure out where we go from here. I'll be home all weekend, so call me if anything comes up before then."

Later that evening, Molly jotted down a hypothetical series of events for her case file:

*Thurs. night*—Sign painted on tribal office bldg.

*Fri. night*—Poison stolen from Green Gardens Nursery. Break-in at Tom Battle's house (window pane broken). Poison planted (where?) and house vandalized to cover up purpose of break-in.

*Saturday*—Tom Battle poisoned, exhibited symptoms upon arrival at museum at 8:45 A.M., died about 9:45 A.M.

*Tuesday*—Black paint and nicotine poison found at museum.

*Wed. night*—Wampums stolen from museum.

Belatedly it occurred to Molly that if the poison was in something at Tom's house, it could be in one of the items she and Daye had packed. She was ready for bed, brushing her teeth at the bathroom sink, when it hit her.

Not in any of the food. Dr. Pohl had said the poison was absorbed through the skin. So the murderer had put the poison in something he knew Tom would handle. Something he would rub on his body. Like what?

She opened her medicine cabinet and stared at the shelves, remembering how she'd stood at Tom's medicine cabinet, removing all the everyday items any man would have. There had been a bottle of cologne, but the seal had not been broken.

Molly closed her eyes, calling up the memory of standing in Tom's bathroom looking into his medicine cabinet.

One thing was missing. There had been no after-shave lotion.

She went to the phone and called Daye Hummingbird and asked if Tom had used after-shave lotion. Of course. Didn't every man who shaved? Had Daye found any among the things she'd packed? No, it should have been among the items in the medicine cabinet, which Molly had packed. What was going on? Molly promised to explain later and hung up.

Molly knew how the murderer had done it. He'd put the poison in Tom's after-shave, something he used every day. That wood panel covering the pane in Tom's front door hadn't fallen out on its own, either. After Tom's death, the murderer had gone back to the house, pushed out the panel in order to unlock the door and take away the after-shave and dispose of it. He'd forgotten to replace the panel before leaving. Or hadn't wanted to take the time, because he thought it didn't matter. Whoever discovered the panel on the floor would dismiss it. As Molly had done—until now.

# 25

Though he tried, Everett Battle, Tom's father, wasn't being very helpful.

"Professional conflicts?" repeating Molly's query. "Why, I can't think of a single problem Tom had at work—" He broke off with an apologetic expression. "I'm not doing you any good, am I?" Battle was a tall man, a full blood, a little stooped now, with grief more than years, Molly suspected.

"Tell me whatever comes to mind," she said. "You never can tell what will be useful."

They were in his living room, which was cheaply furnished but impeccably clean.

"Tom ran a one-man office, you see. His secretary retired two or three months ago and he still hadn't hired a new one. Had a housewife come in part-time," he finished a little forlornly.

"Do you know her name?"

He pursed her lips. "Irene, was it? Alene, maybe. No, it was Earlene. Earlene Watts."

Molly made a note of the name, but she couldn't imagine that a part-time employee would possess any useful information.

"Tom loved his work," Battle said. "The only conflicts—and you can't really call them that—were with other lawyers in the courtroom. But they left it there," he assured her with a solemn look. "They'd take after it tooth and toenail before a jury and then go out for a meal together."

"What was happening in his personal life lately? Did Tom have any enemies?"

He blinked owlishly behind his glasses. "Tom?" He opened his eyes wide, as if the question astonished him. Then he looked down at his hands which rested on his knees. They were boney and prominently veined. Old hands. "Tom always had a lot of friends. People were drawn to him. He got along with everybody. He had no enemies. To think that anybody would want to kill him—well, it's unbelievable." His mind caught up with his words and he looked suddenly bewildered. "But somebody did, didn't they?" When he glanced up, his eyes were full of tears.

Molly said awkwardly, "I'm so sorry, Mr. Battle. The death of a child must be the worst possible loss."

Battle nodded, and a tear dropped on the veined brown skin on the back of his hand. He wiped it away and clasped his hands together.

He cleared his throat. "I miss my wife—you can't imagine how much," he said. "But I'm glad she didn't live to see this."

"Do you know if Tom ever had any dealings with Robert Wildcat or Victor Halland?"

He looked at her, his head a little to one side. "I never heard of them before—before this happened. Oh, I knew Maud Wildcat had a grandson, but I didn't know his first name."

"Do you know Wolf and Josiah Kawaya?"

"I know Josiah, to say hello. He's not easy to get to know. Doesn't talk much. Wolf—" He shook his head. "I know he's been giving Daye some trouble. He wants her back. So you can understand why he didn't like Tom hanging around her, not one bit. But kill Tom? I can't comprehend that. I mean, it hasn't made Daye go back to him, has it? Wolf surely couldn't have thought it would."

"Did you ever hear him mention having any kind of problem with Maud Wildcat, or Regina or Steven Shell?"

"Maud was a close friend of my wife. She's a good woman. Took in her grandson when his mother threw him out. But there weren't any problems between Maud and Tom. The Shells . . . I don't think he knew either of them. I never heard him mention their names. None of those people killed Tom. Why would they?"

Molly didn't think this gentle man could believe *anyone* would kill another human being. It was outside the realm of his understanding.

She was about to mention the other names on her suspect list when he said, with a shake of his head, "Taking a life— even accidentally—is such a terrible thing. When it happened to Tom, I thought he'd never get over it. I'm still not sure he completely forgave himself, though it was the other driver's fault. He'd say to me, 'Dad, if only I'd headed straight for the ditch.' The police said there wasn't time for that. It happened too fast. But Tom went over and over it. If only this, if only that. He couldn't concentrate on his studies and had to take a semester off from college."

"I'm sorry," Molly said, totally confused, "I don't know what you're talking about."

He lifted both hands wearily and let them drop. "I didn't mean to run on. You're probably too young to remember. The wreck happened—" He paused to calculate. "—more than fourteen years ago."

"Tom was involved in a car wreck?"

He bowed his head. "Tom was driving. It was raining and a car pulled right out in front of him. He couldn't stop in time. The other driver was seriously injured. The boy with Tom, another college student, was killed." His troubled expression deepened. "The other driver was permanently paralyzed. Such a tragedy for everybody."

A tragedy that was beginning to sound vaguely familiar to Molly. "What was the other boy's name, the one who died?"

"He was a friend of Tom's from Tahlequah." He sighed. "He planned to be a lawyer too. A fine young man. Douglas Roach."

*Roach?* "Lily Roach's son?"

"That's right. Douglas was the only son they had. Like Tom was my only boy."

"Did the Roaches blame Tom for their son's death?"

He hesitated for a long moment, looking down at his hands, before he said, "Lily did at first. She said some hard things. We never held it against her. She was crazed by grief. We understood that."

"What did she say?"

He shrugged. "I don't remember exactly. Something about it being Tom's decision to drive home that night instead of the next morning after a night's rest. The boys had just finished their final exams. Lily had talked to Douglas early in the week and he'd mentioned an all-night study session. Lily got it in her head that they'd been studying all night every night, not getting any sleep at all."

"Did Tom fall asleep at the wheel?"

"Oh, no. It was just Lily getting rid of some of the pain. She got over it and apologized to us later."

How could he be sure Tom hadn't fallen asleep for a few seconds, long enough to miss seeing a vehicle that was pulling out in front of him? But if Mr. Battle didn't know about it, Lily Roach couldn't have known it, either.

Molly dropped that line of questioning and asked about Brenda Farley. She stayed long enough to make sure that Everett Battle had nothing else useful to tell her. She didn't think he realized he'd moved Lily Roach to the top of the list of suspects in his son's murder.

It was Saturday, the last day of the exhibition. Lily would be at the museum until five, probably later, since the exhibitors would be dismantling their exhibits.

Molly thought about calling Tony, telling him what she'd learned and asking him to come over and go to the museum with her to talk to Lily.

It was after four o'clock. The museum would be closed by the time Tony could get there, and if Lily did leave at five, they'd miss her. But Molly could make it before five if she drove straight to Park Hill from Wagoner.

Lily might be more willing to talk to Molly alone anyway. It was Molly she'd told about finding the paint and nicotine poison. As Molly drove toward Park Hill, it occurred to her, not for the first time, that Lily could have brought the paint and poison to the museum herself. If she'd killed Tom Battle.

But if she still blamed Tom for her son's death, why had she waited fourteen years to do something about it? And would Lily, a TEB member, try to frame another member of the band for the crimes?

Too many questions with no answers.

Days had grown short as October drew to an end and as Molly drove toward Park Hill, dusk settled over the countryside. As the miles slipped past beneath the wheels of her car, her feeling of having discovered some crucial evidence in the case weakened. Too much time had passed since Douglas Roach's death for it to be a motive for murder. And she could imagine no link at all between Lily's son's death and the theft of the wampums.

But as unlikely as it was, it was the only lead she had, so she decided to have a talk with Lily anyway.

She drove into the museum parking lot a few minutes before five, but the only car near the museum was Regina's. Regina herself was loading boxes into the trunk, so intent on what she was doing that she didn't hear Molly approaching. The scene gave Molly a vague feeling of déjà vu. She hadn't seen this before, though. It was something she'd heard.

Not wanting to frighten Regina, Molly called her name from a distance.

"Oh, hi," Regina said, straightening up, adding as Molly reached the car, "what are you doing here?" She glanced worriedly toward the museum.

"Looking for Lily."

"She left early," Regina said and bent to shift the boxes around in the trunk, trying to make room for the one still sitting on the ground, which held a hatchet, a small saw, and a blanket, the same one Molly had seen drying on a rack in Regina's kitchen when she'd gone there to talk to Steven.

"Looks like everybody left early," Molly said.

"We didn't have any business to speak of this afternoon," Regina said, still half in the trunk. "So we took down the exhibits early. Lily and her husband had plans for the evening, and she asked me to lock up for her." Regina shifted another box, then muttered, "Oh, darn," and slammed the trunk lid. She scanned the grounds, frowned, and picked up the box from the ground. "I'll have to put this stuff in front."

Molly opened a car door for her and she set the box in the backseat.

"Something bothering you?" Molly asked.

Regina hugged herself, taking a moment to answer. "It's Steven," she said.

"Is he in the museum?"

"He was," Regina told her. She rubbed her hands up her arms and said, "After everybody else left, I told him I was taking him to the hospital next week." Her face crumpled and she covered it with her hands.

"Hey," Molly said, "you're doing what you have to do."

Regina reached out and grabbed Molly's hand. Regina was dry-eyed but obviously agitated, and there was a tremor in her hand. "He was furious. He said he hated me. Oh, Molly, I'm so afraid he'll do something stupid."

Was Regina talking about suicide? The thought sent a frisson of fear through Molly. She squeezed Regina's hand. "Where is he now?"

"I saw him go into the chapel. I don't know if I should go after him or not. He's so mad at me I don't know what he'll do."

"Are you sure he's still in there?"

"Yes. I've been out here since he went in. I'd have seen him if he left."

"Maybe he needs some time to get used to the idea."

Regina shook her head. Her hand felt like ice. "I don't think so. He hates being in the hospital. If he refuses to get in the car and go home with me, there's no way I can make him."

"Do you think he'd talk to me?"

Regina was clutching Molly's hand with both of hers now. "He might. He knows you. Would you try, Molly?"

Molly hesitated a moment. Was Steven upset enough to be violent? But that wasn't likely. Steven was never violent when he was medicated. "Sure," she said.

Regina relaxed her grip on Molly's hand. "Thank you, Molly. I'll wait here."

# 26

The chapel was dim, the foyer lay in deep shadow. As Molly stepped inside, she peered around for a light switch. But when she finally located it and flipped it to the *on* position, nothing happened. There would be a breaker somewhere, but she didn't see any sign of one in the foyer.

It was chilly in the chapel, and it smelled musty. Lately, the heritage center had had trouble with ground water seeping into the building after it rained. Molly buttoned her jacket and walked to the back of the chapel.

"Steven?"

Silence. Had he left the chapel without Regina's seeing him? Molly thought she heard a faint sound, but she couldn't pinpoint its source. She tensed, but told herself it was probably the building settling.

From where she stood, she could see all of the small sanctuary. Steven wasn't there, unless he was crouched down, hiding between two rows of benches. Molly pictured Steven curled on the floor in a fetal position, and compassion overcame her uneasiness. She walked down the steps between two rows of benches, checking left and right for a huddled human form.

"Steven, it's Molly Bearpaw," she said, louder than before. "I want to talk to you." Steven wasn't there, and her voice echoed hollowly in the empty chapel.

Reaching the lowest level, she looked behind the podium, in the unlikely event that Steven was hiding there, but he wasn't. At the back of the chapel, on the upper level opposite the foyer, there was a small storage closet. Its door was shut. Perhaps Steven had heard her coming and had slipped inside.

She ran back up the carpeted steps to the closet. The door opened easily, but there was nothing inside except a few folding chairs. Steven wasn't in the chapel. Had he run away again?

She heard the chapel's heavy entrance door open and close and whirled around, thinking that Steven had somehow gotten past her and into the foyer.

It was Regina. She stood in the shadowy foyer, both hands behind her, as if frozen in that pose. Molly couldn't see her face clearly, but there was something about her stance that was desperate.

"Steven isn't here," Molly said, "but he must be on the grounds somewhere." She walked toward Regina. "Don't worry. We'll find him."

Even as Molly spoke, she knew that something was wrong, something besides Steven's disappearance. She halted and Regina came a few steps closer, her hands still behind her. How could Regina not have seen Steven leave the chapel? Was there another exit that couldn't be seen from the parking lot?

But Molly couldn't tear her eyes away from Regina to look for it. The interior of the chapel was getting darker by the minute, but there was still enough light for Molly to see that Regina's expression and her posture were uncharacteristically alert, guarded.

Suddenly two things came together in Molly's mind. The first was the yellow blanket in the trunk of Regina's car, the blanket that Molly had seen drying on the rack at the Shell house the day after the middle-of-the-night rainstorm, the same night the wampums were stolen. The second was the yellow fibers the OSBI lab had found on the pieces of glass from the exhibit case that had housed the wampums at the museum.

Coincidence? Maybe, but then something else came back to her. Steven insisting he couldn't answer any questions because Regina had told him not to. Why? Because he'd gone out during the night? Or—Molly's mind raced ahead—had Steven awakened in the middle of the night and discovered that Regina wasn't in the house? Because she was at the museum, stealing the wampums?

But where did the blanket figure in?

Regina must have taken it with her to wrap the wampums in and protect them from the rain. When she got home, she'd spread it on the rack to dry.

These rushing thoughts made Molly feel a little dizzy. Could Regina, Molly's lifelong friend, have broken into the museum to steal the wampums? Impossible. Insane. There had to be some other explanation for the yellow fibers the lab found. Molly knew Regina too well to believe her capable of such a thing.

As seconds passed and Regina didn't speak, the idea seemed less impossible. Because she knew Regina so well, Molly knew that her friend would go to any lengths to help her brother. The brochure from the private Dallas hospital which Molly had seen at the Shell house had contained a list of hospitalization costs. Molly couldn't remember the exact figures, but a private psychiatric hospital was expensive. Why hadn't it occurred to her before to question where Regina would get the money to put Steven there? If Regina had taken the wampums, she planned to sell them to a private collector, possibly somebody she'd met in Santa Fe. Regina had recently told Molly that some of the collectors who came there to buy Indian crafts had more money than brains.

It was beginning to make a horrible kind of sense to Molly, but where did Tom Battle figure in all of this? Perhaps he didn't. Regina might steal to help her brother, but Molly didn't want to believe she would commit murder too.

Where *was* Steven, and what was Regina holding behind her back?

Molly forced her stiff lips to form a smile, but it felt more like a grimace. "We'd better go look for Steven," she said. The words came out sounding shrill and frightened.

"You know, don't you?" Regina said and brought her hands from behind her back. One of them held a gun. An automatic, Molly thought wildly, though she didn't know how she knew. Her knowledge of guns was minuscule, but she did know that as long as you kept your finger on the trigger, an automatic would keep on firing until it emptied itself.

"Regina, I don't know what you're talking about," Molly squeaked, still trying to bluff her way out of the chapel, but she already knew it was futile.

Regina came a few steps closer, the gun steady in her hand. "Yes, you do. I can tell by the look on your face. You put it together when you got a glimpse of the saw in my car."

Saw? What was she talking about? Had dealing with Steven made Regina crazy? No time to figure it out now.

Molly's mind darted frantically for an idea to save herself, while her eyes remained riveted on the gun. She might be able to make it to the storage closet, but it was so small that she couldn't get away from the door, and the door would not stop a bullet. Even as she accepted the reality of the gun in Regina's hand, another part of her refused to believe Regina would actually shoot her. But what if she were wrong?

Molly's heart was beating so hard it felt as though it would jump through the wall of her chest, fracturing bone and ripping skin. She struggled to stay in control of herself. "You don't want to do this, Regina," she said. "If you still have the wampums, you can return them to the museum. I'll tell them how much stress you've been under with Steven. I know you're frantic to help him. Maybe the tribe can contribute something for his hospitalization."

Regina made a harsh sound. "Do you know how much a private psychiatric hospital costs? Three thousand dollars a month, and that's just the basic cost. Medication is extra, and the experimental drug they want to put Steven on runs ten thousand dollars a year. You really think the tribe is going to fork over that kind of money for Steven?"

No, Molly didn't. Even if they had it to spare, the council couldn't pay one tribal member's expenses in a private hospital without obligating themselves to pay for others. There would never be enough money in the tribal budget to cover such expenses.

"I'll organize a fund-raiser," Molly said desperately, wondering if she could make it to the podium. It would at least provide more than one layer of wood between her and Regina. But then what? Regina would come after her.

"I should have taken the saw out of my car, after what happened before. But I didn't, and now I can't let you go," Regina said in a chillingly calm voice. "I'm sorry."

The saw again. And *what* had happened before?

Of course! Tony had described it to Molly the morning after the burglary. The skinny saw in that box in Regina's car was a keyhole saw, the kind that had been used to saw a hole in the museum door.

As for it happening before, hadn't Tom Battle mentioned seeing some tools in Regina's car the day before he died? Molly thought back to the night of the reception, the experience Tom was recounting to Daye, Lily, and Regina when Molly joined them.

Last Friday afternoon, a week ago, Tom had approached Regina as she was removing baskets from the trunk of her car. He'd frightened her and caused her to spill her tools in the parking lot. The keyhole saw and probably a brace and bit had been among them. That explained the odd feeling Molly had had when she found Regina putting the boxes holding the remaining baskets in the trunk of her car. The incident was a mirror image of the one Tom had described at the reception.

Seeing the tools in Regina's car hadn't meant anything to Tom at the time, but Regina couldn't risk his remembering them after the museum was burglarized with a brace and bit and a keyhole saw.

So Tom had to die before the wampums were stolen.

And the odds were that eventually Molly would have remembered on her own how the burglar got into the museum and would connect that to the saw in Regina's car. Regina was in too far to bet against the odds.

All the seemingly unrelated incidents of the past week really did fit together in a logical pattern, just as Conrad had said they would. Now that she was looking in the right place, Molly remembered something else. Regina's mother had grown roses, which was how Regina knew about nicotine poison.

Like Tom, Molly had seen too much, and so she too had to die. It didn't matter what she said now. "You stole the poison from the nursery and put it in Tom's after-shave lotion," Molly said, "and vandalized his house to cover up the break-in. You had to get rid of Tom before you stole the wampums because he'd seen the brace and bit and keyhole saw you planned to use to get into the museum. After Tom died, you went back and removed the evidence—the after-shave."

Regina's eyebrows rose. "You've got it all figured out."

"I helped Daye pack Tom's belongings. There was no after-shave lotion in his medicine cabinet. Besides, the point of the dart that hit Tom at the museum was broken off after impact. There was no nicotine on it, only on the shaft of the dart. Which means you had the poison with you at the museum and managed to dip the dart in it after Tom collapsed. Evidently you didn't notice the tip was gone. But why did you have the nicotine with you? Tom was poisoned before he left his house."

"I guess I might as well tell you," Regina said. "I thought I would be able to hide it in something belonging to Wolf Kawaya."

"Hoping that the police would find it after Tom died," Molly said.

Regina gave a faint nod in acknowledgment of Molly's reasoning.

"Then Robert Wildcat shot the dart," Molly went on. "That must have seemed like an incredible stroke of luck. You'd already left the message on the tribal office building implicating the True Echota Band; that was bound to be remembered when the wampums were stolen. There it was, just lying there in all the confusion, a dart made by Wolf Kawaya, a radical member of the band. Later, I guess you started to worry that the police still wouldn't get it, so you planted the poison and the can of black spray paint in the men's rest room."

"Very clever."

Not clever enough to have suspected Regina before she got herself in this mess, Molly thought. She'd allowed friendship to overshadow logic. "Not so clever that somebody else won't figure it out too," Molly said. "The lab found yellow fibers on pieces of glass from the broken exhibit case. They came from that yellow blanket I saw in your car. You wrapped the wampums in it because it was raining the night you stole them."

"You're a better investigator than I thought, Molly, but I don't believe anybody else knows about the blanket. Because you didn't figure that out until a few minutes ago when you saw the blanket in my car, did you?"

Molly shook her head. "I made the connection when I saw the blanket drying on a rack in your kitchen when I went there to talk to Steven."

Regina's expression didn't change. "Haven't I always told you you can't lie worth a damn, Molly. And even if that's true, I'll get rid of the blanket."

"You're forgetting the after-shave lotion . . ."

"Nobody else could even know that it's missing from Tom's house. You didn't realize the significance of that until just now," Regina pointed out.

"You're wrong. Daye knows. Are you going to kill her too, Regina?"

Regina shrugged, dismissing Daye. "She's too upset to think about what it means."

They sounded like two children arguing, except life and death didn't ride on the outcome of kids' arguments. But it wasn't getting Molly anywhere. Could she appeal to tribal loyalty? "Didn't it bother you to steal the tribe's most cherished relics?"

Regina shrugged again. "Not as much as watching Steven deteriorate before my eyes. I promised Mother I'd take care of him. Commitment to the state hospital hasn't helped. A private hospital is the only thing left. Selling the wampums is the only way I can get that kind of money. I'm meeting the buyer in Dallas next week when I take Steven there."

"I'll say this for you, you're loyal to your brother," Molly said, thinking hard. She no longer doubted that Regina would kill her. From the corner of her eye she could see the pulpit stand. If she was quick enough, she might get behind it before

Regina could take aim. Was it thick enough to stop a bullet? Molly had no idea, but she could see no other possible shelter.

"I would die for Steven," Regina said flatly.

Molly forced herself to hold Regina's gaze. "You may have to," she said and leaped down the steps toward the podium. Behind her, she heard Regina gasp and curse. Then a shot exploded in the chapel and something stung Molly's upper arm.

She fell to the floor and belly-crawled behind the pulpit. The sting had become a deep throb by then and, when she tried to wrap both arms around her legs to make herself as small as possible the pain was so sharp she almost fainted. She'd been shot. Disbelievingly, she touched her arm and her hand came away covered with blood. She stared at it, wondering if Regina knew she'd hit her.

She bit her lip to keep from moaning and the blackness came closer, beckoning her to oblivion and an absence of pain. It would be so easy to let go. She fought against it.

Tip Shaddock was in the security guard's house, watching a program on public television about ancient Chinese healing methods. A man was giving a testimonial about how a mixture of herbs had cured his arthritis. Tip was wondering how he could get hold of those herbs, when he heard something. It sounded like a car backfiring.

He got up and looked out his front window. The only cars in sight were Regina Shell's, parked in the same spot where it had been all day, and that old Honda of Molly Bearpaw's. Tip had seen Lily Roach leave more than an hour ago. Lily had called to him that Regina would lock up when she left the museum, which should be by five-thirty. Evidently, though, Regina was still in the museum, and Tip wondered what was taking her so long. It was getting on toward six o'clock. Probably got to yakking to Molly and forgot the time.

He sat back down in front of the TV. A woman was talking about something called acupuncture, which seemed to involve letting people stick a bunch of needles in you. He switched off the set and went outside. Regina's car and the Honda were still there, but the women weren't in sight.

Maybe somebody had taken a fall over there in the museum, broke a leg or knocked herself out. He'd better go over and check on them. He sighed and rubbed his arthritic hip and headed for the museum with an uneven gait.

The museum door was unlocked and the lights were on, but there was nobody in the foyer. Tip limped through the exhibit area, seeing no one. As he neared the back, somebody flushed the toilet in the men's rest room.

A few moments later, that spooky brother of Regina's came out and blinked owlishly when he saw Tip.

"Where's your sister?" Tip asked.

Steven looked around blankly. "She's here somewhere."

"I saw her a little while ago, loading some boxes in the trunk of her car," Tip said.

"Oh, yeah, that's where she is." He seemed relieved to have figured it out. "She told me to wait here for her."

"Her car's still out there and so's Molly Bearpaw's. Did they come back in here?"

Steven shook his head, his mouth ajar, as though his nose was stopped up. "I didn't see 'em."

Steven's noninformation was beginning to irritate Tip. "Well, where in tarnation are they?"

"Don't know," Steven said helplessly.

"Did you hear a noise a few minutes ago, like a car backfiring?"

Steven looked confused. "I was in the bathroom."

Tip guessed that meant no. "Your sister didn't say anything about going somewhere else?"

"Huh-uh."

Tip had the distinct feeling that Steven would wait in the museum all night, if necessary, for Regina to return. He couldn't seem to figure out anything to do on his own.

"I don't like this," Tip muttered. "The museum ought to be locked up by now. We better find your sister and Molly and see what the holdup is." He turned around and limped back through the exhibit area and the foyer.

"She told me to wait here," Steven called after him.

At the door, Tip whirled around and glared at Steven. "Hey, I'm tellin' you to get your butt in gear and help me look for 'em," he snarled.

"But she said—"

"She might be hurt!" Tip interrupted angrily. With a disgusted shake of his head, he shoved open the door and went out.

After a few indecisive moments, Steven followed him.

# 27

The blackness had receded to the edges of her vision, but the pain was constant and excruciating now. Gritting her teeth, Molly forced her mind away from the pain and cast about for a way to save herself. If she could get on her feet fast enough, she could rush Regina. She considered it for a moment, but she knew it wouldn't work. Regina would shoot her before she could reach her. Nothing more came to her.

The pain was so bad it was hard to think of anything else. So this was how she was going to die, crouched down behind a podium in an empty, musty-smelling chapel.

She heard a creeping sound and knew that Regina was edging down the carpeted steps toward her hiding place. Molly resisted the urge to look and see how close Regina was.

"Molly?" Regina said. "Can you hear me?"

It sounded as though she knew she'd hit Molly and she wasn't sure if Molly was still conscious.

"Molly, I'm sorry," Regina said in a wheedling voice. "I can't believe I shot at you. I lost my head. Come on out now and let's talk about it."

Fat chance, Molly thought as she scanned the narrow area behind the podium. It was carpeted in red, like the rest of the chapel. Here even the walls were covered with red shag. In the corner to her left, red-carpeted steps seemed to end at a blank wall. She hadn't even noticed the steps before, because the carpeting made everything run together in one big scarlet expanse.

Like the red sea in Eva's dream. And she'd left Eva's good-luck charm in her purse in the car.

She pulled her mind back to her predicament. Steps had to lead somewhere. She stared at the wall above the steps. There was something on the far right of that wall. It was difficult to make it out in the waning light, but it looked like . . . Yes, it was! A handle. The steps led to a red-carpeted door. It was at the wrong angle to be a door leading out of the museum. There must be another closet back there. Maybe even a small room.

She heard Regina take another step. "Molly?"

Molly was quiet, and then she thought: I'm going to die, one way or another. I've got nothing to lose by making a run for that door.

What if it was locked? Well, then, Regina would kill her while she was standing erect instead of crouched in a terrified huddle. One way was as efficient as the other. Dead was dead.

Slowly, she positioned herself to make a run for it. Tears filled her eyes at the heat in her left arm. But the pain had lessened a little. Numbness had taken its place and was spreading from her shoulder down her arm. She put her head down briefly, gathering her strength. Time to go for that door, she thought. Can't wait any longer. It's now or never. With her right hand she slipped her right shoe off and tossed it over her shoulder.

Regina fired in the direction of the sound as the shoe hit the wall, and Molly ran for the steps. Then she was grabbing the door handle and pulling it toward her. The door opened and she fell through the opening as Regina realized her mistake and another bullet hit the wall near the door. In a single unbroken motion, Molly got up, pulled the door shut, and jumped away from it as another bullet banged through the door and lodged in the wall. How many shots would it take before she hit Molly again?

Molly looked around wildly. She was in a small dressing room. On her left was a vanity table and a full-length mirror, on her right a bathroom, its door ajar. She closed her eyes and sagged against the wall. There were no windows in the room.

The dressing room must be used for the occasional weddings held in the chapel. She opened her eyes and stared at the back wall. There was a door leading outside. The room was so dark she hadn't seen it at first. Molly raced for it and grabbed the knob. The door was locked.

Oh, God.

She tried to quiet her gasping breath and think. Regina had fired three times. How many shells did the gun hold? Molly had no idea. For once, she wished she knew something about guns. She had a vague memory of hearing that automatics held at least five or six shells. More than three, anyway.

She looked around for something, anything, to use as a weapon on the off chance she could get close enough to Regina to use it before Regina killed her. There was nothing, but as her gaze raked the door that stood between her and Regina, she saw it could be locked from inside with a sliding bolt. Heart pounding, she removed her other shoe and crept along the wall until she was near the door. Stretching out her right arm, she pushed the bolt into the metal casing attached to the door facing.

As she moved back, the door rattled. Regina was standing on the top step, trying to get in. Molly moved soundlessly to the bathroom and locked herself in.

Regina fired again. Molly jumped violently, but the bullet hadn't hit the bathroom door. That made four bullets. Only two more, if the gun held six shells, but Regina may have extras in her pocket. It was just a matter of time before she hit the bolt and took it off. After that, the flimsy bathroom door wouldn't protect her for long.

"Gawd Almighty," Tip cried at the sound of the fourth explosion. "That sounds like gunfire, and it's coming from the chapel." He turned to see Steven following him hesitantly and at some distance. Maybe dealing with Steven had finally driven Regina over the edge. Maybe she was trying to commit suicide. If so, she was a blamed poor shot. And where was Molly Bearpaw?

"Does your sister have a gun?" he demanded of Steven.

"I don't know," Steven said.

Yes, it was definitely possible that Steven had caused his sister to have a nervous breakdown. This was only the second time Tip had ever talked to him, but he could see already that it wouldn't take long for Steven to drive him nuts.

"What *do* you know, dammit?" Tip asked.

"Not much," said Steven in perfect seriousness.

"Can you dial nine-one-one?"

Steven thought about it. "If I had a telephone."

"Great," Tip muttered. "Go back to the museum and dial it. Tell them we've got an incident at the heritage center involving gunfire. They'll know what to do."

"Okay," Steven agreed and started back to the museum.

"Hurry up," Tip yelled. His hip wouldn't allow him to run, but he limped faster toward the chapel. He had no intention of going in. He'd call out that he was the police and order

Regina—or whoever was firing that gun—to come out with their hands up.

But he'd find a big tree trunk to get behind first.

Molly was cornered. There was no place else for her to go, and she was going to pass out. Her skin felt clammy and cold. She shook her head and grabbed the faucet over the bathroom sink and turned it on. Her left arm was almost completely numb now. With her right hand, she splashed cold water on her face. It dispelled the light-headedness a little, but fear was like a winch, squeezing her insides to mush.

Until now, when Molly had thought of dying it was in connection with her grandmother. It hadn't occurred to her that Eva might outlive her. She regretted that she wouldn't have a chance to talk to Eva one more time and say good-bye. She'd like to say it to Moira too. And Conrad. If she could have one more conversation with D.J., she might even be able to say she loved him.

Twenty-eight years wasn't enough time. Too many things she hadn't said and done. Molly felt cheated. She took some deep breaths, trying to keep her mind clear.

Regina hadn't fired again. Maybe she didn't have any extra shells for the gun and she was rationing the ones she had left. Maybe she wouldn't risk another shot until she had some idea of whether Molly was to the right or left of the door.

Through the pain and dizziness, an idea began to form in Molly's mind, an idea born of desperation and probably doomed to failure. But what else was there?

She moved to the bathroom door. Her hand was shaking so hard she couldn't unlock the door at first. It seemed to take minutes to accomplish the simple task, but probably it was only seconds. Gripping the door's edge, Molly eased it open wide enough to step into the dressing room. Soundlessly, she crept along the wall around the room toward the door that led to the chapel. After a few steps, she had to stop and lean against the wall and fight off dizziness. When her head cleared, she took a few more steps.

Her ears rang and she couldn't see. She grabbed the edge of the mirror to keep from falling. Gradually, her vision cleared. She let go of the mirror and moved on. Finally, she stood, hugging the wall next to the door.

She took some deep breaths and strained to hear. Regina was breathing heavily on the other side of the door. Regina had no reason to conceal her position. She had the gun.

Molly held her breath and pressed her ear to the wall. She couldn't be sure that Regina was still standing on the top step. Then Regina muttered a curse under her breath. She was furious. Good, maybe it would make her less cautious.

The door was heavy and it opened outward. If Regina was on the top step, Molly had a chance. If she was down a couple of steps, Molly was dead.

She was dead anyway.

Molly lifted her right hand and was relieved to see that it wasn't shaking anymore. Once you'd accepted that you were going to die, fatalistic calm took over. Reaching out, she gripped the knob on the bolt, eased it down out of lock position, and inched it soundlessly toward her.

When the bolt was half out of the metal cylinder attached to the door, Regina yelled, "Give up, Molly! Why draw out the inevitable?"

Molly's heart lurched in her chest and she covered her mouth with her still-functioning hand to muffle the sound of the scream that was trying to claw itself out of her throat.

Regina's voice was as loud as if her mouth were pressed to Molly's ear. Regina was standing right next to the door, on the top step.

Molly took a moment to let her heart slow down and then she gripped the bolt again and eased it clear of the metal cylinder. Using her right shoulder, she gathered her strength and shoved the door open hard. It hit Regina with a thud. She yelped and grabbed for a handhold, couldn't find one, and started to fall. Having hit the door with all the force she could muster, Molly couldn't stop her momentum. She tumbled down the stairs and landed on Regina's back. She hurt everywhere.

Then everything went black, as Regina scrabbled around on the floor, trying to rid herself of Molly's dead weight. Molly shook her head, cleared it enough to realize where she was and what was happening. The sound of their labored breathing was loud in the silent chapel. Regina's right hand was extended to one side, her fingers clutching frantically at the carpet. The gun! The door had knocked it out of her hand and she was trying desperately to reach it.

Adrenaline surged through Molly. Rolling over, she grabbed the gun, steadying it as Regina leaped to her feet.

It took a little longer for Molly to get up, since her only usable hand was holding the gun. Regina could probably have taken the gun away from her if she'd acted in those first seconds, but she hadn't. She was too stunned.

On her feet, Molly started edging sideways toward the steps leading up to the back of the chapel.

Regina was breathing loudly through her mouth. She took a step toward Molly.

"Don't!" Molly said. "I'll shoot you, Regina."

Regina tried to sneer but it didn't quite come off. "The gun's empty, stupid."

"No, it isn't," Molly said, praying she was right. "You only used four shells." How many were left? One? Two?

But Molly didn't have to find out. Regina stopped and watched tensely as Molly backed all the way to the top level, then walked backward into the foyer. Molly didn't turn around until she felt the door at her back.

She pushed her butt back against the door to open it and then she was outside, stumbling away from the chapel. The adrenaline that had kept her upright until then drained out of her. There was a hammering in her ears and a voice, but it sounded far away.

Someone said, "Judas Priest, what's going on here?"

The gun clattered to the sidewalk and Molly fainted.

# 28

"I knew something bad was going to happen," Eva said darkly. It was after seven and Eva was determined to sit beside Molly's hospital bed all night.

The sheriff and D.J. had responded to Steven Shell's 911 call. By the time they reached the heritage center, the ambulance had taken Molly to the hospital, and Tip Shaddock had brought Regina out of the chapel and was holding her on his front porch at gunpoint. Steven Shell was sitting on the porch steps with his head in his hands.

As soon as they had Regina behind bars, Claude Hobart made a brief appearance at the hospital, and D.J. went after Eva and brought her there. He was standing on the opposite side of Molly's bed, holding her right hand. The emergency-room doctor had removed a shell from the fleshy part of Molly's upper left arm and told her how lucky she was that it hadn't shattered the bone. The wound would hurt like everything for a day or two, but after that she would mend quickly.

"I should have paid more attention to your premonitions, Grandmother," Molly murmured. They had given her pain medication and she was beginning to feel a little floaty. "But I'm not badly hurt, so don't worry."

"Hummph," Eva snorted. "Then how come they put you in the hospital?"

"They want to keep an eye on me overnight."

"I kept having that dream. The one where you were surrounded by a sea of blood."

Not blood, red carpeting, Molly thought, but she didn't want to try to explain it now. "I can go home tomorrow," she murmured.

D.J. squeezed her hand. "I'll pick you up. We need to talk."

D.J.'s face was blurred. Molly's eyes were glazing over. "About what?"

"I want all the details about what happened at the museum today. Claude will want me to take a full statement." Molly had given the sheriff the bare bones in the emergency room earlier. "I still don't know how you figured out that Regina killed Tom Battle."

"It's too complicated to go into now. My brain doesn't seem to be working very well."

"I know," D.J. said, giving her hand another squeeze. "There's something else we need to talk about later. I want you to consider getting a gun."

Molly sensed Eva stiffen and wished D.J. hadn't mentioned a gun in front of her. "You're overreacting, D.J." Molly said. "The chance that I'll get into another situation like this is nil."

"Do you really think Regina meant to kill you?" Eva asked.

What could Molly say? She forced her eyes open and looked at D.J., who shrugged as if to say, It's up to you how much you tell her.

"Yes," Molly said and sighed. "Yes, she really meant to. She's unhinged on the subject of Steven."

"I hope they don't let her out on bail," Eva said worriedly.

"She committed one murder and attempted another," D.J. said. "If they set bail at all, it'll be so high she won't be able to pay it."

"Regina is no threat to me now. She has no reason to kill me, since the police know the whole story," Molly whispered. It was getting harder to keep her eyes open. "Did she tell you where the wampums were, D.J.?"

"Yes, they're hidden in her bedroom. Claude's getting a search warrant so we can go in and get them."

"What will happen to Steven, D.J.?"

"The sheriff's going to talk to Steven's social worker at Eastern State. Maybe they can find a group home for him."

"I hope so," Molly murmured, slurring the words. "The sheriff said Steven is the one who called the police. I want to thank him."

"There'll be plenty of time for that," D.J. said. "Right now we'd better get out of here and let you sleep."

Molly clung to consciousness. "Somebody needs to tell Conrad what happened," she said. "He'll be worried when I don't come home tonight."

"I'll call him," D.J. promised.

"Be sure to tell him I'm okay."

"I will."

"Tony too." She almost smiled. "Tell him I solved the case and saved him another trip."

"You go along, D.J.," Eva said. "I'm staying."

"Grandmother," Molly mumbled, "I don't need you here. You'll wear yourself out. Let D.J. take you home now."

"No," said Eva stubbornly. "I'll sleep right here in this chair."

"I'll take her home tomorrow," D.J. said.

Molly wanted to argue with them, but she drifted off to sleep for a second. D.J. was bending over her when she woke up. She thought he'd kissed her.

"I have to go," he whispered. "I'll be back in the morning."

For a moment Molly was in the chapel again, contemplating her own death. She'd wished for enough time to say goodbye to Eva and tell D.J. how she felt about him. Now that she knew she wasn't going to die, all she could say was, "I'm glad you came."

She gave him a drowsy smile. She closed her eyes, and when she dragged them open again, D.J. was gone and Eva had put her head back in the chair beside Molly's bed and her eyes were closed. She looked so small, sitting there, but strong too. And very determined.

Molly sighed and drifted away to sleep.